AROUSING TROUBLE

He gripped her hard against him. "Do you have any concept of the trouble you have aroused?"

The hum in the air became a roar. She met his fervor with an explosion of her own.

"Tell me, Gideon. Show me."

His lips came down on hers, and this time there was nothing gentle about him. His tongue forced its way inside her and raked the darkness of her mouth. The movement was so completely unexpected, and the resultant thrill, she had to cling to his coat sleeves to keep from falling.

In an instant she became a woman she did not know, a needy creature with hungers only Gideon could satisfy. Understanding little of those hungers, she let instinct take control. Her arms stole around his neck and she pressed hot breasts against his chest, knowing her pleasure would be increased a thousandfold if their bodies were bare. . . .

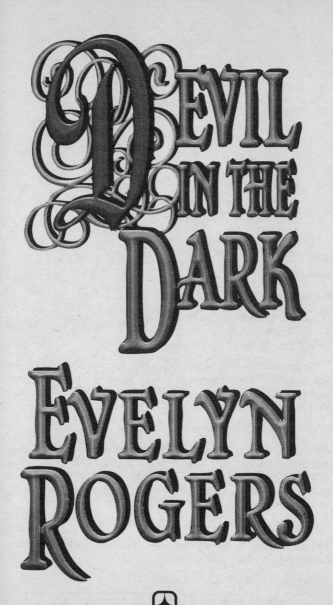

DEVIL IN THE DARK

EVELYN ROGERS

LOVE SPELL   NEW YORK CITY

A LOVE SPELL BOOK®

January 2001

Published by

Dorchester Publishing Co., Inc.
276 Fifth Avenue
New York, NY 10001

ISBN 0-505-52407-4

The name "Love Spell" and its logo are trademarks of Dorchester Publishing Co., Inc.

Printed in the United States of America.

Visit us on the web at www.dorchesterpub.com.

AUTHOR'S NOTE

I have long wanted to write a book about a dark, tormented hero, a man like the classic Heathcliff or Mr. Rochester, and the courageous heroine who brings light into his life. *Devil in the Dark* is that book. It is my tribute to the women writers of Gothic literature and their wonderful books, among them Charlotte Brontë's *Jane Eyre* and her sister Emily's *Wuthering Heights;* Daphne du Maurier's *Rebecca; Nine Coaches Waiting* by Mary Stewart; and the numerous works by Victoria Holt.

This book is dedicated to the readers who also cherish the memory of them, and those of you who have yet to discover what treasure they are.

In addition I would like to thank my editor Alicia Condon and agent Evan Marshall for seeing the possibilities in a new Gothic line and for encouraging me in the writing of this book.

—Evelyn Rogers

Chapter One

He rode out of the Yorkshire mist, a dark figure on a dark horse, black cape flying, the sharp hooves of his steed flashing ominously in the half-light that fell across the road.

Trapped by the sudden danger, Lucinda stood terror-stricken in his path. Instinct drove her backward. She struck her shoulder against the open door of her carriage, narrowly avoiding the hooves as the horse thundered past.

Her own mare whinnied and jumped about in the carriage traces, equally terrified, sending high-pitched squeals into the damp night air.

"Your Grace!" her coachman yelled, as if the horseman, now at the edge of the darkness, had

9

been the one in danger. He hurried to quiet the mare.

Suddenly everything was chaos. The hood of Lucinda's mantle fell away, and the wind caught her hair, sending her ash-blond locks tumbling wildly. Hand pressed to her bosom, she tried in vain to slow her pounding heart.

The black horse reared and pawed the air, then shifted closer to Lucinda with a restlessness that set her heart pounding all the harder. She knew horses. She understood the injury they could inflict.

In the eerie glow from the carriage lantern, the rider stared down in silence at his almost-victim, his gloved hands gripping the reins in masterful control of his steed. As if he controlled her, too, she felt her gaze drawn to his, and she looked into the blackest pair of eyes she had ever seen.

It was only then that she made a sound, a quick gasp she hurriedly swallowed. In contrast, he seemed unmoved by the encounter, his sharp features carved from dusky granite, his mouth set and hard.

Under his perusal, she tried to tame her hair, to hold herself straight and tall. More importantly, she willed herself to breathe. The hooves had missed her. She was a sensible American woman. She was perfectly all right.

Still, her heart pounded and her breath caught in her throat.

Time stopped. His cape, she saw, was lined in red, the color of blood. He nodded once, to what purpose she had no idea; then with a flick of the reins he disappeared into the mist from whence he had come. The sight and sound of him were absorbed by the darkness, leaving her with a chill that crept along the surface of her skin and, equally disturbing, with a stirring in her middle that came close to heat.

He must have been before her no more than a few seconds, yet it had seemed a lifetime. A strange sensation stole over her, a feeling that from this moment on, her life would never be the same.

She gave herself a mental shake. Such thinking was nonsense. Her life was changing, all right, but the phantom rider had nothing to do with it.

"Are ye all right, Miss Fairfax?"

She turned to face the speaker, Arthur Rigg, the coachman who had come to transport her from the deserted train station to her new Yorkshire abode. Short and spare in his dark cloak and tall hat, he was gray everywhere that showed, from the sprigs of hair that poked around the edges of the hat, to his wizened flat face, to the rheumy eyes that stared worriedly at his new mistress.

Rigg had barely introduced himself and loaded her trunk onto the back of the carriage when death had threatened out of the dark.

Sensible Lucinda might be, but she was also realistic. She could put no gentler word to what had just occurred. Death had hovered in the flash of the horse's hooves.

"I'm fine," she said, although the shakiness of her voice testified otherwise.

It wasn't fear that set her trembling, but a far different emotion: anger. It came readily after the danger had passed. How dare this arrogant stranger almost ride her down, then gallop away without a hint of concern? He ought to be soundly chastised—as if, she admitted, mere words would affect the man who had stared at her with such insolence.

She took a deep, steadying breath. The damp air held the scent of the sea some ten miles to the east. When she closed her eyes, she could almost hear the crash of waves on the shore. Somewhere in the distance a dog howled. Around her, the veiled village of Hummersby Bridge slept, ignorant of the drama, and for a moment she wondered if it had all been a figment of her overactive imagination, fueled by her already anxious state. Certainly the waves could not be real.

She rubbed her shoulder, only now aware of the pain inflicted by the hard edge of the carriage's open door. There was nothing imaginary about the condition of her bruised body; her new life had almost ended before it could begin. With a brief nod to reassure the coachman of her well-being, she went on to a matter of more interest than a temporary ache.

"You called the horseman Your Grace."

"Aye. The Duke of Ravenswood, he is." Rigg sounded as if he would say more, but something—discretion? fear?—held his tongue.

"The Devil Duke," she said. "I should have known."

The gray eyes studied her more carefully than before.

"So you've heard of him, have ye?"

"I've heard of him," she said, and let her answer go at that.

In truth, after her fellow passengers learned of her destination, talk in the second-class train compartment had been devoted to little else. Her late father's solicitors had wanted her to ride first-class from London, but, not yet used to having money, she had informed them the added expense was a waste. Besides, she had not wanted to make the ride in what would probably have been solitude. In this strange new world into which she was plunging, already she felt too much alone.

The talk on the train had not been soothing. Gideon Blackthorne was the name the passengers had given, the thirteenth Duke of Ravenswood. Several shuddered at his mention. She was beginning to understand why.

They say he's more devil than human.

A man's life is in danger when he is around.

13

And a woman's virtue. The latter from a pinch-lipped matron who sat in the corner throughout the long night ride and stared at Lucinda as if she were a creature from another world.

Which indeed she was. A New York farm was an eternity away from the North Yorkshire moors she would, at least for a time, call home.

Wanting very much to turn a deaf ear to the train gossip, she had kept to herself a thousand questions concerning the duke. They returned to her now, but again she would not give them voice. She knew only one thing: Despite the talk of danger bordering on the supernatural, nothing had prepared her for the picture the Duke of Ravenswood presented on this stretch of road in the darkness before the dawn.

When she was safely tucked inside the carriage, a blanket over her lap as protection from the damp cold, she leaned back and, with the final segment of her journey begun, gave thought to the duke's sudden, brief appearance. At first she had been stunned by no more than his eyes, but there had been more about him that stayed in a woman's mind, even one as unresponsive to men as Lucinda. He was hatless, his raggedly cut hair almost to his shoulders, as black as everything else about him, his face lean to the point of gauntness, his brows thick over the probing eyes.

And there was, of course, the sensuous mouth

that she suspected could be cruel in ways she could scarcely imagine.

All this she had seen in an instant. He was big, that much she also knew, and strong—he had to be to control the horse as easily as he did—and he gave an impression of height that had nothing to do with the fact he sat astride a monster steed.

Was he handsome? Not in any conventional sense, but there was something about him that would flutter the heart of any woman more susceptible to such things than Lucinda Fairfax, spinster. Her first impression of him had been one of cold distance, of a man who set himself apart from the world. Nothing she recalled could change her mind.

Without warning the carriage lurched sharply, throwing her against the door, bruising what had been her good shoulder. In an instant, the ride came to a halt and Rigg was standing beside the door.

"Are ye all right, Miss Fairfax? I pride meself on a smooth ride, but a dog ran across the road and startled old Bessie. That'd be the horse, you ken. Came from nowhere, he did, black as the night, and disappeared into nowhere just as fast. They say hounds from hell haunt these parts. Never saw one before, but there's those that have."

The somberness of Rigg's tone threatened to strengthen her burgeoning sense of otherworldliness. This was absurd. No one was more realistic than she.

"I imagine he was a very real dog." She straightened herself and tried to smile. "Do me a favor, will you?"

"O'course, Miss Fairfax. You being the late lord's daughter, you have only t'say what you wish."

Lucinda nodded. Giving orders was something else she would have to get used to.

"When we ride upon Fairfax land, will you let me know?"

"Faith, it's a natural enough request. Should'a thought of it meself."

Once more under way, she breathed a sigh of relief. She had devoted quite enough thought to Gideon Blackthorne. Unless he tried to run her down again, she would probably never see him after today. Even if she did, he was quite the least of her worries.

Peering through the window, she watched the first light of dawn tease the edges of the far horizon. She was able to make out little else but rolling countryside coated in a thick mist, broken by an occasional copse of what appeared to be oaks. From the moment the carriage left the village, she had sensed the road was gradually rising, leaving all that she knew and understood behind.

"We'll be on Fairfax land before ye know it," Rigg yelled from his perch.

Fairfax land. Her land. Or so the solicitors said, first through their letters to her home in northern New York, then in the brief meeting held this week in their London offices. She also had holdings in Hummersby Bridge, potentially valuable holdings, but it was the family home and its surroundings that interested her the most.

She would sell it—that had been her first thought when the death notice arrived—and return to the country of her birth, in circumstances vastly superior to those in which she had left. But selling, she had learned, was not an option. That right her father had willed to her first-born son, in the unlikely event such an heir ever existed. But she could reap the profits of her inheritance until the day of her death.

And so she would. There was little chance she would view any part of it with sentiment. Already it had cost her more than it could ever be worth.

Still, she could not ignore a sense of anticipation that kept her on the edge of her seat. Alone she might be, and for the moment, lonely, but for the first time in her life she would be lonely in a house that belonged to her.

The carriage rounded a bend, and she caught sight of a distant structure rising out of the mist, a castle more than a home, turrets rising from every rooftop corner. It covered an entire hilltop, its shadowed presence unwelcoming, almost threatening. She pictured men in mail peering from the corner towers, crossbows clutched in their gloved hands. It was a foolish image. The year was 1860. She read too much.

Another thought struck, this one equally impossible. Hurriedly she lowered the window and thrust her head outside for a better look. Surely this could not be—

"Blackthorne Hall," Rigg shouted from his perch. "The duke's residence. Unfinished in part, so they say, but nevertheless a grand place, it used to be. I'm told most of the rooms are closed off now."

"The duke must have a large family," she replied, embarrassed to have ever thought such a place hers.

"Nay, he lives alone."

Closing the window, Lucinda huddled under the blanket for warmth. *He lives alone.* It was a condition they shared, although the idea did not in itself make her sad.

Living alone anywhere, even in this mist-shrouded countryside, would be preferable to the fate that had awaited her back in New York—the arranged marriage, the feeling always that she was in the way. If only her mother had lived longer, or had made better arrangements than to settle her eighteen-year-old daughter with a distant cousin on a remote farm. The cousin now planned to settle her somewhere else.

It was an uncharitable thought. Anne Fairfax had done the best she could under difficult circumstances. More to the point, her father should not have abandoned his American wife and young daughter to return to England for his unexpected inheritance of title and property. William Fairfax, sixth Viscount Westcombe. He must have been proud.

But that had been a long time ago, so long she scarcely remembered him, proud or any other way. Any resentment she still harbored was not for herself but for her beloved mother, who had been in her grave these past seven years.

Again, the carriage came to a halt. "This be Fairfax land, beginning with the hedgerows," Rigg called out.

With a strange mixture of excitement and foreboding, she settled back and watched as the trees and fields emerged from the mist into the dawning light. The solicitors had mentioned a thousand acres surrounding the house, worked by tenant farmers who lived on neighboring property. The way they put it, this portion of her inheritance had sounded modest. To her, it looked as vast as the world.

The route took them through an open gate, on either side of which rose a tall brick gatepost topped by a sitting hound carved out of stone. The hounds, facing one another, looked coldly forbidding. Nervously she tried to pin her fallen

19

hair into a semblance of neatness and to smooth her wrinkled dress and cloak. Appearance had never been especially important to her, but neither did she wish to look like a sloven justly abandoned all those years ago by the late Lord Westcombe.

The carriage came to its final halt on a curved drive in front of Craven Manor, named for the River Craven that wound across the property. Like a child in a storeroom of toys, she gawked at the sight. She had been assured the manor was quite adequate for her needs.

The solicitors were masters of understatement.

Lucinda knew little about architecture, but she thought the house was of Georgian design, three stories of red brick, the facade broken by a dozen windows, several of them bowed outward so that whoever peered through them could get a better view of the surroundings.

It was all centered by a colonnaded portico, at the back of which waited a carved front door. Over the latter, lit by a pair of flickering lanterns, hounds like those at the gateposts were carved into a triangular pediment, as forbidding as they had been back on the road.

She took it all in at once, then stared in disbelief as she picked out the particulars. Craven Manor was nothing short of a mansion, at least by any standards she had ever known. This could not be hers. Her father could not have lived in such splendor while his wife and only child, long forgotten, struggled to survive.

But of course he had. She took no pleasure in the realization. Instead, her heart turned to stone as hard as the carved hounds.

Someone inside must have alerted the inhabitants to her arrival, for the door slowly opened and two figures walked through the portico and stopped at the edge of the drive: a tall, thin man and a short, equally thin woman, both of middle age, both in black, both rigidly expressionless as they waited for her to descend.

Rigg was down in a flash, opening the carriage door, offering his arm for her to alight.

The waiting couple looked so formal, Lucinda wondered if perhaps they were relatives she had not been told about. But the solicitors had assured her that except for a distant cousin in London, who had inherited the Viscount title but little else, she was the last of the line on her father's side.

The couple had to be the butler John Fenton and the housekeeper. What had the lawyers called the woman? Yes, Athena Pickering, a widow as she recalled. Nothing had been mentioned of Fenton's marital state.

He did not look married, nor likely ever to have warmed to a woman. She wondered if he had ever smiled. She tried to show him how it was done, but her effort at friendliness proved too weak to get any response.

"Good morning," she said, breaking the awkward silence. "I'm sorry to have roused you so early on such a chill, damp day."

"Oh, the weather's right fine, Miss Fairfax," the housekeeper said, then looked as if she could swallow her tongue, giving the impression she did not know whether to be friendly, servile, or even combative toward the manor's new owner.

With eyes downcast, she curtsied; Fenton gave an almost imperceptible bow; and Lucinda, knowing little else to do, stepped forward, her hand outstretched, ready to end this first meeting with a measure of civility and dignity.

She had no chance. From around the back of the carriage raced an animal she recognized belatedly as a huge black dog. The hound bounded between her and the Craven servants and came to a halt half a dozen yards beyond them, his massive head turned to her. Mrs. Pickering cried out, Fenton and Rigg shouted, while Lucinda, surprising herself, simply stared at the beast in amazement, her hand rigid in its outstretched position.

In a land full of surprises, the dog was one more unexpected element.

He stood to the side, watching, never once shifting his unsettling gaze from her. She stared right back.

"Careful, miss," Rigg said, stepping forward.

A growl sounded in the dog's throat, and Lucinda motioned the driver away.

She looked to Fenton. "Does he belong here?"

"Never seen him before."

"First the Devil Duke, and now this," Rigg said. Mrs. Pickering and Fenton stared at him sharply, but he went on. "He looks to me like the hound that ran across the road a ways back. Can't be sure, o'course, but I'd swear it was the same."

The hound of hell, the driver had called him. But the warm dark eyes staring up at Lucinda showed no sign he meant her harm. Rigg must have made a mistake.

The beast had one more surprise for her. Slowly he closed the distance between them, moving with natural grace and silence across the drive, and laid a paw over her still-outstretched hand, as if he would be the first to welcome her to Craven Manor.

She shook the paw. Satisfied, the animal took his place beside her, standing stiff and at attention, his black body brushing against her cloak.

"You've a way with animals, Miss Fairfax," Fenton said. He did not sound particularly approving.

"Horses, yes. But never anything else. I've never owned a dog in my life."

She took a step forward. So did the dog.

"You've got one now," Rigg said.

Mrs. Pickering sniffed in disapproval, and

Fenton gave a slight shake of his head. Their actions helped to make up her mind.

"I'm sure he belongs to someone else. Until we find out whom, if he chooses to stay here, then that's what he will do."

It was a curious first order as the new mistress of Craven Manor, and she was inordinately proud of herself, even while wondering if the order would be obeyed.

"Now," she said, smiling at her greeters though they did not smile in return, "I would very much like to see the inside of my father's home."

She stepped past them all, as if she were brave, as if she weren't close to dropping from apprehension. The hound followed, prompting her to issue a second command.

"Stay," she said sharply, and to her great surprise, the animal lowered himself to his haunches, striking a pose very much like the stone dog carved into the pediment over his head. Very much, too, like a sentinel guarding the home of his new mistress—against what she did not want to consider.

Fenton opened the front door, and she caught the mixed odors of burning oil, waxed floors, and the stale scent that went with a house too long closed to fresh air. Adopting an erect posture that would have made her mother proud, she went inside, her shoes striking against the hard floor of the entryway in time to the pounding of her heart.

24

Chapter Two

The house seemed bigger on the inside.

Lucinda walked across the spacious entryway with its paneled walls and carved wooden ceiling, stared down dark hallways to right and left, and at last gazed straight ahead at the curved stairway leading to the two upper floors.

The sweep of the iron handrail on the stairs, supported by gracefully turned balusters, caught her eye for a moment. She should have swelled with pride from the enormity of what was now hers.

Instead, she felt small and out of place. Her cousin's farmstead home, large by most American standards, would have fit in either the west or east wing of Craven Manor. Or maybe it was

25

north and south. She was completely turned around.

One thought occurred: She could return to the drive, request Rigg to take her back to Hummersby Bridge, and catch the next train to London. There she could instruct the solicitors to send her competency, as they called it, to an address she had yet to determine. Then she could book passage on the next ship home.

The cowardly thought stayed only briefly in her mind. In a life dependent too much on others, she had been meek long enough.

But she was not so brave as to view much of her newly acquired abode right away. Not only was it overwhelming, but somehow taking it in all at once also seemed greedy, as if she had long been counting the money and goods she would receive upon the death of her father.

She would far rather be facing him now, looking for guilt and regret as he met the daughter he had not seen since she was five.

She could not even imagine that he would have greeted her with affection.

"Could I see my room?"

"Of course," Mrs. Pickering said with a brusque nod, then glanced sideways at the butler Fenton, as if asking permission for something. Whatever it was, he must have granted her request, for she walked around Lucinda toward the stairs. "Follow me. Rigg will bring up your things."

Lucinda hid a smile. Her things—all her worldly possessions—fit into the single trunk she had brought with her from America.

Following the fast-moving housekeeper, she paused on the landing of the stairway and stared through the massive window. The mist was dissipating, giving way to a reluctant day. In the distance she could see Blackthorne Hall, resting atop its hill, as dark and forbidding as ever, its corner turrets rising in medieval splendor into the cold air.

Or was it in nineteenth-century decay? Rigg had hinted that the inside of the hall had fallen from its grander days.

Had Gideon Blackthorne returned to his private castle? Or was he still terrorizing the countryside with his hellish manner of riding?

"Met the duke, have you?"

Lucinda jumped. Her housekeeper, standing close by, had an uncanny ability to move without making a sound.

"Not exactly."

Mrs. Pickering was not so easily put aside. For all her servility—an attitude she had difficulty holding on to—the woman had a firm set to her jaw and an unmovable air about her short, almost wiry figure.

"From what Rigg said, I thought otherwise."

"You could scarcely call our encounter a meeting. The man rode past the carriage when I was in town."

"In the night, like the devil himself was at his heels, I'll be bound." Mrs. Pickering sniffed. "You'll scarce see our Devil Duke in the light of day."

"Why is that?" Lucinda asked, unable to control her curiosity any longer. "And why is he called a devil? Has he harmed anyone?"

The housekeeper's faded blue eyes settled on Lucinda for a moment, then shifted away.

"These are questions no Fairfax should be asking. Like as not, you'll get your answers soon enough. The best advice I can give you—if you're of a mind to take such from the likes of me—is to stay off His Grace's property and away from his presence. If you want a long and happy life."

With that, the housekeeper turned and continued up the stairs, leaving a startled Lucinda to hurry after.

It seemed as if everyone was playing a game with her—Let's Scare the American Intruder—and that included the Devil Duke himself. She would not be intimidated. Practical she had always been. Now she had to be tough.

The bedchamber to which she was led was wide and deep and dark, the furniture equally dark and massive; heavy draperies over the window closed out the light and air. Gaslights mounted on either side of the fireplace sent out a muted yellow light, and a fire blazed in the grate.

All this she took in with a single glance. As much as she wanted to ask more about her dangerous neighbor, she took one look at the canopied four-poster bed and forgot all else save the fact she had not slept in more than twenty-four wearying hours.

Inelegantly she tossed her cloak aside, kicked off her shoes, and directed to the general vicinity of Mrs. Pickering the most coherent thought she could manage:

"Please, I'd like to rest awhile before seeing anything more."

"I will bring tea."

"Later," she said, then added, after catching the grim look on the woman's face, "I would very much appreciate tea and something to eat later."

With that, she climbed onto the high mattress and rested her head on the plump pillow, barely aware of the door's closing.

Lucinda awoke in a sweat, fighting the bedcovers, imagining them to be a heavy black cape that was suffocating her. With a start, she sat up and glanced wildly around, but there was no Duke of Ravenswood sitting at the edge of her bed attempting to smother her, as she had pictured in her dream.

Sleep-drugged, she took a moment to compose herself, then shifted her feet to the side of the bed and gave a more thorough study to her surroundings. A chair and footstool were placed at an angle in front of the dying fire, a wardrobe and desk were against opposite walls, a thick Chinese carpet covered the floor. The same mustiness she had smelled on first entering the house permeated the room. She stood, caught her balance, and moved in stocking feet across the carpet to throw back the draperies blocking the window.

To her surprise, she discovered not a window but a pair of glass-paneled doors that led onto a small iron balcony. Beyond the doors, night was falling. She must have slept through the day. Feeling foolish and not at all like herself, she flung open the doors and stepped outside to view her land. But her attention was drawn to the distant hill where Blackthorne Hall rose ominously in the half-light.

It seemed her fate in this new land always to be confronted by either the castle or its owner. Everywhere she turned, one or the other accosted her, even in her dreams. She had been warned not to ask about him. But how could she not? What was it she would find out soon enough?

And why must she stay away from Blackthorne land and its owner? Did he have guard dogs like the one that had attached himself to her?

If this was truly a game, it was one she could never enjoy.

A knock sounded at the bedroom door. Drawing a steadying breath, she turned to watch Mrs. Pickering enter with a tray. She set it on the table beside the hearth chair.

"I took it upon myself to bring tea and sandwiches," the housekeeper said. "I hope they're to your American taste."

She sounded as if her new mistress were used to less delicate fare, raw beef sliced off a freshly slaughtered calf, perhaps, and a tankard of dark ale to wash it down.

Lucinda smiled sweetly. "It all looks delicious."

"It's simple fare. Cook can do better when she has the challenge of a solid Yorkshire dinner."

"I'm sure she can."

Mrs. Pickering stood rigidly silent, clearly waiting for her new mistress to do or say more. What that something might be, the new mistress had no idea.

"I won't be expecting dinner tonight, of course."

Mrs. Pickering sniffed.

"Rest is what I need, really. Please give my apologies to the cook."

"No apologies necessary, Miss Fairfax. Craven Manor is now yours. You can do whatever you please."

The words came out solemnly, filled with a meaning Lucinda could only guess at. Whatever it was, the housekeeper, a woman obviously of strong opinions and a tongue as sharp as her features, was not pleased that Lucinda was here. Lucinda thought of several responses, but since each was tinged with either irritation or apology, she rejected them all.

In the past, she had called no one a confidant, but in her daily existence she got along with everyone. She would do the same with Mrs. Pickering if it killed her.

"Your belongings have been brought to the dressing room," Mrs. Pickering said, nodding toward a shadowed corner door Lucinda had not noticed before. "I did not take the liberty of hiring a lady's maid, thinking you would want to make the selection yourself. Until then, I'm here to serve in any capacity you wish."

How about being my friend?

It was not a request likely to bring a warm smile to the woman's lips. A crazed American, she would think, and at the moment she would be right.

"I'm not used to being waited on," Lucinda said.

"I imagine that will change."

She said it under her breath, as though she had not wanted to be heard, then hurried past Lucinda to the dressing room door.

"Your trunk has been unpacked. I hope you've no objection." She hesitated. "We've a fine dressmaker in Hummersby Bridge. Good as anyone in London. Should you find the need."

Lucinda nodded. Consisting of plain black dresses and even plainer petticoats, the wardrobe of Craven Manor's new mistress must have been a great disappointment to the woman.

"Also there's warm water for bathing, if you've a mind."

"You brought all this through the bedroom while I was sleeping?"

"There's stairs from the dressing room down to the servants' area. A viscountess of some years past insisted on it."

Anne Fairfax had been a viscountess. Lucinda could never remember her mother insisting on anything, though she had yearned in silence through the years for her husband to return.

"If you've nothing more you need, I'll get along," Mrs. Pickering said. "There's much to be done with a new mistress about the place."

What? Lucinda wanted to ask. *Your new mistress plans to make no demands remotely resembling building stairs or even preparing huge meals.*

But it was too early in her stay for such honesty.

Thanking the housekeeper for her thoughtfulness, she went to investigate the dressing room. Mrs. Pickering was clearly displeased by her presence. Why? It was something else she would have to find out. She could not help wondering exactly how much her father's legal representatives had failed to reveal, either through ignorance or design.

The bath soothed the worries from her mind, and the food gave her a burst of energy she had not expected. The pattern of the dishes caught her eye, a pair of now-familiar hounds sitting rigidly in the midst of softening scrolls. She set them aside. They reminded her of another door to her inheritance, one she must soon pass through, when she returned to Hummersby Bridge. For now, the house and grounds and the people she was meeting were all that she could absorb.

Despite the immensity of her bedroom, the walls began to close in on her. From her balcony she had observed what appeared to be a garden directly below her room. The moon was high, the mist showing no signs of returning. She was used to evening walks and even rides on the beloved mare she had been forced to leave behind. Perhaps a brief stroll in the night air would clear her thoughts. What could be the harm?

How to get from here to there was another problem. She chose what seemed the most direct route: down the stairs leading from the dressing room and out a back door. The bedside lamp was too unwieldy to carry, but she found a candle and holder in the nightstand, tossed her cloak over the clean black dress Mrs. Pickering had unpacked—one very much like the garment she had worn on the journey—and was on her way.

At the base of the stairway, she found herself in a large, deserted kitchen. Breathing a sigh of relief—she was in no hurry to meet any more of the staff or run into any she had already met—she found the back door she was seeking. It opened onto the garden, which at ground level was as unkempt as it had appeared from the balcony, the ivy at her back growing thick and untamed up the brick manor wall, the shrubbery in front of her untrimmed, the flowerbeds gone to weeds.

Lucinda adored flowers. She fought the urge to dig her hands in the dirt, beginning the preparation of the beds for whatever would grow in this northern clime. Roses would be nice, peonies, and banks of lilac to scent the air.

She pulled herself up short. Very likely she would not be here in the spring to see the result of her work. But she could not keep herself from considering what she would do if she actually planned to stay.

A sudden breeze snuffed out the candle, but the moonlight provided sufficient light for a slow stroll down the twisted paths. A high, ivy-choked fence surrounded the area, and she felt protected. What harm could there be for her here?

No sooner did she assure herself of safety

than she heard what sounded like the creak of a gate at the back of the garden.

"Who's there?" she called out.

The only answer was the hoot of an owl perched unseen in one of the trees beyond the fence, a liquid wooing call that hung for a long moment in the night.

Attributing the creaking noise to the wind, she continued her stroll, but the peacefulness of solitude had fled. She was halfway down the walkway, no longer quite so eager to partake of the night air. Once again a mist was settling over the land. She felt the clammy moisture on her cheeks and on her hands.

Mist and moonlight. It was a curious combination, one that seemed to fit only in Yorkshire.

At the back of the garden a shadow moved.

"Who's there?" she called again, showing far more courage than she felt.

This time she got a more definite response. The shadow stepped into the moonlight, and her heart stopped.

She recognized the tall, powerful figure in an instant—the black hair, the black cape with its blood-red lining, even the black eyes, though the latter were imagined more than actually perceived. Not imagined were the harsh lines of his face, the strong features, the air of being absolutely in control.

Gideon Blackthorne, the Devil Duke of Ravenswood, stood a dozen yards away, as forbidding and as imposing on foot as he had been in the early morning hour astride his galloping steed. He was not resting in his castle, as she had supposed, or riding wildly about the countryside. He was here with her, at the beginning of a new night, and they were very much alone.

Chapter Three

Lucinda waited for him to speak.

From the far end of the garden, Gideon
Blackthorne stared at her in silence. In the
moonlit mist, he appeared ghostlike, but she
knew he was all too real, flesh and blood and
will, the latter focused on she knew not what.

The only fact she knew was that he was here
and he was staring at her.

He had no business being where he was, no
legitimate reason she could think of. The warnings she had received about him on the train
came back in a rush, along with the ominous
words of her housekeeper. She should retreat,
back to the safety of the house. Any sensible
woman who knew his reputation would do ex-

actly that. If he had anything to say, he could say it through the bolted back door.

Instead, summoning more courage than good sense, she held her ground.

"Is it a Yorkshire custom to call upon new neighbors in the middle of the night?"

She heard the quaver in her voice and hated it. She wanted to be firm.

"It is hardly the middle of the night."

His voice, floating to her across the dozen yards separating them, was deep as the shadows, insinuating, goading. It went with the rest of him. Nothing about the duke gave a woman confidence that she was safe in his company.

Or wanted to be.

Lucinda shook herself. She was no schoolgirl confronting a grown man for the first time. She was sensible. She was immune to masculine appeal. Until this morning, she had not been sure there was such a thing.

"You have not answered me," she managed.

He took a half-dozen steps in her direction, his stride long, his boots inaudible as they struck the hard ground. The breeze died, and all was quiet. Even the owl seemed to have deserted the scene.

"You speak bluntly," he said. "Are you not terrified of a man, a stranger, coming upon you like this on your own land?"

Yes.

40

She fought to keep from backing away. "Should I be?"

"No more than I."

The words sounded harsh, almost pained, and were unfathomable to her. What was there about her that could possibly terrify such a man? He had to be mocking her.

As they stood looking at one another, the moonlight softly diffused in the dampness, she got a sense of the body beneath his cape. He was leaner than she had thought when he sat astride the horse, but just as strong, just as powerful, pulsing with a leashed energy she could only imagine.

As before, his head was bare, his black hair thick and coarse as it fell to his shoulders. In his darkness, he seemed as much a part of the night as the moon and the mist.

She trembled inside.

"I forget my manners," he said with a slight bow. "Allow me to introduce myself."

She caught a glimpse of a pointed collar against his neck and pictured what he would look like without the cape, the white shirt full-sleeved and open at the throat, tucked inside a wide black belt and tight black trousers, his black boots fitted halfway up his well-formed calves.

She thought a moment about the boots and the calves before hurriedly shaking off the image. She wasn't a fanciful woman. What had come over her?

"I know who you are," she said, then added, "Your Grace." The latter sounded strange on her tongue.

"Of course you do. I'm sure you have been told much about the Devil Duke."

His self-mockery surprised her.

"Perhaps I should be terrified, as you suggested. Unless the stories about you are wrong." She surprised herself by adding, "Is my life truly in danger? Or is it my virtue?"

"Which is it you fear most to lose?"

Lucinda could never have imagined such a question would be put to her, or that she would ponder the answer. But she had only herself to blame that it had been asked.

She looked away. "I cannot answer that. You would know too much about me."

"Yes, I would. For now I know you are the Honorable Miss Lucinda Fairfax of the United States, arrived only this day to claim her rightful inheritance from her late, unfortunate father."

"Why do you say unfortunate?"

"Surely you've been told about the accident that caused his death."

"Only that he fell while walking in a heavy mist. The solicitors said he had been warned about the dangerous path he chose."

"They said nothing more?"

"What more is there?"

"What indeed."

He stepped closer, until he was a few scant feet from her, staring with an intensity that rooted her to the ground. Something flickered in the dark depths of his eyes, then was gone, leaving her puzzled, shaken. If she did not know the idea was absurd, she might have believed he was as shaken as she.

"Is it the custom in your country to wear your hair loose in such a manner? It is the color of the moonlight, you know, and the mist catches in its strands like beads of crystal. You'll be taken for wanton if you are not careful."

Nothing could have stunned her more. Self-consciously, she stroked her hair away from her face.

"I have been called many things in my life, but never wanton." She struggled for dignity. "Is it the custom in your country for a titled gentleman to insult a lady as you are doing tonight?"

"Nothing I have said was intended as an insult."

Another step. She could see the deep lines between his thick black brows. Such lines were the mark of the devil, she had once been told.

"What are you doing?" she said, not trying to hide her confusion, her concern. "Why are you here?"

"I was . . . riding by and saw a light through the trees."

She looked at the dead candle in her hand and felt a chill. She found no comfort in knowing he had been so close when she chose to explore her new home. It was as if he had summoned her from the sanctity of her room, and not her own restlessness that had sent her out of doors.

"What made you think it was I in the garden and not one of the servants?"

"I knew."

"But that doesn't—"

"I came to apologize."

Concern became astonishment. "Apologize? Whatever for?"

"I almost ran you down this morning. Or do such things happen to you so often you have put the incident out of your mind?"

She pulled her cloak tight around her, hoping he could not hear the hard beating of her heart. "Nothing like that has ever happened before. Besides, I was standing in the road in the dark on the downside of a rise. You could have had no idea I was there."

"You are being reasonable."

"I have had some time to consider the incident. Whether you realize it or not, it is a custom in my country to be reasonable."

"And in mine to be contrary."

He closed the distance between them, moving

swiftly, quietly, looming over her with such arrogance of power and confidence she almost cried out.

He looked her over, studying her hair and her face and the cloak-covered length of her in a way she had never been looked at before. She could not tell if he approved of what he saw. She was ashamed because she wanted him to.

"You have fine eyes, Lucinda. Blue, I would guess. It's hard to tell in the night." The devil lines deepened. "Lucinda means light, does it not? You have come to a dark place in the world. I doubt you truly belong."

Of course she didn't. But she was not of a mind to tell him so.

"Are you deliberately trying to frighten me into leaving?"

No quaver. His boldness made her bold as well.

"If so, I fail in my task. What would it take to send you running? This?"

He touched her hair, so lightly she could barely feel the weight of his fingers, yet they seemed to crush her.

He was left-handed. It was another devilish mark.

Devil-like, he went on.

"Or this?" he said.

He stroked her cheek.

Her skin burned where he had stroked.

Duke or no duke, she should have slapped

him. But her heart thrummed all the harder, her breath caught, and a hundred protests lodged in her throat.

"Perhaps this," he said, bending his head.

His lips, always so set and firm, parted as they neared hers. She stared at them in fascination, the last of her will gone.

A growl broke the silence, deep and menacing, shattering the moment. For once his stony face gave way to expression. It was a look of pain, but it came and went so quickly she was not sure she was right.

He pulled away and glanced beside her. Shaking herself, she followed his gaze. As silently as the duke, the black hound of the morning had come to her side. He stood with hackles raised and teeth bared, so tall she did not have to stoop to touch his head. One stroke of her hand and the growls died, but the teeth remained in evidence.

"You have a protector," Blackthorne said. He showed no fear of the hound, a man used to threats and danger.

"It seems I need one," she said, barely above a whisper.

His gaze returned to her. "Nothing can protect us from ourselves and from our fate. You are a brave and beautiful American, and I suspect an innocent, for all your outspokenness. What you are could be your ruin."

"You talk nonsense."

He seemed not to hear. "Tread softly. Heed little that you see and hear. Then leave. For God's sake, leave."

With black cape swirling, he turned from her. At the same moment a cloud passed over the moon, and the night swallowed him. She did not hear his footsteps on the garden path, nor the creak of the back gate, but she knew he was gone.

She swayed dizzily in the void, leaning against the hound for support, hearing the pounding of a horse's hooves as he rode away.

Eyes closed, she could still see Gideon Blackthorne looming over her, the lines of his face sharp, the eyes burning, the mouth taunting. He had almost kissed her. She had wanted him to. Her cheeks burned as she admitted just how much she had wanted it.

It would have been her first. At twenty-five, what a foolish spinster she was.

She hugged herself. The kiss would have meant nothing to him. He had not come for that purpose, nor even to apologize, but rather to warn her. Of what, she had no idea.

For God's sake, leave.

A devil summoning the Almighty. Did he wish her far away for her own safety or for his? It was a lunatic thought, but she could not rid herself of the idea that he was a tortured soul and she a partial cause of his torment.

With the hound close beside her, she hurried

toward the back door. More lunacy. But the concept of his deep distress would not go away, even though she knew him to be one who would inflict more torture than he would suffer.

You have fine eyes.

He had been taunting her. He had called her beautiful. Another taunt. She was too thin, too tall, her features too strong to be considered beautiful. Innocent, yes, she was as he no doubt had meant it, sexually. And most certainly outspoken. But all of these things, even if true, could scarcely bring about her ruin. Or her loss of virtue. She was far too sensible. He forgot to mention that.

Arrogant Yorkshire dukes, it would seem, had a definite flair for the dramatic.

So deep in thought was she that the sight of a figure standing just inside the doorway brought a startled cry, and the candle holder fell to the floor with a clatter, breaking the candle in two.

"Don't be afeared, Miss Lucinda," a high-pitched voice croaked. "It's just old Jenny."

On a shelf next to the woman rested a burning lantern, its light barely bright enough for Lucinda to study her. She was short, hardly reaching five feet, her back bent, her gray hair wiry and wild. Her face was narrow and deeply lined, her nose thin and sharp, her lips invisible in the surrounding wrinkles. She looked as old as the moors.

What disturbed Lucinda the most were the eyes, deep and colorless. She had never seen such eyes.

"I thought I was alone." She tried to smile, then said to the hound close beside her, "You were supposed to warn me."

"He will if there's harm coming. Ye'll get no harm from me."

"Who are you? You seem to know me."

"Everyone in the country knows the new mistress of Craven Manor, or knows of ye. There were eyes peering from dark windows in the village as the carriage passed."

Lucinda shivered. The image of curious eyes watching her in the night was not soothing, not after all she had just gone through.

Jenny hurried on in her high, thin voice. "No more'n a few months past, none in these parts had so much as heard yer name. Until the letter come. But Jenny knew. Jenny knows everything."

Lucinda felt a sickness in the pit of her stomach. It would seem that her father had not talked about her through the years, not rhapsodized about the precious child he had been forced to leave behind. She had not expected him to do so, but once or twice he could have said her name.

Her eyes burned. She blinked the tears away. Jenny was an old woman. She could be wrong.

"And the dog? You know him?"

"I cannot be sure. There's hounds enough that roam these parts."

"So how do you know he will keep me from harm? That he knows when danger is near?"

"He kept Blackthorne from his lustful intent, did he not?"

"You were watching?"

"Old Jenny is always watching." She lowered her voice to a broken whisper. "Beware the duke. He's a bad 'un. Ye'll not be wanting to meet the same fate as yer father."

"My father—" Lucinda began, but the old woman had already turned from her. Long, twisted fingers grasped the handle on the lantern, and she shuffled away, her bent back almost hiding the wild and wiry gray hair.

Lucinda was left in the dark. A cold fist clutched her heart. More than ever she felt alone. With all her being she longed for a bright sunny day, a field of wildflowers stretching before her, a carefree ride on her beloved mare.

Wanton or not, she would wear her hair loose and her heart would sing.

Instead, she stood in a secret-filled land in the dark doorway of a strange house with gloom at her back and unwelcome strangers before her, and no one in all the world in whom she could confide.

Foolishness. She must not give in to such weakness. Because she was alone, she must inevitably feel lonely on occasion. But it was a small price to pay for being beholden to no one, as she apparently now was. Especially a man. For the first time in her life she could truly take care of herself.

The dog whined and rubbed his damp nose against her hand.

"You're sleeping in my room, hound," she said. "It will be sort of like stabling a pony on the hearth, but I'll clean up after you if there's a need. The first thing I must do is find you a name. I'll be talking to you a great deal, I imagine, and an identity will make the conversation go easier."

Scrambling about the kitchen, feeling through strange drawers in the dark, she found a match and lit the larger end of the broken candle. Holding it aloft, she made her way back up the stairs.

No one followed, but she could imagine Gideon Blackthorne watching her in taunting silence and Jenny cackling dire warnings in her wake. Neither the man nor the woman played games. Everything they said and did was far, far too real.

Chapter Four

"There's those who say Jenny Patchell is a witch."

Mrs. Pickering set a pot of tea down firmly on the breakfast table.

"Not me, understand. I don't believe in such nonsense."

She glanced at Lucinda, then looked away, as if meeting her eyes brought too much strain.

"You're best off paying no mind to aught the woman says. We've long learned to ignore her in these parts. You're new and not aware of the way things are."

Lucinda refused to take offense, though it required effort. Being new, and also powerful, she brought change, which, she understood all too well, was not necessarily a welcome thing.

She did, however, grow weary of her inquiries being met with half answers and dire hints.

"What was she doing in the kitchen last night?"

"It was natural enough. Jenny lives at the manor. Most of the time. There are days and sometimes weeks when she disappears. Where she stays she never says, and we never ask."

"Why is she ever here?" Lucinda asked, determined this time not to be put off. She very much wanted to know about the woman who had confronted her with insinuations concerning her father and the duke. She had mentioned old Jenny's appearance as soon as she came downstairs to begin her day.

Gideon Blackthorne's visit she kept to herself.

Mrs. Pickering thought a moment. "Jenny's just here, that's all. She does the mending and helps when Cook's in a taking, even with those gnarled old fingers of hers. She's been here since long before I came, and that was . . . let me think . . . twelve years past."

She stared beyond Lucinda, her pale eyes seeming to see herself in a distant place and time—one that had been, if the solemnity in her expression meant anything, not a happy one.

"I was newly widowed and needy of employment. Very needy."

"And my father hired you."

"That he did." The solemnity died, and she

pulled herself up straight. "A good man, Lord Westcombe. He told me I could have a position at Craven Manor as long as he was around." She sniffed. "Of course, he's not around now."

"No," Lucinda said, "he is not around." It was something she could have repeated again and again since she was five.

Mrs. Pickering walked stiffly from the private dining parlor, returning shortly with a breakfast tray, an egg cup with toast at the side, and a pot of marmalade. It was the light breakfast Lucinda had requested when the housekeeper was in her room an hour earlier, serving a wakeup cup of tea.

Mrs. Pickering was nothing if not efficient. It must be an English trait. Lucinda knew so little about these people, though English blood ran in her veins.

She took a sip of tea. The heat burned her tongue.

"Did you have any children?"

Mrs. Pickering looked down at her in surprise.

"I meant no offense," Lucinda said. "I was just wondering. You spoke of being widowed, and I thought there might have been children. . . ."

Her voice trailed off, leaving unsaid the rest: children who had been left behind when the woman had to move on.

The housekeeper smoothed her skirt over her

narrow hips. "We were not so blessed." A note of sadness crept into her voice. "My late husband and I were in service from the time we wed, and it was enough for us."

"What about Mr. Fenton? Was he ever wed?"

"Not so as he ever said. Wouldn't make a hair's difference whether or no, he's been here since long before I came and is a good man. He knows this house better'n anyone who ever lived here, I'll be bound."

"I'm sure he does," Lucinda said hastily.

"And since you're inquiring, it's time you met Cook."

She bustled away and returned shortly with a tall, motherly-looking woman who, Lucinda noticed with both satisfaction and surprise, smiled at her pleasantly. Her dark hair, streaked with gray, was partially bound beneath a white cap; her brown eyes were settled amid crinkles that looked familiar to the smile. Middle fifties, Lucinda guessed, a few years older than Mrs. Pickering, though not nearly so gray. She wore an apron over a plain blue dress. The color was a relief from all the surrounding black.

Twisting a cloth in front of her rounded stomach, she curtsied.

"This is Mary Rigg, the coachman's wife and cook for Craven Manor," Mrs. Pickering said.

"Good morning, Mrs. Rigg. I hope I didn't take you from your chores."

"Oh, no, mum." The cook's eyes widened as she looked at the breakfast table. "You've scarce touched your food. I'll boil another egg. This one's grown cold."

"Please don't bother. The breakfast is fine."

Mrs. Rigg did not look convinced.

"I was telling Arthur, I'm sure the lass doesn't eat enough to keep a bird alive, that's what I said, being so thin and all. Of course, not too thin, but perhaps needing a little flesh on the bones. I got a peek at you when you come in early yesterday, waiting up for Arthur as I was."

She caught Mrs. Pickering's eye and fell silent.

"Could I ask you one favor?" Lucinda said. "Have you anything that might be appropriate to feed Baron?"

"Baron? Have you brought someone with you, mum? No one told me we was having guests, and him a member of the peerage and all."

"The dog," Mrs. Pickering said. She spoke with evident dislike. She had been most distressed to find him in her mistress's bedchamber when she served the morning tea, even though he had not shed or made a mess.

All in all, Lucinda thought, he must be far easier to care for than a peer.

"I'm sure we can find some scraps for him," Mrs. Rigg said. "Will you be wanting luncheon

57

at noon? When Lord Westcombe was about, it was his habit."

"If that's your routine, please. Noon will be fine."

"And tea at five?"

"Of course."

"If you'll wait a moment," Mrs. Pickering said when the cook had gone, "I'll get the account books. You'll be wanting to go over them as soon as possible."

"Not right now."

Lucinda thought of Jenny Patchell. It was time she got to what was weighing heavily on her mind.

"When did you know I existed?"

"I beg your pardon?" Mrs. Pickering made no attempt to hide her astonishment.

"When did you know Lord Westcombe had a daughter?"

The woman looked from right to left but not at her mistress. "I'm sure it was none of my business."

"Nevertheless, when did you know? Was it no more than a few months ago?"

"Jenny's been talking."

"It doesn't matter where I heard it. I simply want to know if it's true."

Mrs. Pickering finally looked at her. "Aye. We learned about you when the first letter came from the solicitors in London. We knew he had wed, but there was no mention of a child."

58

For the first time since Lucinda had arrived, the woman's voice was soft, as was the expression in her eyes.

"Lord Westcombe was not a man for talking, understand. He kept to the library when he was home, sometimes took his meals there, especially in the evening when there was no one else about."

"You've been here twelve years, you said."

"More or less. I'm not being exact, understand."

Twelve long years in which the sixth Viscount Westcombe could have talked about his wife and child at least once. He could have commented on his wife's death. Lucinda had made sure he got word. She would not have expected him to wear mourning clothes, but he could have acknowledged her passing in some other way.

She clasped her hands in her lap. The sickness she had felt last night when she talked to Jenny returned, along with the burning at the back of her eyes. She had thought her father could not hurt her ever again. He was dead and buried. Nothing could be done about the past.

She had been wrong.

She sighed. What she was feeling could be considered nothing but silly, inappropriate, and certainly uncalled for. Mrs. Pickering might think her father had been a good man, but his daughter saw him in a darker light.

She thrust herself away from the table. "If you've the time, I'd like a tour of the house now. We can look at the accounts later."

"If that is your wish."

The housekeeper left and in a few minutes returned with Fenton, as stiff and formal as ever. They began to the left of the entryway, walking through a drawing room crowded with dark, heavy furniture and bric-a-brac, then into a more sparsely decorated library.

In both rooms she longed to throw open the brocaded draperies, open the windows, air out the mustiness. Instead, she looked and nodded, asking few questions.

The drawing room held no hint of her father's having lived there, but in the library she got a small sense of him. His oak desk was wide and deep, his desk chair of leather and high-backed, both desk and chair wearing an air of frequent use. Another leather chair faced the brick fireplace. The scent of tobacco hung in the air. She pictured him, his features vague, in a smoking jacket, pipe in hand, staring into a roaring fire.

The most striking feature of the room was the bookshelves that lined the walls, some of them glass-covered, others open, all the volumes neatly arranged, some of them new, some, more interesting, worn and obviously well read.

"He stayed in here a great deal, didn't he?"

Neither Fenton nor Mrs. Pickering spoke for a minute.

"In the last year or so, yes," the housekeeper said, almost reluctantly. "Now that I think on it, since the time of his fiftieth birthday."

"Was he ailing?"

"Troubled, I would say. Though, understand, it was none of my concern."

"And should not be mentioned now," Fenton put in.

Mrs. Pickering looked as though she wanted to say more, but fell silent under the butler's sharp eye.

Lucinda studied the room once again. Both the desk and the books would bear a closer inspection, but some other time, when she was alone.

The tour continued. To the right of the entryway were the private dining parlor where she had been served breakfast, and beyond, a large dining room that could, according to Fenton, seat up to twenty-five guests and had, on more than one occasion, done exactly that.

At one time her father had entertained, though not in recent years, since he took to solitude. Had he done his entertaining lavishly? Did he toast his guests and good times? Did he have a special lady friend?

She turned abruptly from the room. Some questions were best left unasked and unanswered.

On the far side of the dining room lay the

kitchen, pantries, and a wine cellar, all of which she declined to investigate.

One flight up to the left was the Great Hall—"We call it the salon, though some insist otherwise," Mrs. Pickering said—and to the right, four bedchambers, including the one where she had been placed. Only the salon drew more than a cursory look. The floor was mosaic tile, the ceiling and fireplace elaborately stuccoed, reminding her of pictures she had seen from Italy. The room was, she had to admit, lovely.

"Your grandfather was fond of dances," Fenton said.

"Was he?"

"His portrait is in the family gallery," Fenton added, "if you would care to look. Not your father's, I regret. He postponed a sitting too long."

Fenton nodded toward a loft overlooking the far side of the Hall, access to which was provided by a corner stairway.

She shook her head. "What about the upper floor?"

The nursery and schoolroom, accommodations for the teacher and nanny, and rooms for the servants, she was told, including quarters for themselves.

"And Jenny Patchell?"

Mrs. Pickering sniffed. "Sometimes she stays up there. Other times, when she's about the manor, she chooses to sleep in one of the cottages on the grounds. Lord Westcombe gave her the freedom to choose, as, I believe, his father had before him. There's been no reason to arrange otherwise."

"We've more servants' quarters in the attic," Fenton said, "but they've long been closed off."

Not because of economic necessity, according to what Lucinda had been told, but at the whim of her father. He preferred to hire extra help as needed and keep the number of servants down to a minimum, choosing instead to concentrate his resources on his holdings in town. Or so the solicitors in London had said.

He must have been a practical man, ridding himself of all he considered unnecessary.

"Where is my father's bedchamber? Did I see it and not know?"

The housekeeper and butler glanced at one another.

"Lord Westcombe's private rooms are on the ground floor," Fenton said. "We were not certain you wanted to see them. They have been shut off since his . . . passing."

"They will not upset me. Do not forget that I hardly remember the man."

They led her back down the main stairs, past the drawing room and library, and into the far corner of the house. Throwing open the last door, Fenton stepped inside and lit an oil lamp on the wall immediately to his right. A yellow light flickered across the high, wide poster bed, the chests, the chairs, the heavy drawn draperies, all of which could be seen from the hall.

"His bedchamber and dressing room," the butler said, stepping aside for her to enter.

A sudden dread came over Lucinda. She had wanted to learn more about the distant man who had sired her, but now that she was about to do so, something, an eerie and undefinable sensation, made her wary.

She had no choice but to walk inside. Mrs. Pickering followed close on her heels.

"All his personal belongings, clothes and such," the housekeeper said, "have been distributed to his staff and to the poor, according to his will, you may be sure. We've made no decision on our own. Otherwise, the rooms are exactly as he left them the day . . . well, as you have been told, the day of his passing."

Only a short distance into the room, Lucinda felt as if a wall had been thrown up around her. The wariness became alarm. She could not move forward, but neither could she move back. Reaching out, she touched cold emptiness.

"What's happening?" she asked, her voice shrill.

Fenton and Mrs. Pickering glanced at one another.

"In what way, Miss Fairfax?" the butler asked. "You don't feel anything?"

"Nothing except that the place needs a good airing," Mrs. Pickering said.

Chilled, she rubbed at her arms and tried to calm herself.

"If I didn't know better, I would think he died in this room." She looked to Fenton for confirmation, and then to Mrs. Pickering.

"Lord Westcombe was brought here," Fenton said, "but he was beyond knowing or caring what was done to him."

"You're overtired," the housekeeper said with a shake of her head. "We should not have shown you so much."

"I'm not tired. I'm . . ."

She had no words to describe how she felt. Threatened, perhaps; crowded by the presence of forces unseen. But that was impossible. She did not believe in ghosts.

Yet there was definitely something in the room that could not be seen, something—or someone—that had been nowhere else in the house. Unable to breathe, she turned and hurried past the two blocking the exit into the hallway.

The change was immediate, warm and welcoming in comparison to where she had just been.

She drew a deep breath. "I'm sorry. I don't know what came over me. You felt nothing different in there?"

The two looked at her almost pityingly, as if grief over losing a beloved father had suddenly strained her emotions and good sense.

They could not be more wrong.

Suddenly everything became too much. The duke last night, and Jenny; then today viewing the way her father had lived while she and her mother, and finally just she, struggled to get along.

And now his ghost. She could put no other word to describe the presence she had felt.

Suddenly knowing more about her father went beyond curiosity; it became an imperative. Someday she would have to go back into his private room. But not today.

"I would like to see where he died."

Both servants stared at her in astonishment.

"You speak of Lord Westcombe?" Fenton said.

"Oh, Miss Fairfax," Mrs. Pickering pleaded, "that's not a safe place for you to go."

"My father walked there often, did he not?"

"Yes, but he was used to the moors and the steep scar," Fenton said. "And you see what happened to him."

"Is it far?"

"A brisk thirty-minute walk if you know the way."

"Describe the path. If he went there often, surely there is such a thing."

Both housekeeper and butler continued to protest. Lucinda was not of a mind to listen.

"He fell from a high point overlooking the river on a misty night, isn't that right? I've got a clear day to see it. You can't guarantee when I'll have one again. Besides, I'm used to going about by myself." She gave her ultimate argument: "I'll take Baron. Nothing will happen to me."

Half an hour later, her warm broadcloth cloak wrapped around her and her sturdiest boots on her feet, she and Baron set out on her mission. The dog trotted on ahead, as if he knew her destination, sniffing the ground to the right and left of the path as it wound across the rolling, rocky landscape, darting to a distant tree when the opportunity arose to lift a leg, then running to rejoin her if she got too far ahead.

It was not a joyful journey, yet she felt her spirits rise because she was out of doors and there was no dampness in the air. And she was far, far away from her father's chamber. The longer she walked, the more foolish she felt about her reaction to his room.

Gray clouds drifted in patches across the pale sky, and she got a glimpse or two of the sun. This was ordinary. It soothed her like a balm.

Her hair was bound beneath the hood of her cloak. She fought the urge to set it free.

You'll be taken for wanton if you are not careful.

Gideon Blackthorne's voice wrapped around her, and his image stood before her on the path. His warnings, his touches, the sense of him as his head bent low to hers came in a rush.

She slowed her step, lest she catch up to the image. Squeezing her eyes closed, she opened them to find him gone. But she could not feel relief. Why was he tormenting her? Except as a curiosity, he could not find her interesting.

Could it have anything to do with her father's death?

Absurd. Until she got to Yorkshire, there had been no hint that his fall was anything other than an accident.

She hurried her pace. The terrain gradually altered, becoming more uneven, rockier, with strands of trees to right and left, small forests of scattered evergreens, a few trees in autumnal hues, some of them already bare in the early autumn, their naked branches twisted in the air.

Breaking through one such forest, she walked on twenty yards and found herself standing at the edge of a high cliff, looking down at the River Craven, which ran shallowly over a rocky bed twenty feet below. This must be the scar to which Fenton had referred.

The river looked small compared to the rivers of home, but through the centuries it had been powerful enough to carve out the gorge.

There was no path leading down to the water. Instead, the steep cliffside was studded with huge boulders and smaller rocks, stubborn evergreen shrubbery clinging to what little soil could be found. It would have been a nasty fall.

Two scenes assailed her: the one before her and the one in her mind.

Whirling from the edge, she covered her face. It had been night, the mist falling, and no one to answer a cry for help. What had brought him here? Was it merely a need for fresh air as he had reportedly told Fenton before he left? Had a troubled mind sent him out of doors?

Or had it been something more sinister, like a summons from a powerful neighbor? The possibility that he had been murdered would not leave her mind. Why was she here on this cliff? What had drawn her to this dreadful place? Was it her father's spirit forcing her to repeat his fatal mistake?

No. She did not believe such spirits existed. Neither were there ghosts. If she reminded herself often enough of those beliefs, she might feel them in her heart.

The dog growled. Lucinda jumped, and her heart caught in her throat. Lowering her hands, she forced herself to look through the trees. The Devil Duke stood in the shadows, watching her.

And here she was, close to the ridge where her father had met his death.

Gideon's presence made no more sense than did hers. He was out in the daylight and he was on foot, contradicting what she knew of him.

But that did not make him seem less dangerous. She ought to run, but that might spur him after her, or so she told herself. The truth was she had no urge to separate herself from him. Not right away.

"Your Grace," she called out, and then, she knew not why, "Gideon."

Slowly he shook his head, but he gave no other response.

In the distance he looked almost insubstantial, but that had not been her sense of him last night, not after her first glimpse. When he'd walked toward her in the garden, she had never seen a man so pulsing with life.

This time it was she who took the step that would close the yards separating them. Baron stayed close by her side, his growl like a rough hum in his throat.

"The river winds through Blackthorne property, doesn't it?" she said loudly. "Am I on my land or yours?"

His answer was a motion for her to draw closer. Something in the gesture, something in his silence, stopped her progress. But only for a moment. He drew her to him as if she were bound by a leash. Reason told her she had a right to approach him. He was an English nobleman, and she his new, if temporary, neighbor. But it was not their adjoining properties that drew her on; it was something darker, something she could not name.

The dog gave her confidence. Once again she began to walk forward, no calmer than she had been a moment before, but more determined.

"Maybe you did not understand me," she said when she stood at the edge of the trees, a dozen feet from the shadowed duke.

He gave no response.

"Is something wrong?"

"Nothing," he said in a hoarse whisper that barely carried to her. "And everything."

The dim light in which he stood kept her from seeing his eyes, but she could picture them, black as his cape, and watchful.

"You should not have come here."

Again he spoke in a whisper, as if he did not want them to be overheard.

"Why not? Why do I get so many warnings and never a reason behind them?"

He looked at her for a long moment, then with his usual dramatic flair, whirled and walked deeper into the trees. She stared at his retreating figure until he disappeared.

Running after him would be another act of foolishness, though that was exactly what she wanted to do. The impulse almost made her laugh. Because of her position in life, that of a poor spinster cousin, she had always been a little timid. And always, always, reason ruled.

She would not be timid again. But she could not forsake all reason.

With a sigh, she made her own retreat, walking thoughtfully along the cliff's edge, then, quickening her step, hurrying toward Craven Manor. She was late for Cook's noontime

71

luncheon. And she had to work up courage to follow through on the plan that had formed in her mind.

Gideon Blackthorne seemed more accessible by night than by day, if accessible was what she wanted him to be. Something about him called to her in a way no man had ever done. It was not his darkness alone, or the rumors about him. More than anything else, it was the torture in his eyes. And, she admitted, the gentle manner in which he had touched her hair.

They were reasons she could never reveal to another living soul.

When everyone was settled down for the night, she would go once again to the garden, this time with a candle protected from the wind. There she would wait for him. When he came, she would ask him about his curious behavior today, saying it was the reason she was there just as he had said on his first visit that he had come to apologize.

Both of them lied, but she was no more certain of his motivation than she was of her own.

One more thing. She would leave Baron in her room.

She shivered at the thought, not entirely because she knew the potential danger of isolation with Gideon. There were other possibilities to consider. The loss of virtue, for one—the willing loss.

A week ago she would have sworn such an event was impossible. And so it still must be.

Yet she would wait for him. Eventually he would come.

Chapter Five

All went as she'd thought it would; the garden was deserted, the night brightened by a half-moon, this time its light undiffused by mist. With a lantern in her hand, she watched as Gideon Blackthorne stepped from the darkness at the far end of the garden, a shadow moving out of a shadow, until he was far enough along the path for the moonlight to grace him with its gentle force.

Slowly he walked toward her, in the elegant, confident way he had, the cape scarcely moving, his riding boots silent against the ground. She stood and waited for him to approach, hoping she had made the right choice in planning the evening as she had.

In the hours since she had last seen him, she'd decided that no lonely spinster's fantasies motivated her to be with him again. She wanted to understand him, the way he reacted to her, the way she reacted to him. She could not leave Yorkshire without satisfying this curiosity, although curiosity was an inadequate word for the obsession that had taken hold of her.

"Have you come to apologize again?" she asked when he was no more than ten feet away.

"Of course. Of that you should have no doubt, Lucinda of the night."

Ah, the voice, and the English intonation he put on every word. Especially her name. It was enough to send a susceptible woman to her knees. She managed to stand.

"I most humbly apologize," he said. "But you might tell me what I have done that has given you offense."

"I was referring to this morning."

He hesitated, and she could sense a sudden tension in him. Strange that she could do so when she had rarely spent much time in the company of men. She knew so little of their personal ways.

But Gideon Blackthorne was different, and in his company, so was she.

"What about this morning perturbs you?" he asked.

"In the woods by the scar. Where my father had his accident."

76

"Ah, yes. There."

"I know I'm not supposed to ask about what happened to him, but I wanted to see the place where it occurred. You surprised me, standing deep in the trees. Surely you remember."

He took a step forward. "Of course. I remember everything about you. You looked fragile, standing too near the cliff's edge."

"Why did you barely speak? Why did you keep your distance? When I walked toward you, after you had beckoned, you turned and walked away."

Another step.

His eyes narrowed. "I must also remember that it is disturbing for you if I retreat when you are near."

She stirred uneasily. "You put an interpretation on my words I did not mean."

"I doubt it. You are here, are you not?" He glanced around her. "And without your protector."

She had no response. Baron was locked safely in her room. In all her considerations of the meeting, she had not thought of how obvious such a precaution would appear.

She was grateful that she had not worn her hair loose, as she had for a time considered. She was not wanton. She was . . . curious.

"I have only to call and someone will come." She hoped she spoke the truth.

"But the fallacy there is you must choose when and whether to do so."

"I will give you warning."

"And I will heed whatever it is you want."

If his words were meant to give comfort, they had the opposite effect. She dropped her gaze from his, fearing he might read in her eyes the stirrings she did not want him to see.

Turning the conversation onto a new track seemed her best defense.

"You have been neighbors with my father for a long time, have you not?"

If he caught her ploy, he gave no sign.

"All my life a Fairfax has lived in Craven Manor. And after a few months' absence, one does so again."

She almost told him it would not be forever, but it seemed unfair not to reveal her plans first to her father's loyal staff.

"A very different Fairfax," she said. "One not in the least English."

"Though by blood you are English as much as American."

Somehow he had turned her simple question—designed to learn more about him—into an interrogation concerning herself. Gideon Blackthorne's effect on her grew stranger: she did not mind his manipulation.

"I'm a Yankee through and through," she said with pride. "I knew very little of my father. He had no influence on me."

"Your mother? She is dead, too, is she not?"

"A fever took her seven years ago."

"Your voice softens when you speak of her."

"I loved her very much."

"But not so much your father."

"As I said, I knew little of him. He left when I was only five," she said, then added, as if giving a reason for his departure, "I was a sickly child."

Never before had she thought of her condition as an excuse for him, and she did not think so now. Still, she had made a point of mentioning it.

"And tonight? Do you remain sickly? I think not."

Another two steps, and he was standing before her as he had done the previous night, the devil lines deep between his eyes.

"No," she said, her voice weak, "I'm not sickly now."

"And you are not a child."

Was that a smile that played on his lips? Surely not. She sensed he was a man who rarely gave in to the gentler emotions.

"You don't care much for the English, do you?" he asked.

"I've been given no reason to."

"Then I must change your mind. And men? What about men?"

"It must be clear to you that my father abandoned his wife and daughter to claim his Yorkshire inheritance. Perhaps I should defend him to you—one should not speak ill of the dead—but honesty keeps me from doing so."

"Please believe me when I say I understand."

"I doubt it. As for other men, my mother was born to wealth, but her father squandered everything on horses, cards, wherever he could place a wager. My grandmother apologized for him, saying it was an illness. Perhaps it was, but a costly one. I can make no such apology for William Fairfax. He did what he did of his own free will."

Why she was telling him so much, she had no idea. When she began to answer his questions, she had not meant to, but once she had started, the details of her pathetic past came out in a steady flow. It seemed right and natural, and, strangest of all, he was proving to be a sympathetic listener. It was a trait she had not seen in him before.

Or perhaps he used a ploy of his own. Perhaps he sweetened her with sympathy to take away whatever fears and inhibitions she might have concerning him.

If so, his ploy was working very well.

"Please forgive me for burdening you with my story. I do not feel sorry for myself. On the contrary, all that has happened to me has made me strong."

"And desirable."

Her heart rose into her throat.

"You go too far."

"And yet not far enough. Have you no man waiting for you in this United States of yours?"

"I broke off a betrothal after my father died and I decided to travel to England."

There was no need to explain that the betrothal had been arranged, that her not-quite beloved was twenty years her senior, his only interest a passion for getting a younger woman in his bed. Even her matchmaker cousin had not bothered to deny it.

"He must be desolate to lose such a prize."

Before she'd left, he was already courting a woman younger than she. It was another explanation she kept to herself.

"He survived."

"Then he is a fool."

Lucinda suffered a momentary loss of words. "Do not make light of me, Your Grace."

Whatever pleasantness had been on his face darkened to something far different.

"Do not call me that."

"I'm not used to titles. Did I say something wrong?"

"Not as far as the world is concerned. But here, in the night, it is just the two of us. I mean you no harm, that you can believe. But I would very much like you to call me Gideon. And I will call you Lucinda."

"As neighbors."

"As man and woman."

To her embarrassment, the lantern she held in her hand shook. She lowered it to the ground, where it cast an upward light on his strong features, giving him still more the look of a devil.

"Are other Englishmen as bold as you?"

"We are what our lives make of us. No matter where we live. You have already said yours made you strong."

"It also made me cautious."

"If you truly believe that, you do not know yourself. Admittedly, I have spoken boldly to you, yet you have not fled. And there have been times when you have spoken boldly to me."

He put a hand upon her shoulder. The touch was light and warm, and she felt his strength and something else, almost a trembling that did not go with any other part of him.

If this kind of touch was part of his plan, he was very clever indeed. She would do much to still the trembling. It had started another kind of trembling inside her, one that, like his, ought to be stilled.

When his head bent, once again she lifted her lips to him. The darkness whirled around her. This was a fairy tale, and she a princess. Nothing could harm the princess in such a story, certainly not the prince.

The lips that brushed hers were not of fancied royalty, but of a flesh-and-blood man. Her first kiss was not a disappointment. Light as it was, and warm and damp, it shook her to her toes.

She placed her palms against his chest, covered by cape and shirt but still solid against her touch.

She was not a princess. Such creatures did not feel the earthy, primitive emotions that were clutching at her, a swirl of eagerness and desperation that blended into panicky need. The strange, arousing feelings spread through her like liquid warmth, and she leaned into the kiss.

He broke away, leaving her dizzy, and for a moment held her against him, lightly, in the way he had touched her shoulder. This time she did not lean into him, but waited until she could stop shivering and draw a deep breath.

The panic remained, but the need for his touch died a quick death. She wanted to fall through a crack in the ground and never be seen again.

He stood back from her, hands at his sides, leaving her to steady herself. She forced her gaze once again to his.

"For the third time in our brief acquaintance, I must apologize. If I have been less than fervent before in expressing my regrets, believe me that I am not so now."

"There is no need for apology."

"You are wrong. I should be a man of honor." His tone was bitter. "I have proven once again that I am not."

"It was a very light kiss," she said, as if she

were experienced in such intimacies. "You barely touched me."

She amazed herself, defending him as she did.

His look was worldly, and regretful, as if he were having to rebuke a child.

"But I wanted to do much, much more, Lucinda. You are right to distrust men."

With a bow, he turned and hurried down the path, once again a shadow, disappearing into the darker shadows that bordered the far end of the run-down garden.

Cold shame crept in where moments ago warmth had pulsed. In what had passed between them, it was not the man who should have talked of honor, or rather the lack of it. It was the woman's place.

She had told him she would warn him if he went too far, and then call out for someone to join them. And what had she done? Pressed her lips as firmly as she knew how against his.

Honor had not been a consideration. Like him, she had wanted much, much more. A loss of virtue would not have been a tragedy. Innocent though she was, she suspected it would have brought great joy.

Earlier in the evening—could it be so recent as a half hour ago?—she had told herself she was no lonely spinster fantasizing over a dark and incredibly arousing man. But that was exactly how she saw herself now.

And so must he.

She had not understood the afterwards of such a tryst, and the recriminations she would heap on herself even if he were the only other person in the world who knew what had happened between them.

Picking up the lantern, she turned to go inside. This time, Jenny did not meet her at the door with more vague warnings of a dreadful fate. It was the one thing about the night she did not regret.

Hurrying up the back stairs, she opened the door of the dressing room to find Baron watching her with reproach.

"You're right," she told him as she threw more coals on the dying fire. "Why don't you bite me on the ankle? I deserve far worse."

His answer was to settle his bulk once again at the edge of the hearth, his deep, wise eyes focused on her.

Quickly she changed into her nightgown and crawled beneath the covers, her fingers on lips that still felt their first touch of a man. For a moment she could forget herself and think about that man, who was turning her life upside down.

More than ever, she felt convinced that Gideon Blackthorne was a troubled soul. The proof—probably too strong a word—lay in the tension that took hold of him, a tension an unsophisticated woman such as herself could hardly arouse, and in the bitterness with which he had made his final apology.

That she had done nothing to ease his mind brought a feeling of distress to mingle with her shame. Women were natural nurturers. And she had wanted to nurture him.

How he would laugh if he knew.

Tonight must be the last of their secret meetings. Never again would she enter the garden after dark.

Her last thought as she drifted into sleep was that he had not explained his behavior of the morning. He had apologized, but he had said nothing else.

By morning she had decided to take her long-delayed trip into town. She had reasons aplenty for not wanting to go, but sitting around brooding was doing her absolutely no good. She had people to see and things to do; she had postponed her duties long enough.

She called herself up short. Nothing in her timing showed she had been remiss. She had been in Yorkshire less than a week. Somehow it seemed she had been here a lifetime.

Starting down early to order the carriage, she heard voices in the entryway below, their anxious tones obvious even from where she stood. It was Mrs. Pickering and John Fenton in conversation, talking low but not so quiet their voices did not carry. She stopped on the landing of the front stairway to listen, though she knew it was not an honorable thing to do. She could not see them, and they could not see her.

"He was here again last night, I tell you." Mrs. Pickering fairly hissed out the words. "She met him with lantern in hand. And without the hound."

"You saw them?"

"Aye. He touched her, too, though as to what purpose I could not see from my window."

"I think we can assume his purpose," Fenton said.

"If so, he was quick about it."

Lucinda covered her mouth with her hand, fearful the horror she was feeling might come out in a cry.

"It is not His Grace who should concern us. What is our new mistress up to?"

"No good," Mrs. Pickering said, "for any of us. You don't suppose she has her eye set on the duke as father to the son she needs, do you? It's too preposterous, but it's just the sort of thing an American might think of."

"She would be more likely to succeed if she chose one of our queen's royal princes," Fenton said.

Mrs. Pickering chuckled softly; then her voice turned harsh. "Whatever her purpose, we were right to fear her presence. We must proceed cautiously."

They moved away from the entryway,

through the door that would take them to the dining rooms and on to the kitchen. Lucinda held her place, drawing a slow, deep breath. When she was a child, her mother had told her that nothing good would come of eavesdropping. Her mother had been right.

A new disquiet took hold of her, one sharper, more invasive than the other worries had been.

. . . a father to the son she needs.

The Devil Duke? The idea was enough to send her into hysterics.

We must proceed cautiously.

Proceed with what? Her head throbbed as she struggled to come up with an answer that made sense. Nothing occurred.

Putting on a face that was as untroubled as she could manage, she went down to breakfast, determined as soon as possible to get out of the house she had never wanted to enter in the first place. More than ever, she felt that she did not belong.

And now she knew without a doubt that neither was her presence desired.

Chapter Six

"Oh, Miss Fairfax, you cannot be going into town." Mrs. Pickering set a pot of tea on the breakfast table. "It would be a terrible mistake."

Lucinda looked up at her in surprise. She had been prepared for subtle difficulties from the housekeeper, but not outright opposition. If the woman truly planned to proceed cautiously, as she had so furtively whispered not fifteen minutes past, she had a strange way of going about it.

"Is something wrong with Rigg?" Lucinda asked. "Or with the horse Bessie?"

Mrs. Pickering sniffed. "I beg pardon, Miss Fairfax. I spoke too bluntly. I meant you shouldn't go unchaperoned. It's not my place to interfere, but you not being familiar with our ways, I thought you should know people will talk."

"I sailed from New York alone."

"And a brave thing it was, I'm sure. But this is Yorkshire. We're a different sort of place from your country."

Lucinda agreed wholeheartedly.

Knife in hand, she cracked her boiled egg sharply and reached for the salt.

"People will just have to think I'm an undisciplined American."

It was, she knew, a charge the woman would believe.

Within the hour, under a soft gray sky, she was settled in the carriage and under way. Rigg set Bessie into a fast clip. The ride into the village was accomplished in far less time than it had taken to reach Craven Manor, after the near disaster of that first early morning arrival in Yorkshire.

Just as Lucinda had kept closed the draperies of her chamber balcony, she averted her eyes when the carriage rolled past the view of Blackthorne Hall in the distance. It was but half past nine in the morning and already she had more to contend with than she could manage without a turreted castle stirring up unwanted memories.

Was she truly turning into a coward? As far

as the Duke of Ravenswood was concerned, most definitely yes.

At her request, Rigg helped her down in front of the bank, which stood apart from the row of small specialty shops that fronted on High Street, the main thoroughfare of Hummersby Bridge. Were eyes on her, peering out of those dark shop windows? Probably.

Were they friendly eyes? According to Mrs. Pickering, people would be scandalized to see her all alone. The coachman, it would appear, did not count for much.

After identifying herself to the clerk, she was immediately escorted to the office of Carlyle Winston, the trustee of her estate. The half-dozen customers stopped what they were doing and watched—subtly, of course. It would be rude to gawk openly.

The same feeling she had experienced in the London law office overcame her now. In her plain cloak and bonnet and with her farm-country ways, she was very much out of place.

Winston met her at his office door. He was a tall and stately man of middle age, with a large nose and thin lips, his short brown hair neatly trimmed, as were his side whiskers and small moustache. From his chestnut-colored frock coat to his highly polished side-buttoned shoes, he showed himself to be a man of substance, one whom any customer could trust.

He greeted her with a warm smile and a firm handshake.

"My dear Miss Fairfax, what a pleasure this is. You are as lovely as I have heard, if you will permit me to say so." His voice was loud so that everyone could hear.

She had no idea how to respond except to ask that he keep to the truth. It made trust come so much easier.

She limited herself to a nod.

"Do come in," he said.

She took a deep breath. When she invaded his inner sanctum, she would be taking the last step in establishing all of this as real, all of it as official. And that would be true whether she stayed here in Yorkshire or in New York or moved to the South Seas.

If she wanted to be prideful and deny what her father had arranged for her, now was the time.

She thought of her mother and walked inside. She did this for Anne Fairfax more than for herself. The door closed with a thud behind her.

"Mr. Winston," she said and cleared her throat. "I know you have much to tell me. And I would very much like to put a few questions to you."

An hour later Lucinda walked out of the office in a state of shock. She was rich. By any standards of which she was aware, she already had enough money to last the rest of her life. And that did not include future income from the thousand acres surrounding Craven Manor and from the china factory a great-grandfather had started in town.

She had not wanted to be an heiress; she had felt guilty because her mother had been denied an easy life; she had not wanted to honor her father by accepting his wishes as laid out in his will.

But that was before she knew the amount in question. If she denied the bequest, all the funds and property would go to the Crown. It was not something that she as an American was prepared to allow. Nor would her mother want her to. Already she had lost her husband to the British. Victoria should get nothing more from her.

Lucinda sighed. She was rich, far more so than the solicitors had indicated. Or perhaps it was that their legal jargon had confused her. Or that she was already confused after enduring the long journey and suffering the bustling streets of London.

Whatever the case, she had not been prepared for what Carlyle Winston had to present.

If there were any bank customers watching her departure, she did not see them. All she could think of was that her father had been hoarding money for years, most intensely the past two. Combined with the Fairfax family fortune he had inherited at his father's death, all that he had saved was now in her name.

It did not matter that she could sell none of his property. She could bankrupt all of it if such were her choice. Not that she would, of course— she was far too frugal, too sensible—but she had the power to do so if she chose.

It was a heady thought.

In a daze, she emerged onto the sidewalk outside the bank and promptly collided with a very solid gentleman, sending his towering top hat skittering into the street. In an instant she came back to earth.

He hastened to retrieve the hat, then hurried back to her side.

"I'm sorry—" she began.

"Please, there is no need to apologize. I am the one at fault for not looking where I was going."

She heard the smile in his voice and looked up into a pair of brown eyes as warm as a puppy's. His hair, worn longer than the banker's, was, like hers, fair, though his was more golden. His face was clean-shaven, his features even. He was one of the handsomest men she had ever seen.

She put his age at not much above hers. It was impossible not to warm to his friendly countenance.

"I do not, however, apologize for our accident," he said. "Otherwise I should have missed meeting the lovely Miss Fairfax, newly arrived from the colonies."

The compliment flowed smoothly, sounding far more sincere than Carlyle Winston's similar remark. Lucinda was charmed. There was no other word for it. He was so filled with open goodwill and humor, she could do nothing but smile right back at him.

In her rare good mood—after feeling troubled and gloomy for far too long—she could not imagine a more perfect person to meet. He seemed . . . simple, though the description had nothing to do with intelligence. He did not look tortured and mocking, he did not send chills up and down her spine or create heat in her belly, and he most certainly did not inspire her to throw her arms around his neck.

He made her smile. Good. At the moment, she had much about which to smile.

"Allow me to introduce myself," he said with a bow. "Sheridan Pettifore. Sir Sheridan, please be informed. It pleases my mother very much to claim the distinction of a baronetcy, and I must admit it pleases me. You smile. Do I amuse you?"

"A little. Is that all right?"

"It's perfect. It's what I do best. Amuse others, I mean."

"You live in Hummersby Bridge?"

"The family home is a short ride from the village, in the opposite direction from Craven Manor."

"You seem to know a great deal about me."

"Everyone does. You've been the primary topic of gossip since your father's dreadful fall."

She was glad he did not soften his voice or try to extend condolences, as Carlyle Winston had done. The banker had openly admitted that her father had not once mentioned her existence until a few months ago when he made out his will. She had assured him that his sympathy was unnecessary.

Sir Sheridan glanced past her, then up and down the street.

"If you're looking for a chaperon, I don't have one," she said.

"Shocking."

"So said my housekeeper this morning when I ordered the carriage."

"You need a lady's maid," he said. "No protests. You most certainly do. Otherwise you will be taken as a savage."

"It's possible I already am."

"Let's not give the gossips more grist for their mill, as they say, although I'm never quite sure what the expression means. Mother will help. She can send you candidates from which you may choose."

"I'm not sure—"

"I am, if you will forgive my forwardness. Should I ever journey to America, you can advise me in much the same way."

Try as she might, Lucinda could not picture the baronet on the farm in New York.

"In the meantime," he said, "might I offer you a spot of tea? Only a few steps away there's a tea shop I think you will find quaint."

After the barest nod, she found herself in a small room with frilly linen cloths on the table and matching curtains at the window, and a wide-eyed waitress who hovered very close. Sir Sheridan ordered two servings of tea and a plate of assorted cakes and waved the woman away.

"Don't reveal any dark secrets," he warned. "We're sure to be overheard."

"I promise I won't."

She had thought she was not hungry, not after all that had happened to her last night and this morning. But in the jovial company of Sheridan Pettifore—Sir Sheridan—she became ravenous and consumed more than her share of the cakes.

He watched her and occasionally reached for one of his own. At the same time, he filled her in on the gossip of the village—about the farmers, the squires, the powerful men, the women who stayed in the background but exerted an equally powerful force. All the while he spoke he was seemingly oblivious to anyone who might be listening.

She remembered the dour words of the banker Carlyle Winston, about the demonstrations for the rights of women raising rancor among the men in England. The comment had come when he was elaborating on all she owned and the rarity of such an inheritance being passed on to a daughter, and on the possibility of her wielding power as a result.

It did not matter that she was an only child, the lone direct heir. By custom if not by law, the bulk of the estate should have gone to Lord Westcombe's distant cousin, now the seventh Lord Westcombe, a very wealthy man in his own right.

Sir Sheridan seemed not to mind in the least the possibility of a woman in control.

In truth, he did not seem to mind anything, which added to his charm. She was thinking how pleasant he was. And how wonderful it was to be mindless for a time.

"For a small place, Hummersby Bridge certainly provides a great deal to talk about," she said.

"Every place does, if you scratch beneath the surface. Bear in mind, I do not scratch deeply, but only so far as it interests me. One must somehow pass the time."

"Can I add to your store of gossip?"

"Please do. It's what I live for."

She leaned close. His handsome features settled into serious interest.

"I'm rich."

"Of course you are."

"I mean very rich."

"You did not know? I had heard—and do not

ask where, because I do not remember—that Lord Westcombe had become practically a miser in recent years. He used to give dinners, rather elaborate ones for dozens of guests, but they came to a stop."

"You didn't happen to hear what brought on the change? I asked Mr. Winston, but he could not give me an answer. He said my father had no known confidant."

"This is true. Whatever the cause of his change, it was a secret."

"As was his American daughter."

"We knew he had married while he was abroad, but the status of that marriage was a subject never mentioned. Trust me, Miss Fairfax, if it had been, I would have heard."

"I'm sure that is so."

His face brightened. "I have an idea. You need to celebrate. And you simply must meet the people of your village. Have you considered giving a soiree?"

"A party? No. Such a thing hadn't occurred to me."

"Let it play in your mind. We haven't had such a gathering since Rebecca Atterbury held a ball last spring when she came out of mourning for her late, unbeloved spouse."

"I'm supposed to be in mourning, too, remember? A ball is out of the question."

Sir Sheridan's high, smooth brow furrowed. "Ah, yes, there is that. A year is the accepted period for a parent, and yours has been gone only half that time." He thought a minute. "But you were not very close—"

"We were estranged."

The smile returned. "Then six months ought to do. I was thinking only of a modest reception, an assembly, an evening of introducing yourself to your new neighbors and letting them do the same to you. You can't expect everyone to barrel into you on the sidewalk of High Street."

"They could not be so fortunate, right?"

He caught her small smile. "Right. I must add there are many who have been dying to call on the young American who has suddenly appeared in our midst."

"The rich young American."

"Money always helps. Rebecca has been interested most of all. I warned her we must give you time to catch your breath. Life here must seem very strange."

A pair of watchful black eyes swam in Lucinda's mind, eyes very different from the friendly ones regarding her now.

"Strange? You have no idea how strange."

She considered the soiree suggestion. Her residence at Craven Manor was temporary and did not require such an undertaking. Yet she could not help thinking of the only social gatherings she had attended since reaching her majority: rare dinners for neighboring farmers and their wives, held in her cousin's dark dining room, the talk devoted to weather and crops. The prospect before her was as different as onions from daffodils.

Sir Sheridan went on prattling about whom she should invite and the entertainment that could be provided without shocking the doyennes of the county. Before she knew it, she had agreed to his fast-developing plans.

His eyes grew hooded, alerting her to serious matters to come.

"Something is wrong," she said.

"Perhaps. The guest list suggests another problem. I have yet to mention our most notorious resident. Surely you have heard about our Devil Duke."

Lucinda set her cup into its saucer, lest it begin to shake.

"On the train coming down, there were comments made."

"His reputation has spread beyond these moors. I myself have heard him spoken of in London."

She tried to keep her response to a nod. Under no condition should she question Sir Sheridan about Gideon Blackthorne. It was unworthy of her to talk about him when he was not present, and especially to give the impression they had not met. Reason and ethical concerns ought to keep her quiet.

Reason and ethics were not enough.

"I heard that he was dangerous," she said.

"No one bothered to explain in what way."

Her response was not in the form of a question, but the query was certainly implied. All right, she was unworthy. It went along with lacking honor, a flaw she had exhibited with the Duke of Ravenswood more than once.

"He shuns the world beyond his estate."

"That hardly makes him dangerous. I might do so, too, if I owned as much land as he."

"Fifty thousand acres. He rides about when most folk are snug in their beds, like a creature from a darker world, for what purpose God—or perhaps I should say the devil—only knows. And, too, while he has a bailiff, he serves as his own land agent and thus handles all his income himself. My dear Miss Fairfax, while you may not know it, such a condition is totally unacceptable."

Lucinda thought Blackthorne's actions made him seem conscientious and responsible. It was the first positive trait she had connected to him . . . other than the way he looked and the way he kissed.

She sighed. She simply had to quit thinking such thoughts.

"According to Carlyle Winston," she said, "we share this bailiff, as well as a half-dozen tenant farmers. I'm to meet with the bailiff this week, if it can be arranged."

She was also supposed to meet with Hudson Smedley, who ran the china factory, though that was an appointment the banker thought might be more difficult to set up.

Sir Sheridan shuddered. "When you meet with the bailiff, we can hope His Grace is nowhere around."

"Yes, we can hope." The man had no idea of the sincerity of her words.

Sir Sheridan was not done with the Devil Duke.

"He even refuses to take his seat in Parliament. He remains in Yorkshire year round instead of going to London from January to July, as any respectable peer knows one must."

"Is any of that really evil?"

"Frankly, no, though it goes against custom and we're a country that lives by its rules, written or otherwise. Far worse is the rumor that he killed a man. Shot him down, is the talk in the pub, though no body was ever found."

"How did such a rumor get started?"

"Who knows? I can assure you that for all my faults, I have never openly created a false story and passed it on. But there are those who swear it is so."

"Who was the victim? I mean the supposed victim."

"A derelict, a trespasser on his land. He had been in Hummersby Bridge asking for work, then declared he was going out to the country. He had word His Grace was hiring."

"He wanted work? That was all?"

"Several of the tavern regulars heard him declare so. Of that, there can be no doubt. He was never seen again, though one or two men offered to buy him a drink if he returned to report on what was happening on His Grace's land. The man was not, you may be sure, one to pass up such an offer."

"The death is still just speculation."

"Shots were heard one night by a passerby on the road. It was far too late for hunters to be about, and there are no poachers fool enough to go on Blackthorne land. And then there came the sound of a horse galloping fast, away from the road in the direction of Blackthorne Hall. It's slender evidence, I know, but the fact remains the derelict was never again seen."

Lucinda fell into a silence. She remembered the hints that perhaps Gideon had been involved in her father's death. She had questioned the banker about the possibility that the fall had not been an accident, carefully avoiding the use of anyone's name. Whether it was murder or suicide she had in her mind, Winston had appeared shocked that she would think of such a possibility.

But she had gotten the impression that his shock, like his compliment, was not entirely sincere.

"And then there are the rumors about women," Sir Sheridan said.

Lucinda picked at the crumbs on her plate and remained silent.

"They say His Grace has by-blows scattered like sheep across the countryside."

"By-blows?" she casually asked, as if she did not care.

"Children. If you will pardon me for being rather crude, bastard offspring left to fend for themselves." Sir Sheridan shuddered. "I am admittedly a shallow man, but even I would not do such as that."

The fact that women would have a weakness for Gideon Blackthorne came as no surprise, nor that he would take advantage of them. Suddenly the joy went out of the morning. Through the tea shop window, even the sky appeared a darker gray.

"I really must be going," she said. "Thank you very much for the tea."

"Have I distressed you in some way?"

Sir Sheridan might be shallow, but he was not, she noticed, insensitive.

She said the first thing that came into her mind.

"It's just that I suddenly remembered I have nothing to wear to this soiree I'm giving."

Most men would have ignored her womanly plaint. Sheridan Pettifore seized on it.

"You must see Hummersby Bridge's dressmaker. Mother says she does fine work, and

Mother does not pass compliments around freely."

Lucinda got a definite picture of Lady Petti-fore, a widow she assumed, a figure of stately proportions, tall as her son with a warrior's glint in her eye.

Sir Sheridan told her where this wondrous dressmaker could be found, and as soon as he departed, she went there before she could change her mind. She truly did need clothes, she could afford anything she needed or wanted, and selecting them would take her mind off thoughts about mysterious shots in the night and bastard children running about unclaimed.

Inside the shop, studying the model clothing and the pattern books, along with the samples of fabrics, she embarked on a spending spree that would have sent her into apoplexy the day before, ordering a half-dozen dresses in varying shades of gray with more colorful trim, petticoats, a new bonnet—the dressmaker proved to be a haberdasher as well—and a riding habit in midnight blue.

The last was done on impulse. Before leaving Craven Maner this morning, after her argument with Mrs. Pickering, she had taken a quick tour of the grounds, with special attention given to the stable and to the horse that her father used to ride. She yearned to do the very same; riding was the thing she missed the most about home.

The dressmaker agreed to start work on the habit right away.

Lucinda smiled to herself when she thought about what she was doing. She had come a long way from the cautious Miss Fairfax who had refused a first-class passage on the train up from London. It might not be the right way to change, but at least she was moving on.

Finally it was time to order a gown for the soiree. Everything else she had chosen was modest, high-necked and long-sleeved. And, except for the riding habit, gray.

Under the dressmaker's influence, she picked a more feminine style, off the shoulder, tight-waisted, with full sleeves that ended tightly at the elbow. For such a dress, only the forest green silk would do, the dressmaker said.

Lucinda agreed.

A quick trip to a nearby shop provided slippers to go with the gown, two pairs of gloves, and a sturdy pair of riding boots. Carrying the packages with her, she strode toward the small church at the opposite end of High Street from the bank. It was here that Rigg was scheduled to meet her, but she saw no sign of him, and she found herself in the churchyard cemetery close by. Most of the headstones were small, their engravings barely readable, but toward the back there was a fenced-off area that was far grander, with statues of angels and towering monuments.

She went back and found that it was the Fairfax family plot. Not only were angels prominent, but also the family crest: two sitting dogs forever facing one another, heads held high. She read the names of the men and women who were her ancestors. They stirred nothing within her, not even the newest plot, which held the remains of William Fairfax, sixth Viscount Westcombe, a noble and kind man according to the marker, 1808–1860.

She could not help noticing that the area enclosed by the fence was filled to capacity. Should another Fairfax wish to be interred with the family, there would be no room.

Footsteps sounded behind her. She turned to watch the approach of a round, soft woman with a pleasant smile.

"Hello, my dear," the woman said in a voice that could not possibly give anyone offense. "You are, of course, Lucinda Fairfax. I am Mrs. Hanson, the vicar's wife. I was in the chapel considering the flowers for Sunday's service when I saw you through the window. I knew you would be here eventually at your dear father's grave."

"Actually, I was waiting for my carriage. I didn't know the grave was anywhere around."

Mrs. Hanson touched Lucinda's hand briefly. "There must be so much for you to learn about your father. Lord Westcombe is remembered most fondly by everyone in Hummersby Bridge."

She spoke softly, her voice filled with respect. She had such a kindly air about her, her smile settling comfortably into the lines of her face, that Lucinda could not imagine her ever frowning.

"I'm sure he is remembered fondly," she said, and could not help adding, "because of the factory."

She spoke from her heart. Winston had told her the factory had been started by an earlier Viscount Westcombe to alleviate unemployment in the village. Shocking it was for a peer to be in trade, but that had been the way of it. Winston himself had sounded slightly disapproving.

"Such a good man," Mrs. Hanson said in a tone far different from that of the banker. "He did not have to do all that he did."

Lucinda glanced at his headstone. "No, he most certainly did not."

She was not of a mind to listen to paeans of praise to her father. It was difficult to feel gratitude toward the man who had broken her mother's heart.

She glanced beyond the Fairfax plot to an area of the cemetery shadowed by trees.

"Is that a crypt back there?"

"The Blackthornes'." Even Mrs. Hanson's natural cheeriness could not keep a note of somberness from her voice.

"I have heard of them." Lucinda spoke in an equally somber tone, finding as she did so that when one became unworthy, it became easier—even if only by omission—to lie.

"What a sad tale it is," Mrs. Hanson said.

"What tale?"

"Why, the tragedy. Have you not heard of the manner in which the former duke and his firstborn son met their deaths?"

"No, I haven't." In this she was completely sincere.

Mrs. Hanson spoke in a conspiratorial whisper. "Would you like to?"

Lucinda fought temptation. With so many matters on her mind, she should not care about this one. She ought to decline and walk away.

Instead, she nodded her assent.

"My husband says I am a terrible gossip, but, Craven Manor lying so close to Blackthorne Hall as it does, you have a right to know."

Lucinda looked up and down the street. Rigg was still not in sight.

She turned to Mrs. Hanson. "You say I have the right? I'll trust in your judgment."

The woman led her to a stone bench at the edge of the churchyard where they had a view of both crypt and roadway. Setting her packages on the ground, Lucinda closed her eyes for a moment and pictured the flashes of despair she had seen so very briefly in Gideon Black-thorne's eyes.

"Please," she said softly, "tell me everything that you can."

Chapter Seven

"There were two of them, you know."

Lucinda stared stupidly at Mrs. Hanson.

"Two?"

"Two boys. Two babies. Twins, as alike as peas in a pod, so they say, yet different, though how one can tell such fine points in a newborn I cannot determine."

A cloud passed over the sun, casting shadows across the Blackthorne mausoleum. Looking up, Lucinda spied the only witness to their conversation, a lone raven perched high in a leafless tree, as still as any gravestone, a natural part of the black branch it clutched.

Gideon had a brother. It was difficult to picture him being close to anyone. She wanted to hurry Mrs. Hanson along, but she could see in her eyes the woman's enjoyment in the telling, and hear it in the conspiratorial quickening of her voice.

"It was then that the tragedies began."

"So soon? When they were born?"

"I fear so. The first nursling, Geoffrey he was called, began life with ease, though his own troubles were to strike soon enough. The second came a half hour later, a surprise, or so the midwife said."

"That would be Gideon."

"Yes. His Grace, the present duke. There were, as you have guessed, difficulties. His mother, the late duchess, did not survive his birth. They say the duke was beside himself with grief, unable even to look upon his children, not for days."

Lucinda's heart went out to the two little boys, motherless and, for all intents, fatherless as well. It must have been an unkind entrance into an unkind world.

"What happened to Geoffrey?"

"I'll get to it all in its proper order, my dear, if you have the time. Theirs is a story not quickly told."

She said it gently, meaning no offense. It must have been a while since she had found a newcomer who could hear the story fresh.

Lucinda glanced toward the road. No carriage awaited her.

114

"I have the time."

Mrs. Hanson picked up her cadence as if no interruption had occurred.

"Eventually, of course, as is the nature of things, the late duke came to welcome the boys, Geoffrey most certainly. He could not help feeling that the second son, the unexpected infant, had caused the death of his duchess. It was a feeling shared as well by the woman charged with the care of the boys. She made no secret of her partiality."

She shook her head. "I report only what was believed at the time, but it comes from those who served at Blackthorne Hall. It does not speak well of the father, nor of the nanny, you might think. There are those who would agree. But ours is not to judge in this world, as the vicar would point out."

Lucinda tamped down her impatience with an agreeable nod.

"They grew to boyhood, strapping youths both of them, Geoffrey wild and full of his oats, his younger brother more serious, given to solitude, much as he is now. You know what they say: As the twig is bent, so grows the tree. It's true as Scripture where our present duke is concerned, if the Good Lord will forgive such a comparison."

"The brothers did not get along?"

"Oh, no, my dear, there you are wrong. Devoted to one another they were, the older admitting guilt for his own scrapes when the father was inclined to punish the younger, and the younger looking at him with an open admiration one does not often see in siblings. Except, I suppose, in twins, though I have no personal knowledge of them but only what I have read and been told."

Lucinda tried in vain to imagine Gideon Blackthorne as a boy looking adoringly at anyone. But she could see the solemn part. Even as a lad, he would not have smiled.

"And then, sad to tell, the accident occurred. Poor Geoffrey. A riding mishap it was, much like the one that took your own grandfather and uncle." Her eyes widened. "Oh, dear, I had not considered this might be painful for you. I'll hush this instant and get back to the chapel flowers."

"No!"

Lucinda had not meant to sound so insistent. "I mean, it's all right, really. Please, go on. You said there was an accident. Geoffrey was—"

"Injured, badly. He was attempting to bound over a hedge that was far too tall and wide for his youthful skills. The horse almost cleared the branches, they say, but for one hoof. It was enough. The lad came down hard, head first."

She hesitated, as if the memory were too painful to recall. But when she again spoke, her voice was as strong as ever, and Lucinda remembered the woman was relating only what she had heard.

"The injured horse was destroyed immediately. The poor lad lay unconscious in his bed for weeks. His father was in an agony; then joy rang out in the old hall when Geoffrey came round. It was thought all was well. Over the next months his strength returned, his brother at his side. When he was allowed, you know. The late duke said that knowing the madcap ways of his twin, Gideon should have prevented the ride. Unfair you will say, and perhaps it was, but that was the way of it."

"I take it Geoffrey eventually died of the injuries?"

"Not in any way you might think. May the Lord forgive me, but it might have been better if he had, and right away. The Reverend Hardcastle—vicar here before my own dear husband—said that ever afterwards he was different. One minute as wild and joyous as ever—even wilder if it can be believed—then in a rage the next, which before he had never been. His Grace—Gideon, if I may be so bold as to call him—was almost always by his brother's side, same as ever, only more silent than before, as if he should set aside all youthful ways and become his brother's guardian. As so he should, according to the father, who refused to admit any change in Geoffrey."

She shook her head sadly.

"Such responsibility must have been difficult to shoulder for one so young. The lads were but twelve when the fall occurred. The tragedy went on for so long, so very long, and continues still, some believe."

She stared at the stone angel atop the Blackthorne crypt.

"Geoffrey's remains have been interred here these ten years past, along with those of his father. So many accidents; so many one would think a curse lay over the peers of Hummersby Bridge."

She glanced past Lucinda.

"Oh, there's Mr. Rigg now, much to your relief, most likely. I'm sure you'll be wanting to end the blather of a gossipy old woman and get to your own fine home."

Lucinda started at the alteration in Mrs. Hanson's voice and tempo. She could not let the narrative end, not with so much left untold.

"How did he die? Please, tell me that."

"Why, he drowned, of course, along with his father."

"But you said his death was connected to his injury."

"And so it was. My, what an attentive listener you are." A pat on the hand. "Please come for tea some afternoon, will you not? I'm sure we will find much to talk about."

There was about the woman a determined

sweetness that was impossible to fight. Lucinda reluctantly gave up.

"I'm sure we will."

Watching Mrs. Hanson make her way back to the chapel, Lucinda could not shake off the spell cast by the story. A curse on the Blackthornes, and on the Fairfax family as well . . . or so Mrs. Hanson had said. She thought of Mrs. Pickering's ominous words about proceeding cautiously. Because of a curse? The vicar's wife could very well be right.

Here in a Yorkshire graveyard Lucinda had never felt so far from the New York farm.

At the carriage she half listened to Rigg's apologies for his tardiness—something about the horse throwing a shoe. Assuring him all was well, she climbed into the carriage, tossed her packages carelessly on the seat beside her, and considered what she had learned.

That Gideon had been a solemn boy she had no doubt; that he had been thoughtful and caring put him in a new light. He had been treated badly. Was that treatment the source of the distress she had sensed in him? It seemed a sufficient cause, and yet she wondered.

Strangely, she felt a bond with him. He had lived his life in wealth, she most of hers in genteel poverty, yet they had each been troubled by those who should have given love. Each in his own way, they had been cursed. It seemed a strong word for her situation, but not for his.

This time as the carriage passed the stretch of road where Blackthorne Hall rose in the distance, she did not avert her eyes. Nothing she had heard—nothing she might ever hear—should change her feelings about what had happened between her and Gideon Blackthorne, yet she no longer thought of last night with shame.

He had wanted much, much more than the brush of lips against lips, and she had shown him with her actions that she felt the same. It was a momentary giving in to weakness, and it must not happen again.

That did not mean she should never see him. Knowing a little about the solemn child who became a solemn man, she wanted very much to look into his eyes and see what else was there besides distress and—she admitted it—heat.

An evening walk in the garden was beyond consideration, both because she shouldn't and because, coward that she was turning into, she knew Mrs. Pickering would be watching from her upstairs window. So how to meet him again? Clearly, he did not care to talk to her by day.

The party. The soiree. Sheridan Pettifore had volunteered to help her with the guest list. Though he would probably protest, she already had one name she would add: the Duke of Ravenswood.

The only question was how soon such a gathering could and should be arranged. She must of necessity ask Mrs. Pickering. Surely whatever animosity the housekeeper felt toward her new mistress would not keep her from giving good advice.

Two weeks, she hoped; two weeks at the most.

When she returned to Craven Manor, it was to find a message from the banker Carlyle Winston saying Hudson Smedley, overseer of the china factory, was away in the coastal town of Whitby, arranging the shipment of essential materials, particularly calcified bones from the factory supplier in South America. He could not meet with her until the end of the week, and so the time had been set for Friday at ten in the morning.

Late in the afternoon she had her first visitor, the bailiff she shared with Gideon, a leathery-skinned, brawny young man named Joseph Dent, who introduced himself at the back door.

Lucinda met him in the library. Hat in hand, he seemed as ill at ease indoors as she had been at the bank.

"Did Carlyle Winston get word to you so quickly? I thought you would not be here for several days."

Dent frowned. "His Grace sent me."

"Gid . . . the duke?"

"Aye. He said you'd be wanting to hear exactly how Lord Westcombe's land is worked. You'll be needing to decide if you want the same arrangement."

"That was very thoughtful of His Grace."

He shrugged and studied his hat. If she hoped to get a response, more information to add to her small store of what she knew about her neighbor, she wouldn't get it from their shared bailiff.

She listened, sitting forward behind her father's desk, while Dent talked about her thousand acres, the crops they yielded, the cattle they supported, and the tenants who worked the fields while living on Blackthorne land. The major portion of their time was spent on His Grace's needs, as was only right, since he paid most of what was due to the families.

It was much as the banker had told her, only Dent provided the details.

"I'd best be getting back," the bailiff said. "I can find me own way out. I've been here before, reporting to Lord Westcombe, as it were."

"Of course. Please, tell me one thing if you can. In the last months of my father's life, perhaps the last couple of years, did you notice anything different about him?"

"In what way, miss?"

"Others have said he seemed troubled."

"He was not one to talk, not to the likes of me. He did seem more serious, if you will, though that's not the right way o' putting it. He was very much interested in making a profit, as who is not in these times? He went over the figures careful-like, though he was never one to be careless, not Lord Westcombe."

He started inching backward. "If that's all—"

"Yes. Thank you for your time."

He paused at the door.

"His Grace asked me to tell you one thing, if you don't mind me saying it."

"Not in the least."

"I'm a plain farmer, Miss Fairfax, risen above me station, and I know only one way to put things, and that's as they are. Should you take to wandering about your land, as you've every right to do, he says, take care. You've a mind of your own, he says, and might go about foolishly, but there are dangers in the country that can strike without warning."

Would His Grace be one of the dangers? I've heard he killed a man.

"How am I supposed to take care?"

"I'm telling you all I know, and that's no more'n the truth. His Grace is a rare 'un. He loves this land as no man I've ever seen. He knows every acre of it well. I'm thinking you being a woman"—she thought he blushed—"you might be going about where you shouldn't be."

"Does he give all women this same advice?"

Dent crushed his hat between his massive hands. "I wouldn't be knowing."

She relieved his distress by thanking him and

sending him on his way. For the next hour she stared into the fire and thought of all she had heard today, all she had learned, all the questions that had been raised.

Over the next two days, restlessly she walked about the house, studying the books in the library, finding most of them technical and historical works that did not hold her interest long. Whatever had been worrying her father, she would not discover it in his reading.

She even went to the gallery to see the portrait of her great-grandfather. He had been friends with the famous Josiah Spode, maker of the finest bone china in England, according to the banker. As a result of that friendship, he had begun his own china factory in Hummersby Bridge. His act had taken courage. Most, even those in his own family, sneered when he went into trade.

Apparently, viscounts did not do such things.

There were also likenesses of her grandfather and grandmother. Only the latter aroused an emotional response in Lucinda. Staring at the fair-haired, slender woman was like looking at a portrait of herself.

When the weather allowed, she worked in the garden, mostly weeding and digging up dead plants that had not survived neglect, though she gave up on trimming the thick stalks of ivy that covered the manor house's back wall. Between the two of them, Rigg and his wife tended a small vegetable garden next to the stable, but neither had energy for anything so frivolous as ivy or flowers.

And she walked about the grounds, never straying far, with Baron at her side. She spent much of her time in the stable and in the field where Lancelot, her father's white gelding, cropped the last of the deep green autumn grass.

She itched to go for a ride. When a package came for her at midday on Monday, she opened it to find the midnight blue riding habit and the first of her new gray dresses. A note from the dressmaker indicated that work had been done on the garments over the weekend so that she might have them as soon as possible.

Lucinda yipped for joy, bringing Mrs. Pickering running into the private dining room where her mistress was dawdling over lunch.

"I believe there's a saddle at the back of the stable that will do for me," she said with a broad smile. "Tell Rigg to get Lancelot ready. I'm going for a ride."

The riding habit fit her wonderfully well. Sir Sheridan's mother had been right: The dressmaker was fine indeed. Lucinda liked the way the garment made her look almost voluptuous, as if she had full breasts and hips instead of what nature had so parsimoniously provided. She also liked the way the color brought out the blue in her eyes.

They were silly considerations—she should have been wondering how well the fabric would wear—but they pleased her feminine heart.

With a high spirit, she went to watch as Rigg led the gelding from the stable. The horse was magnificent, long-legged, broad in the chest, his head held high as he pranced about in place. Like her, he was eager to be gone from all that would confine him. She calmed him with gentle pats and mounted.

With Fenton close behind, Mrs. Pickering came out to tell her she would need a companion, a groom if no one else, since a lady never rode alone.

"She does in New York," Lucinda said with a smile. "Besides, we don't have a groom."

"Nevertheless—"

"Mrs. Pickering, I've been walking over the grounds for two days now. I know the lay of the land, at least as far as I'll be riding. I'll be perfectly safe." She almost added that even Gideon Blackthorne would find nothing to criticize in her chosen route.

She glanced down at Baron, who stood panting beside the horse. "I certainly won't be alone."

With a gentle touch of her new riding boots, she urged Lancelot forward.

Jenny came out from one of the thatched cottages behind the stable to give her advice as Lucinda passed.

"Ye'll not be wanting t' ride past the moor yonder," the old woman said in her cackling voice, her long, twisted fingers gesturing toward the north.

"Why? What's beyond it?"

"Blackthorne land."

Lucinda's heart caught in her throat. "The boundary is not marked, is it?"

"There's a natural barrier, a hedgerow thick fer sure, but if ye were of a strong enough mind, a way through it could be found."

"What would happen if I did so?"

"Ye might meet the owner."

"But it's daylight."

"Gideon Blackthorne's a strange one. He might be out on this sunny afternoon."

Though it seemed absurd, Lucinda got the idea the old woman was directing her to exactly where the duke was. But that made no sense. It was from Jenny's lips that she had heard the direst warning about the duke, an admonition to beware of him lest something terrible occur.

He's a bad 'un. Ye'll not be wanting to meet the same fate as yer father.

The old woman must have a mind as twisted as her hands. Unless she was, like Mrs. Pickering and John Fenton, proceeding cautiously, for whatever reason Lucinda could not guess.

When it came to being strange, Gideon Blackthorne had nothing on Jenny Patchell. Nor, perhaps, on anyone else at Craven Manor.

And that included its new mistress. She knew exactly where she must ride. After a workout to get used to Lancelot and get him used to her, she struck out across the moor.

On this stretch of land, the drainage was poor, the ground unpleasantly spongy, and the damp peat, half covered by moss, sent up a sour smell. She was not to be deterred, though she slowed her rate of progress. Gradually the ground under Lancelot's hooves became firmer and she clicked the horse into a faster pace.

Impatient with the hat that matched her jacket and skirt, she pushed it away from her head, letting it bounce against her back. Conditioned as she was to riding with her hair unbound, she took out the pins and thrust them into a pocket, then shook her head until she could feel the sun's warmth in the free-blowing strands.

Ahead of her loomed a wall of thick shrubbery and scattered trees, much like the barrier that grew around her garden. Here was the marker Jenny had warned her about.

A cruel thought hit her. Was this the hedge over which twelve-year-old Geoffrey had tried to jump? It must have been much lower all those years ago, but it still would have presented a formidable challenge.

She pictured the foolhardy boy, a miniature Gideon, laughing in the face of danger as he soared in the air, and then the soft cry as the realization of disaster struck, the flash of hooves, a whinny of terror, the crash to the stony ground in a tangle of horse and lad.

Last came the gunshot that ended the horse's misery, while the boy lay still beside the slain animal, unseeing and unhearing.

Her eyes burned, and she cursed an imagination that was much too keen. The fall had happened a long time ago, and the tears over it had long since been shed. Forcing herself to study the barrier, after a moment she found what she was looking for: a break in the shrubs a dozen yards to the right. This break was all she should consider, and the possibility of what and whom she might find on the other side.

With a nudge, she got the gelding through the break. The land beyond seemed firmer, darker, but that was probably because she was so close to the trees. She faced a gradual rise that blocked out the rest of the Blackthorne estate. From her position she could not make out the turrets of the hall.

Riding slowly, she topped the hill and saw Gideon scant yards away. He stood with his back to her, his left hand on the wooden post of an iron pick resting against the ground at his side. The cape was not to be seen. Instead, he wore the white, full-sleeved shirt that she had once imagined, and, too, the wide belt and the fitted black trousers. Today he wore heavy work shoes instead of the sleek riding boots.

A pile of large boulders and smaller stones lay close beside him. It was obvious he had been clearing the field in which he stood. The work must have been arduous. He was covered in sweat.

The bailiff had said the duke loved the land. She could see it was true, in a manner she could not have guessed.

As if she had called out, he turned in her direction and saw that she was watching him. Her heart slammed against her chest, from nothing more than the meeting of their eyes.

And then she saw a fury she had not seen in him before, a storm that threatened to rain thunder and lightning down on her head. How dare she ride upon his land? He did not want her there; surely she had been warned to stay away.

Suddenly she felt cold, even with the unusually warm sun beaming down on her. And embarrassed. She wanted to ride away as quickly as she could.

The fury in his eyes lasted no more than a second, replaced by the thorough study that he had so often given her, as if he could undress her with his eyes.

Her mouth grew dry, but her palms began to sweat.

"Baron," she whispered, "if you growl at him, I promise you will spend your nights leashed next to Lancelot's stall."

The dog slapped his tail against the ground, silent, his attention focused on the Devil Duke.

It was her turn to go to Gideon. Let him run from her if he could.

Under her guidance, the gelding moved carefully down the hill, seeking sure footing with each step. He was, Lucinda knew, far more cautious than she.

Chapter Eight

She reined the horse to a halt a shadow's length away from Gideon. He held his ground, feet apart, the pick clutched like a scepter in his gloved hand.

The front of his shirt caught against the contours of his sweat-dampened chest, and she could see the short dark hairs in the opening at his throat. His thighs were strong, his stomach flat, and the sun glinted in the silver buckle at his waist.

She had always thought he looked elegant in his flowing cape and calf-high boots. Dramatic, too, as he'd stood before her in the moonlight. On both counts, he looked even more so under the harsher glare of the sun.

And, too, he seemed more masculine, though that was something she would have called impossible.

"You're not backing away this time," she said, uncertain of her voice, grateful it did not come out in a squeak.

The world would call her a fool for saying such a thing to a man accused of despicable acts. But this was her Gideon of the garden. She did not know how else to speak.

"It would do little good to run," he said in the deep, liquid voice that wrapped around her like a glove. "You have the advantage. This time you're the one on horseback."

"Do you think I would chase you down?"

"I doubt it. But then I'm not certain what you would do. You surprise me, Lucinda. Most people do not, but you are . . . different."

"I'm not sure that's a compliment."

She saw something flicker in his dark, dark eyes, something indefinable that made her remember the fit of her clothing and the blue of her eyes. And, too, belatedly, her wantonly unbound hair.

"Be sure," he said, and then in a harder tone, "Did not Joseph tell you to take care where you rode? Of course he did. He is a good man. You should have listened to the advice."

"It sounded more like an order."

"You do not take orders well."

"I thought I did."

"But not from me. Or perhaps it is that I have not given the right one yet. What would you do for me, Lucinda, if I asked you to?"

He would not believe the answer that sprang to her mind. She hardly believed it herself.

Right then, she would do anything.

A breeze brushed against her cheek, but it could not cool her. She was very much aware of being out in the middle of nowhere with no inquisitive housekeeper as observer, caught between two watchful pairs of eyes, both pairs belonging to dangerous creatures: Gideon Blackthorne in front of her and, behind, the hound that had mysteriously attached himself to her.

"I don't know what I would do," she lied. "If I surprise you by my presence, it is nothing compared to the way you confuse me. Do not ask me what I am doing right now. I don't have an answer for you. I don't have one for myself."

"It's enough that you are here."

"I thought at first you were angry."

"I changed my mind."

The air crackled between them. Unable to breathe, she looked beyond him for a moment to the pile of boulders and rocks.

"I've interrupted your work."

"You'll not hear a complaint."

She studied the chest hairs at his throat and the muscles molded by the clinging shirt. Suddenly aware of her boldness, she jerked her gaze back to his glinting eyes. He knew exactly what she had been doing; he could read the scandalous thoughts racing through her mind.

And he understood what he could order her to do.

She tried to speak lightly. "Is it common for men of your position to work in the fields the way you're doing? Joseph Dent spoke of your love of the land, but I had no idea it went this far."

"I am, as you have heard, an uncommon duke."

"I did not have to be told. I knew it when I saw you for the first time." She smiled. "Or at least I thought I knew it. I understand as much about dukes and viscounts as I do the surface of the moon. In this culture of yours, you're special and far, far above lesser folk, and you pretty much get to do what you want."

"Wrong, Lucinda. I am really an ordinary man—"

She stared once again at his chest and almost laughed out loud.

"—and the best, strongest, most special folk I know work on what is inaccurately called my land. They know it well, and they possess it in ways I never can."

He dropped the pick, removed his work gloves, and tossed them on the ground.

"As for doing what I want, if that were true, you would be off the horse and on the ground beneath me in an instant. But I have vowed to be honorable where you are concerned, and so there you sit, provocatively above me, warm and vulnerable and as distant as a star."

Lucinda gripped the reins to keep from throwing herself from the saddle and into his arms. She very much needed Baron to bark and show his fangs, but instead, obeying her original command, he sat quietly on his haunches halfway up the hill.

She remembered Sir Sheridan's referring to Gideon's effect on women. She remembered all that he'd said.

"Do you really have blow-bys scattered like sheep around the countryside?"

"By-blows," he said. "You continue to surprise me."

She flushed with embarrassment. "You know what I mean. And I'm sorry I asked. It's just that I am absolutely impervious to the charms of men, and completely shamed by my behavior the other night, yet, as must be far too obvious, I am having a terrible time keeping my distance from you."

"No," he said.

"No?"

"No, I have no bastards scattered like sheep around the countryside."

"If you did, you wouldn't admit it."

"Probably not."

An uncomfortable silence fell between them.

At least it was uncomfortable on her part. He looked, as always, perfectly at ease.

Except for the devil lines between his eyes. They seemed more furrowed than ever. He enjoyed this kind of talk, this teasing about sexual matters that no decent woman would tolerate.

Lucinda was learning far more about herself than she wanted to know, and far less about him.

"If a . . . a soiree were held at Craven Manor, would you attend?"

The question came out of nowhere, which, considering the hard way he was staring at her, was exactly where she would like to thrust it now.

"Probably not," he said.

"Oh. I thought you might consider it."

"I don't attend soirees. Or teas, or balls, or social occasions of any kind."

Expecting his response, she was far more disappointed by it than made good sense.

"I shouldn't have asked you," she said, trying to speak airily. "Sir Sheridan said you would turn me down."

That got a reaction from him. It was only the slightest twitch of his lips, but in any other man it would have been an exclamation of disgust.

"You've met our fair young baronet."

"In town, when I went to meet with Carlyle Winston."

"A necessary encounter you did not enjoy, I

take it. The meeting with the banker—not, of course, Sheridan Pettifore. He must have been the one to tell you about the blow-bys."

"You're making fun of me."

He watched her in silence for a moment. Nervously, she smoothed her hair away from her face.

"If I am"—again the liquid voice—"I should be whipped. And you, of course, the one to do the whipping."

Again his lips twitched, though not quite in the manner of before. She expected another apology to follow, but she did not get it.

"What did you think of Pettifore?" he said.

"He was pleasant."

When compared with Gideon Blackthorne, he was also a swallow of tepid water taken after a goblet of rich red wine.

"And he suggested the soiree," her drink of claret said. "It does not sound like anything you would come up with on your own."

"I didn't have to agree."

"Perhaps you are a woman too easily persuaded to a man's will. At least to that of a gentleman."

"That's a terrible thing to say."

For a moment she thought he really might apologize. This time he should, but he proved her wrong.

"I am a terrible man, Lucinda. Do not forget it."

"How can I help it when you keep reminding me? First the talk about what I would do for you, and now about what I think of Sir Sheridan. I think you said such a thing about him to keep me at a distance."

She flushed even as she said the words. They sounded presumptuous, as if an unsophisticated woman such as herself could strike fear in the heart of such a man. She had spoken without consideration. Yet despite her embarrassment—a common emotion when she was around him—she thought her accusation might hold a trace of truth.

With no more than words he pulled her close, then pushed her away, but not because she disturbed him. She was an oddity, an amusement. He was truly a Devil Duke.

"If I had once been tempted to bend to your will, or follow any order that you gave, I no longer feel that way. Don't think, Your Grace, that you can persuade me to do so much as blink."

He stared at her almost blandly, as if she were not about to explode with anger.

"I prefer you call me Gideon."

She almost spluttered in indignation. "When I talked to Mrs. Hanson today, I felt a sympathy for you and a yearning to understand more about who and what you are. Both the sympathy and the yearning are gone."

The change in him was instant, subtle, yet apparent to her. He was angry. She had said something wrong.

"What did she tell you?" His voice was harsh.

She looked away. "It doesn't matter. I am sorry I intruded on you today. You probably don't believe me, but it will not happen again."

She did not bother to wait for a *good riddance* or a fervently whispered *at last*. A tug on the reins and pressure from her heel sent Lancelot at a fast trot back up the hill. Baron, still silent, ran close behind. As she rode across the moor to her manor house, she half expected the day to dim and the mist to rise. Instead, the sun continued to shine from a sky still cruelly clear.

Was Gideon Blackthorne the killer he was rumored to be? She could not believe it so. But he could wound deeply, with no more than a look or a phrase.

. . . *a woman too easily persuaded to a man's will.*

Stung by injured pride, she had responded quickly and angrily to his words. The truth of the insult did not strike her until she was brushing down Lancelot in the dark confines of his stall. She had let Sheridan Pettifore talk her into something she did not want.

And of course she had let Gideon kiss her, after making sure he had the opportunity to do so.

In her American home, such weakness had not been in her character. Though she had lacked serious young suitors, her want of funds keeping them from an honorable approach, more than one had hinted that she might be interested in meeting with him alone. It was as if being needy and dependent on others had also made her more readily available.

Always she had declined the young men in very emphatic terms, or, when they were more subtle, pretended not to understand. In the ten days or so that she had been in Yorkshire—so short a time and yet it seemed forever—she had changed.

The alteration went far deeper than she was prepared to admit. She was supposed to fear Gideon, to shun his presence. She had as much as told him she would do exactly that.

She had spoken too wildly. He was a complex man, far more so than anyone had indicated, though everyone seemed quick to express an opinion about their Devil Duke.

She thought of him as only Gideon. He did more than warm her physically and awaken hidden yearnings until they made her dizzy. His power over her also touched her heart and soul.

About that change, she had no idea what to do.

Sir Sheridan came to call the following afternoon, with a freckle-faced, auburn-haired young girl who blushed a bright red when he led her in the front door. Lucinda had just come into the entryway after a restless walk around the immediate grounds. He promptly introduced her prospective maid Alice.

Eyes downcast, the girl curtsied and muttered, "Mum."

She could not have been more than fifteen, a fact Lucinda commented on after Alice had been led away by Mrs. Pickering.

"She's much too young to be out working on her own."

The handsome baronet's brows raised a fraction. "You think so? Not by Yorkshire standards. Nor anywhere else in England, I don't believe. We have laws about this sort of thing, but they would not affect one as old as she."

She led him into the library, where the fire was lit, its warmth a welcome relief after the dreary outside cold. It had become her favorite room. She had even grown fond of the history books.

"Mother thought you would find Alice suitable. She's been in service for two years. Don't raise your brows, dear Miss Fairfax. She's not been beaten. Indeed, Mother tends to spoil the servants. She hopes you will do the same."

"I probably will, since I've never had a lady's maid before. What is she supposed to do?"

Sir Sheridan threw back his head and laughed. "She doesn't come with written instructions, although she herself will probably let you know soon enough what her duties should include. I can be of no help. I have no idea what is expected of a lady's maid. You should—"

"I know, ask your mother."

"One thing I can tell you. Alice can accompany you on your ride into town Friday."

"You know about my appointment with Hudson Smedley?"

"Everyone knows. I told you earlier, you're the talk of Hummersby Bridge."

"I still can't imagine why."

"We've had falls and riding accidents, a mysterious disappearance, and, not long ago, even a fire that turned several cottages to ash. You are the first new event, if you can be called such, that isn't a catastrophe."

"I could be. I haven't left yet."

"Oh, dear, don't tell me you're giving up on us already. I thought you couldn't sell any of your property."

Lucinda rolled her eyes. "I'm afraid to ask what else you know about me."

As quickly as the words were out, she regretted them. Staring into the fire, she waited to hear the sound of Gideon's name. He had become so much a part of her daily life, if only in her mind, that she could not believe others did not know it.

"Only that you enjoy riding and, like most of your family before you, you're very good at it."

"I took Lancelot out for the first time only yesterday."

"Our methods of communication are very thorough." To her look of puzzlement, he added, "Mrs. Pickering rode into town to purchase supplies."

Lucinda hadn't known, but then she had been thinking of other matters when she returned to the manor house.

"I don't suppose she said where I rode."

"Not that I heard. Was it someplace scandalous?"

She dug her nails into her palm. "Not in the least. It was just that I rode alone, something I simply must not do, she said. She put it on the level of going into town unchaperoned."

Sir Sheridan leaned forward. "You do not fool me, Miss Lucinda Fairfax. I suspect it was somewhere truly scandalous. Please tell me where."

The door opened, saving her from a response. It was Fenton, serving a tray of tea and cakes. She could have kissed him on the cheek, but it would have been the talk of the village for the next six months.

"Cook suggested you might want refreshments," the butler said.

"Oh, yes," she said with a little too much enthusiasm.

She poured the tea much as she had seen her mother do a long time ago in Albany. Not as

Evelyn Rogers

smoothly as she would have liked, but still, she did not spill a drop on either herself or her visiting baronet.

When cups and plates had been set aside, she sat at the desk, paper before her and pen in hand, to begin the invitation list for her soiree. Sir Sheridan sat opposite, ready with his advice. She did not say anything about inviting Gideon Blackthorne. She did not want to say his name where anyone else could hear, for fear of revealing feelings that were no one else's concern.

But she did intend to ask him in writing, if for no other reason than to demonstrate that their most recent conversation had not bothered her for long. And that she was not impressed by the fact that he had already declared he would not attend.

"I'll see that you get stationery appropriate for invitations," Sir Sheridan said. "I don't suppose you have any at hand. Of course not. Lord Westcombe was hardly a sociable man."

He went on to discuss the food she should consider laying out, the musicians she should hire—strictly for background music, not dancing—and the additional servants necessary for such an evening.

Her parsimonious side started to protest, but another, more liberal, part of her bade her to keep quiet and write whatever he said. She was rich, a condition about which she had to keep reminding herself, and this was her introduc-

146

tion to Hummersby Bridge society. She ought to show this part of the world that though she had been denied the influence of the viscount, her mother had raised her properly.

And she liked the idea of challenging Gideon to visit her through the front door.

After the departure of her friend and advisor—for that was how she had started to view him—she went upstairs to begin her life as a woman with a lady's maid.

Right away, Alice proved amiable and experienced, despite her young age, although she kept casting doubtful eyes at the pony-sized Baron. By Friday, life had settled into a not unpleasant routine, the invitations written and posted, Lucinda taking daily rides about the estate when weather permitted, the routine chores seen to by her small staff of servants.

Alice accompanied her on the ride into the village to meet with the manager of the Fairfax China Factory, Hudson Smedley. Tall and thin to the point of emaciation, he settled his cold, pale gray eyes on her as she walked into his sparsely furnished office, extended a cold, bony hand, and welcomed her with a thin, cold voice.

She had seldom met anyone whose various parts went together so well to form the whole. She corrected herself. There was one man who came to mind, but with him everything was darkly virile, not chillingly spare.

The meeting was brief.

"Carlyle Winston has assured me you wish for the arrangements here to remain as Lord Westcombe determined," the manager said.

"That's true."

"I will, of course, make regular reports to Mr. Winston concerning the finances." His thin lips flattened into what she took to be a smile. "You will be pleased with the reports. Our profits have never been higher. I expect them to rise even more."

Clearly, he felt his management was superior to that of her father. She was in no position to contradict him.

"Could I look around? I know nothing about the work done here."

The cold eyes narrowed. "Unfortunately, that will not be possible today. The kilns are fired to capacity, and the heat is unbearable to one unused to it."

She started to protest.

"Another time, perhaps," he said, "when I can present in comfort what we are able to accomplish, though we are far from the regular factory towns to the south."

Lucinda could do nothing but agree. Following the quarter-hour meeting, she set out on the carriage ride home. Arriving earlier than expected, she decided on a quick ride before Cook could put a luncheon together.

Thinking of her father and the work at the factory, she chose once again to ride down the path to the high point of her land, where the precipice of the cliff overlooked the small but powerful River Craven. It was also one of the few places where she had seen Gideon Blackthorne, standing in the shadowed woods at her back, but that was no reason for riding there. At least, that was what she told herself.

She had been avoiding the scar ever since that first viewing, but today it most definitely called to her. The destination had the added allure of being one the duke would not like.

This time she stayed far from the edge, choosing instead to rein Lancelot into the trees. The branches seemed more bare than they had before, the ground more littered with dead leaves Lancelot's hooves rustled through them as she led him slowly into the stand.

An animal scurried through the grass somewhere to her left, and a covey of birds—pigeons, she thought—landed in the trees, then with a flurry of wings promptly flew away. Otherwise, there was no sign of life.

Suddenly Baron began to bark and took off through the trees—after the animal, she supposed, probably an elusive rabbit.

She sighed. It was time to ride back to the manor house. She leaned down to stroke Lancelot's neck and tell him so.

Without warning, a loud crack rent the still air. Lancelot reared, and Lucinda, caught unawares, felt herself slipping to the ground. She hit hard, and her head exploded in pain. She tried to cry out, but, like a sudden fall of night, darkness descended, and she was aware of nothing save the inability to speak or, blessedly, even to feel.

Chapter Nine

When Lucinda regained consciousness, she was lying awkwardly on the ground, twisted and sore, her head pounding. It took a minute for her to realize where she was, and to remember what had happened.

She had fallen. But that was impossible. Never had she fallen from a horse, not even in those first long-ago days of lessons when she was a sickly child trying to regain her strength.

She refused to open her eyes. The pain would be too great. How long had she been lying like this on her bed of leaves and packed dirt? Not long, she guessed; a few minutes at most.

She felt Baron's cold nose nudge against her cheek and heard his whine.

He had barked and run away. That she remembered. And there had been another sound, a sharp crack of some kind, like the report of a gun.

Surely not. She must not let her imagination run wild, else she would be thinking her fall had not been an accident.

Slowly she opened her eyes to let in a sliver of light. Pain made her dizzy, but she forced herself to sit upright, to open her eyes wider, to look at the small, quiet forest surrounding her. Lancelot stood a few feet away, nuzzling the dead leaves in a search for grass. Closer, the dog trained his warm brown eyes on her.

Her head throbbed. She touched a knot close to her temple and winced. Like Geoffrey Blackthorne, she had suffered a head injury in a fall from a horse. Was this the way Gideon's unfortunate twin had felt when he finally came to after his fall?

Her heart went out to him. He had been but a boy.

Pulling herself to her knees, she managed to stand. The trees whirled around her. She reached out to the nearest one for support, glancing higher up on the trunk, staring at a split in the bark, in its center a small, round recess. Idly her finger probed the discovery. The recess was more like a hole in the trunk, its sides splintered, and at the end, a half-inch deep, was something hard and cold and metallic.

A nail? A bolt?

No, nothing so innocent. Her heart jerked. As surely as she knew anything, she understood exactly what the metallic object was—a bullet—and from the rawness of the cut, one that had been recently fired.

Memory returned in a flood, the split-second events preceding her fall crowding one on top of the other. She had been riding peacefully, moving cautiously through the trees. Then came the report of a gun. Not a branch. A gun. Baron had taken off through the woods after a rabbit, and she had leaned forward to stroke Lancelot's neck. Otherwise she would have been sitting upright when the crack rent the air. The bullet could easily have . . .

She shook her head vehemently, ignoring the pain. It couldn't be. Impossible. She stared up once again to where a great force had gouged out a part of the iron-hard trunk. Bile rose in her throat. She hugged her middle and clasped a hand over her mouth to keep from throwing up.

Minutes passed before the nausea eased, leaving her with a different sickness, a sense of horror over what might have been. She began to tremble. Baron had not been after anything so benign as a rabbit. He had been trying to protect her from her enemy.

153

But who could that be? Who? She meant no harm to anyone.

She studied the woods more carefully, but all was peaceful and quiet. Just as it had been before the fall.

We must proceed cautiously.

Mrs. Pickering could not possibly be the culprit, nor the straight-backed John Fenton. But someone else, someone she had not met? Whom had the housekeeper meant by *we*?

Beware the duke. He's a bad 'un.

Jenny Patchell had further warned her against suffering the same fate as her father. And here she was, far too close to the precipice where he had met his death.

But Gideon? The man who held her gently and brushed his lips against hers could not mean her harm. And if he had, more than once he could have found a simpler way to hurt her. He could have taken his pleasure and gone his way.

Yet she knew of no one else.

Once the ugly thoughts started, she could not stop them. In each one, Gideon was at the heart of her suspicion.

He had sent Joseph Dent to warn her about wandering into danger. Was he the danger? Could he have been warning her about himself? His darkness had been a part of his nature since he was born, or so said the vicar's wife. Was there a weakness in him like that in his late brother? Had he truly been involved in her father's fall, as had been hinted?

Had he harmed the derelict that Sir Sheridan had mentioned?

Was he now after her?

It could not be. This was insane. He had stroked her cheek too gently, and his kiss had been torturously sweet.

Why was she assuming that anyone intended to hurt her? The shot could have been an accident, if there was a shot. A careless hunter. A misfired gun. These were far more likely causes for the almost tragedy than attempted murder.

And yet . . .

She could not think clearly, not with her head throbbing as it was. A whistle brought Lancelot to her side; the horse waited patiently while she cautiously, painfully maneuvered herself into the saddle. From her high position, she should have studied the tree trunk, the splintered bark, the cold piece of metal in its dark recess. The thought of so much as a glance brought a renewed threat of nausea.

At last she began the long ride home. Lancelot knew the way; she scarcely had to guide him. Rigg met her outside the stable.

"Faith, Miss Fairfax, what happened to ye?" he said as he took the reins.

She glanced down at her soiled habit. Too late she remembered her hat, hanging limp against her back, and the tangled state of her hair.

"I fell."

It was all the explanation she could or would give. For now.

He called out for help. Her head pounded as she heard others arrive—Cook, Mrs. Pickering, Fenton, each exclaiming in horrified tones as news of the accident spread.

Fenton helped her to the ground, then carried her in his arms inside and up the stairs. He was surprisingly strong and gentle. Embarrassed and grateful at the same time, she gave herself up to him. Alice must have been watching from the chamber balcony, for by the time they entered the room, she had the bed turned down, the pillow plumped, a fire stoked high in the grate.

"I'm covered with dirt and leaves," Lucinda said, trying to make light of her condition. "The bed will be a mess."

"Never you worry about that, mum," Alice said. "I'll take care of everything."

Lucinda sighed and did not argue.

"You've got a nasty bump on your head," Mrs. Pickering said. "I'll get a cool cloth."

"I'll send Rigg right away for the doctor," Fenton said.

"No." Lucinda closed her eyes. "No bones are broken. Nothing's sprained. I'll be all right. All I need is rest."

Mrs. Pickering started to argue, but she waved the woman to silence.

"I've got a bump on my head and a great deal of injured pride. But that's the worst of it. The cool cloth sounds wonderful. Otherwise Alice can take care of me." She tried to keep her voice light. "I do believe, however, I'll be wanting supper in my room."

"This is what comes of a woman riding alone," Mrs. Pickering said with a sniff as she headed for the door. "Against the laws of nature, that's what it is."

What would the woman say if she knew what Lucinda suspected? Did she already know?

When Lucinda was left with only Baron for company, after Mrs. Pickering had brought the cloth and Alice had eased the soiled clothes from her body and replaced them with a freshly laundered nightgown, she lay in the dimness of her room, listened to the crackle of the fire, and remembered.

The bullet had been meant for her. She pressed a fist against her mouth. Someone meant to do her great harm.

But that made absolutely no sense. Her death would benefit no one. The shooting must have been an accident, a careless hunter after grouse.

Perhaps there had not been any shooting at all. She hadn't actually seen the bullet. It could be that the fanciful nature Yorkshire had brought out in her was the only culprit here . . .

along with the pride that refused to accept an awkward fall.

Lucinda rubbed her pounding temples. Which answer fit? She honestly did not know.

Two days later, when her aches were greatly eased and she felt like her old self, she settled on a plan of action. It might not be a particularly brilliant plan, but at least it required her to do something besides sit around and think.

As with so many of her plans, this one involved Gideon. All her dark thoughts when she had been in the woods seemed foolish now, hopelessly dramatic, brought on by panic and pain. She could not bring herself to believe him guilty of anything worse than obsessive solitude. When she told him of her suspicions about a stray bullet, he would investigate and learn the truth.

If the hand on the gun truly belonged to a hunter, most likely he was a tenant farmer on Blackthorne land, one who likewise worked a portion of her own property. He had been far too careless. He needed to know what his carelessness had almost caused.

And if she was wrong—if no gun had been fired that day, and it wasn't a bullet buried deep in the tree trunk but a nail as she had at first supposed—Gideon would find that out, too.

He would not laugh. He would give her an inscrutable look that would make her feel fool-

Devil in the Dark

ish. But she would no longer be afraid.

The excuse she used was the personal delivery of a second invitation to her soiree—"so that he can't claim one was never received."

Her plan met with strenuous opposition. She had expected nothing else.

"No one calls at Blackthorne Hall, not these ten years past," Mrs. Pickering said over Lucinda's untouched breakfast. "Outside of a few tradespeople, and even they are never invited inside." She waved at the envelope on the table. "The post has served just as well. He won't accept, mark my words, no matter the manner in which he is asked."

Fenton came along to offer his own displeasure, not so forcefully stated but clearly visible in his frown. Even Rigg, the only member of the staff who never opposed her, raised his eyebrows sharply when she ordered the carriage readied for the morning ride.

Lucinda remained adamant. Wearing underneath her cloak one of the new gray dresses, having leashed Baron in the stable, she settled back in the carriage and thought about the man she would soon face. She thought of the set of his mouth when he looked at her, and the occasional glint in his black eyes. It seemed a lifetime since she had seen those eyes, yet it had been less than a week ago that she had approached him as he worked in the field and he had told her he was a terrible man.

159

She had almost forgotten his words, but she remembered how the elegant Duke of Ravenswood had been covered in sweat.

Anticipation sent a shiver down her spine, and her heart quickened in a way that had nothing to do with her quest. Alice should have accompanied her, but the girl had come down with a mild congestion in the chest and Lucinda ordered bed rest, much as it had been ordered for her. As always, she would face Gideon alone.

Drawing a steadying breath, she closed her eyes and let the carriage take her along the main road, then down the turnoff that led to Blackthorne Hall. The day was gray and blustery, with a low mist hovering over the moors. It seemed perfect weather for a first, and probably last, ride to the hilltop castle that Gideon called home.

The route was winding and gradually rising, with tall pines blocking her view most of the way. Nearer the summit the road became a series of switchbacks, the turrets visible first through the left window of the carriage, then through the right, until she was swept through a large brick gatehouse, empty except for a roost of pigeons high in the arched roof, and the drive leveled out to a straight line.

Though the hall and the manor house were within sight of one another, the journey from Fairfax stable to Blackthorne driveway took close to an hour. Stepping down from the carriage, she studied the towering dark masonry front of the castle. No light shone in welcome from the closed windows; no face appeared to observe her approach.

Over Rigg's protest, she insisted on walking alone up the dozen stone steps to the massive wooden front doors. She lifted the heavy brass knocker. It fell with an ominous bang. Getting no response, she knocked again, but in vain. One of his servants—he surely had servants—should be answering the door, even if he said nothing more than no one was at home.

There was, she decided, nothing subtle in Gideon's desire to be left in solitude.

She felt foolish standing there in the cold like a rejected mistress whose affections were no longer desired. Slowly she retreated down the stairs. Rigg stood by the open carriage door, and I-knew-it-would-be-like-this expression on his lined gray face.

She glanced beyond him to an expanse of lawn that appeared surprisingly well tended. Beyond the lawn rose a six-foot stone wall that extended to both right and left as far as the eye could see, its line broken only by the drive and the gatehouse. She was not surprised that Gideon had fenced himself away from the world.

A faint but raucous sound came from the left side of the castle, an inhuman, unpleasant noise that startled her. Motioning Rigg away, she followed the sound, hurrying past the front of the hall and rounding the corner.

Shadows fell across the narrow drive and the half-dozen outbuildings that met her eye. She could barely make out the figure of a woman standing some thirty yards away. The woman held herself as still as a post, her arms hanging straight at her sides.

"Hello," Lucinda called out and began to close the distance separating them. "I hope everything's all right. I couldn't rouse anyone at the front door."

The woman was tall and big-bosomed, her dark, gray-streaked hair pulled severely back in a bun, her black gown hanging loose on her ample figure. Her lips were pinched, her skin papery and pale, and her small dark eyes like those of the raven Lucinda had seen on her first journey into town.

Her attention focused on one of the woman's hands, almost obscured in the folds of her gown. She was holding something, casually, forgotten. With a sharp intake of breath, Lucinda realized what the something was: a pullet suspended loosely from the fingers that were wrapped around its twisted neck. In an instant, she recognized the squawking sound that had brought her here. It had been the death cries of the fowl as the woman snapped its neck.

Such a killing was something she was familiar with, from her years on the farm. It was the coolness of the woman and, despite the dead bird in her hand, the dignified picture she presented that caused the surprise.

The woman parted her lips. Lucinda half expected her to cackle in the manner of Jenny Patchell. Instead, her voice was strong and smooth, almost fluid.

"You're Miss Fairfax, are you not? I'm Irene Littlewood, if I may be permitted to say it. Mrs. Littlewood, they call me, though I never was wed. You mayn't have heard of me. Most folk do not know I still dwell in these parts."

She paused, not really to give her visitor a chance to speak, but rather, Lucinda was sure, to gain dramatic effect.

"I was nursemaid to the twins." Mrs. Littlewood's eyes narrowed. "Aye, I know, it's been a long while since my services were needed. But His Grace knows he owes me, that he does. Don't look surprised. He's got you fooled, I'll be bound. He has you coming around ready to do his will."

"I beg your pardon?" Lucinda asked, certain she could not have heard right, not any of it, not a single word the woman had said.

"No need to play innocent with me. Though why any woman would be interested in him is beyond reasoning. Like a thundercloud he is, full of moods and scowls. Not like Geoffrey. There was a lad for you. Sunshine he was, and laughter. Aye, I know, he was a bit of a wild one, but there was no harm in him, and I don't care what anyone says. And where he is now? Moldering in the family crypt, beside his dear father, and no one to mourn 'em but the nanny who served him faithfully for years."

Her voice had turned strident, the words coming faster one after the other, as if she seldom got the chance to talk to anyone and could not let the opportunity pass. Lucinda glanced around, but she saw no one else in the shadows.

"Mrs. Littlewood, I don't think—"

"Ask His Grace why he never visits the graveyard. Ask why he never so much as whispers his brother's name. I'll tell you the answer. Ashamed he is to be the one who lived. I've said it before, and I'll tell you now, the sea chose the wrong brother to take from us. It was the evil one who survived."

Malevolence came off the woman like a stench. Lucinda backed away.

"Please, no. You shouldn't be saying such things. I'm a stranger to you."

"But not to Gideon, that's my guess. Has he got you with child? That's the way of him. If you think he'll help you now, you're a fool. He's got secrets too dark to see the light of day; places he goes; women, of course, that goes without saying. He's a bane to womanhood, that he is. He came into this world in a river of his mother's blood, and his hands were stained with it. In all these years he's not been able to wash the blood away."

Lucinda squeezed her hands over her ears. "Enough," she cried and turned, running around to the front of the hall, toward the carriage and to Rigg, who stood open-mouthed as she hurried up to him.

"Get me away from here," she said, scrambling into the carriage without waiting for his help.

Hurriedly he climbed to his perch and grabbed the reins and whip.

Her eye fell to the envelope lying at her feet. Grabbing it up, she tossed it out the window onto the front drive, then threw herself against the carriage seat.

"Hurry," she whispered, as if the coachman could hear.

It seemed an interminable time before the carriage began to move, the wheels crunching as loud as thunder against the gravel of the drive. Over the noise, the words of the nursemaid resonated in her mind. The words shook her like the report of the gun. She looked out to see one of the massive front doors of the hall slowly open. Gideon stepped into view.

Heart pounding, she shrank into the darkness of the carriage interior, but he knew she was there. With a dim light at his back, she could not see his face, but she imagined his watchful eyes. And she felt the pull of him, as if he willed her to stop her departure and return to him.

Bessie, the normally placid mare, fought the reins, slowing the turn that would direct her path back toward the gatehouse and home. Lucinda wondered if Bessie was in league with the Devil Duke.

Gideon came down the steps, staring in her direction as he drew closer, until he was scant feet away from the carriage door handle. He had only to reach out, grasp the handle, and . . .

His gaze dropped, and he knelt to pick up the white envelope a fraction of a second before Bessie's hooves would have trampled it. The carriage completed its turn. Stepping back, he watched Lucinda ride away.

And she, unable to do otherwise, foolishly thrust her head out the window and stared back at him, until the carriage rumbled through the gatehouse and dropped down the hill, toward the thick blanket of mist that lay across the valley below the hall, toward the house she was beginning to think of as home.

Chapter Ten

He wasn't coming.

Lucinda knew it in her heart. Though common sense screamed she should feel relieved, there was little relief in her reaction.

She looked around the large salon of Craven Manor, at the trio of musicians playing in the gallery, at the food laid out at one side—*à la française*, as Sheridan Pettifore called it—and last, at the sparkling assembly.

Everyone on the guest list was in attendance: Sir Sheridan and his mother Lady Pettifore; Carlyle Winston; the mayor and two members of the Town Council, together with their wives; the county's wealthiest squire, whose name she had trouble remembering; Vicar Hanson and his wife, and the beautiful, dark-haired, voluptuous widow, Rebecca Atterbury.

All were the recommendations of Sir Sheridan. The one guest she had invited on her own, against all advice, even that of her serving staff, was not here. He was, unfortunately, the one she most wanted to see.

Gideon—the unwanted infant, the unloved child, the guilt-ridden youth burdened with responsibilities beyond his years. So much ugliness thrown at her by the hate-filled nanny had sent her running from him; contemplation of it drew her to him again.

"You keep casting furtive glances toward the door," Sir Sheridan whispered into her ear. "Pray tell there's no one else you were expecting."

She smiled into his handsome fair face, and thought of the dark, scowling countenance she would have preferred.

"No one," she lied. "All is exactly as I hoped it would be."

For the most part, she spoke the truth. Under the guidance of Fenton and an uncharacteristically fluttery Mrs. Pickering, the extra help had performed beautifully. She had even ceased worrying about the incident in the woods. Already she had made far too much of a one-time accident.

Nothing anywhere close to threatening had

occurred again. She felt confident nothing would.

He's got secrets too dark to see the light of day . . .

If Irene Littlewood had spoken the truth, of what importance were the secrets to Lucinda? Everyone had them, certainly most everyone she had met since leaving America. And that included herself.

. . . places he goes . . .

How had the nursemaid made such a simple statement seem ominous?

. . . women, of course, that goes without saying.

Words not so easily dismissed and, worse, *Has he got you with child?*

Lady Pettifore's laughter rang out over the buzz of conversation, pulling Lucinda back to where she should be. This was supposed to be a night of enjoyment and education; she would make it so if it killed her.

Sheridan's mother stood across the room by the side of the banker Winston, a widower, Lucinda had learned. Whatever Winston was saying seemed to amuse the widow Pettifore very much.

They made a handsome couple, the banker in black tailcoat and blazingly white shirt, Lady Pettifore in a black silk gown sprinkled with spangles that caught the light from the chandeliers. The woman had paid the same compliment to her son and Lucinda not a half hour before.

"What a fine pair you are," she had proclaimed, loud and clear, as the two were conferring over the progress of the evening.

Could Lady Pettifore be matchmaking? Perhaps she had learned from Carlyle Winston exactly how well off the American newcomer was.

Like Winston and the rest of the men, Sir Sheridan wore a black tailcoat and matching trousers, and a high-collared white shirt. He did, indeed, look fine. About herself, she was not so sure. Alice had insisted on pinning up her hair in a manner far too complicated for her own taste, with curls around her face and tendrils trailing against her neck.

And she had a major complaint about her forest green gown. It came far too low off her shoulders and across her bosom. Outside her bath, she had never exposed so much flesh.

Perhaps it was just as well that Gideon had not put in an appearance, since he tended to be inspired to forwardness even when she was covered from chin to toe by her cloak.

Her skin prickled at the thought of his eyes raking over her. It was a prickling not entirely unwelcome.

She ought to be ashamed. She was no better than the duke.

"How wonderful it is at last to meet the Honorable Miss Fairfax," a voice trilled in her ear.

Lucinda turned to smile at the widow Rebecca Atterbury. Older than she by a half-dozen years, Mrs. Atterbury had skin the color of milk, slanted blueberry eyes, lips a cherry red. She also boasted breasts as full as muskmelons.

The best word Lucinda could come up with to describe her was ripe.

"You are as handsome as I had heard," the widow added with a blink of her thick-lashed eyes. "And as mysterious, too."

"There is absolutely no mystery about me, Mrs. Atterbury. At least, not that I am aware of."

"Oh, but of course there is. Six months ago no one in Hummersby Bridge knew of your existence. No one, that is, but your father, may he rest in peace, and that naughty Carlyle Winston, who insists on keeping every tidbit of gossip to himself."

"Is that what I am?" Lucinda responded more sharply than a hostess should, wanting to ask exactly what was being said. She warned herself not to get ruffled. This was chitchat, party talk at which she was absolutely no good.

Sir Sheridan came to her defense.

"Of course you are, Lucinda. Haven't I already told you so? You really must listen to me. You're a foreigner. All such creatures, especially one as lovely and, I have to confess, as wealthy as yourself, provide us poor provincials with something to talk about through the long rainy evenings that pester us far too often."

He looked so earnest she had to laugh. She also had to quit fighting the concept that people talked about her. An English heiress in New York would have been regarded in the same way, without a hint of scandal. The talk could have nothing to do with the Devil Duke. Thank goodness he had chosen not to attend. Life was simpler when he was not around.

It was at that moment the door to the salon slammed open and Gideon strode into the room. Right away his tall, dark figure dominated everything and everyone around him. Even the fiddlers ceased to play.

As always, he wore the black cape and his head was uncovered, leaving the world to see the hard angles of his face, the fine, firm mouth, the deep, black eyes.

And as always, he was a sight to rob a woman of her sanity.

In his wake scurried John Fenton, struggling to get to the fore and announce him as he had done the other guests. Such was Gideon's stride that the butler could not have caught him had he been on a horse.

All laughter in the room died, all eyes turned to the duke.

"The missing guest cometh," Sir Sheridan said softly.

"Yes," Rebecca Atterbury whispered in a voice that had thickened like clotted cream. Then louder, "What a delightful surprise."

Lucinda kept her silence, devoting her strength to remaining upright while she faced Gideon Blackthorne straight on.

"Your Grace," Mrs. Atterbury said in a throaty voice. "It has been far too long since we last saw one another."

He paid her no mind. His eyes bore into Lucinda's. It was as if no one else was in the room.

"We must talk."

He did not speak loudly, but his words echoed from wall to wall.

For her, the world receded. "I—"

"Now."

The glint in his eyes was harsher than any she had seen before, a flash like that of lightning in an ebony sky. It was, she supposed, meant to frighten her. Instead it made her angry.

"I will await you in the library downstairs."

With that, he whirled and retraced his steps, his boots snapping sharply against the Italian tile floor.

In his wake, the silence was deafening. All eyes turned to the hostess, but she was barely aware of them. Her cheeks burned. She absolutely should not run after him, like his dog or his horse. He had been rude, incredibly so. His dark reputation was justly earned.

In defiance of his command, she should stay right where she was, laughing and talking with the pleasant man at her side, tamping down the gossip that was sure to spread like wildfire. She

173

knew it, and so did everyone else in the room.

How reasonable she was, and righteously angry, yet she had no voice, no heartbeat, no breath. She would not regain them until she found out what had brought him out on this evening, before a crowd of people he did not want to see, making a show of his appearance when she knew it was what he hated most.

The distance between where she stood and the door stretched as wide as the ocean. She wasn't aware of negotiating it, but suddenly she found herself hurrying down the front stairs, past the landing window through which she could make out the distant dark turrets that marked Blackthorne Hall, and on down into a darkened library lit only by a few burning coals.

He was standing close to the hearth, watching for her entrance, waiting for her to come to him. Taking a deep breath, she stepped inside before she could change her mind, then closed the door firmly behind her, putting the two of them in clandestine seclusion, in a world all their own.

The low flames sent shadows licking across the angles of his face, lighting the fire that already glimmered in his eyes. He had thrown aside his cape. To her surprise, he was dressed much as the other men, the tails reaching the back of his knees, the white shirt stark against the brown of his skin, the trousers fitted in a way that hinted strongly of the shape and the length of his legs.

He wore everything as well as he had the simple linen shirt. When compared to him, all her other gentlemen guests were wearing rags.

Slowly he looked her over, lingering for a tormenting time on her bosom. His eyes burned; there was no other word for it, they burned. The heat from them penetrated to her bones. She did not know whether to jerk the low-cut neckline up to her chin or tug it down to her waist.

And then the heat in his gaze died, replaced by the enigmatic expression she had so often cursed, the look that shut her out of his thoughts. The distress he had shown in the salon did not reveal itself, but she knew, despite his pretended insouciance, that it simmered beneath the surface of his stare.

She found her voice, as well as a racing pulse.

"For a man who likes his privacy, you made a very conspicuous entrance upstairs."

He gave no sign he heard. "One week past," he said, "when you came to Blackthorne—"

"I was delivering your invitation. I wasn't sure about the reliability of the post."

"There was no other reason?"

"None that matters now."

He stared at her for a moment.

"You met Irene Littlewood. Did you hear her speech about the river of blood? No need to deny it. I can read the truth in your eyes. It was she who sent you running from the brutish duke. From the one who should have died."

He spoke scornfully, but the disdain seemed directed toward himself.

The fireglow flickering devilishly across his face proved too much for her to watch. She hurried to light the lamp on the desk, then stepped away, putting the desk between her and Gideon. If he knew so much, he had to understand his effect on her. He had to know she wanted to touch him very, very much.

"You don't need me to take part in this conversation, do you?" she said. "There's no reason for me to swear the woman's story had little effect on me, though that's the truth of it." She took off her gloves and dropped them beside the lamp. "Since you know so much, just fill in what else I would say."

"If you were being honest, or if you lied?"

"A little of both. I like to vary my responses to you."

"The trouble is, my dear Lucinda, you do not lie well. It is one of your charms."

The air between them hummed. She looked away from him and stared at the fire.

"Don't play with me, Gideon. If I have caught your interest, it is because I gave you little choice."

"There, my dear, you are right. At the moment, I am most interested in your fall from the horse."

Lucinda started. Of all the things he could have said to her, this one was the least expected.

For a moment she was back on the ground, returning to consciousness, in pain and then in fear. But there was little purpose in describing that moment for him, though she could have done so with meticulous detail. She would have to reveal her suspicions. She would have to include him.

She forced her gaze back to him. "You heard?" Good. She sounded almost casual. "Of course you did. Everyone from here to the North Sea coast knows the brash American woman rode recklessly close to the ridge where her father met his death."

"Is that what they're saying?"

She waved her hand. "That or something very similar. I'm beginning to understand the way of things here."

"Unfortunately, I have been occupied of late. I learned of it only today."

"Regardless of what you were told, I was not riding recklessly. I was barely moving."

"So why did you slip from the saddle? I have seen you ride. You sit a horse well."

She stirred uneasily, too late seeing the workings of his mind.

"Lancelot was startled."

"By what? This?" He tossed an object onto the desk in front of her. "I dug it out this afternoon."

Her blood ran cold. She looked at his find for

177

a moment, then turned away. The time for lies was past.

"I assume it was still in the tree trunk," she said.

"You knew it was there."

She let silence be her answer.

"Is that why you came to Blackthorne Hall? To confront me? To ask if I knew anything about a shooting that had endangered your life?"

"I wanted to tell someone about my suspicion that I was fired on. You came to mind." She could not resist another glance at the desk. "However did you locate it? Whatever made you think to look?"

"Desire, Lucinda. It is a powerful stimulant for a man."

Her heart pounded. "Desire is a very strong word."

"It's not one I use often."

He paused, and in the silence she heard his breathing and she sensed the beat of his heart.

"When I learned of the . . . accident, I wanted very much to know what put you in danger."

"Why?" she said, unable to meet his eye. "What am I to you but a troublesome American?"

"That is a question you must not ask."

Another *why* sprang to her lips, but she kept it to herself. His refusal to answer hurt too much.

She reached for the bullet, then jerked her hand away.

"Did you see anything untoward when you were riding?" he asked. "Did you hear anything?"

"A sharp report, nothing more. I wasn't sure of its significance."

"But you rode to tell me of it."

His voice was thick and soft. He made her reaction to what had happened, to her fears and her hope that he might help, seem intimate.

"Have you told no one else?" he asked.

"No one. I already admitted you came to mind. You and you alone."

The warmth of her words affected her in a deeply stirring way; she had no idea if they affected him. In that moment she was no longer cold.

She braced herself against the desk. "I thought perhaps a hunter, one of the tenant farmers we share, had been careless."

"No one has come forward to confess."

"They wouldn't."

"My tenants would."

"You speak very confidently."

"I am confident about very little in this world. Do you not know this by now?"

He was around the desk in an instant, his hands gripping her arms, his gaze easing like hot honey from her eyes to her throat to the swell of her breasts.

"Did you like Sheridan Pettifore staring at you? He is someone you can tease, Lucinda. I am no such man."

His thumb traced the hollow of her throat. Eyes closed, she turned her head away from him. The thumb trailed lower. Her breasts tightened and seemed to swell, until she thought the hard tips would slip from the confines of her dress.

"Why did you come here?" His voice was at once husky and sharp. "You do not plan to stay. Why couldn't you have demanded that the money be shipped to you far away?"

"But that—"

He gripped her heard against him. "Do you have any concept of the trouble you have aroused?"

The hum in the air became a roar. She met his fervor with an explosion of her own.

"Tell me, Gideon. Show me."

His lips came down on hers, and this time there was nothing gentle about him. His tongue forced its way inside her and raked the darkness of her mouth. The movement was so completely unexpected, and the resultant thrill, she had to cling to his coat sleeves to keep from falling.

In an instant she became a woman she did not know, a needy creature with hungers only Gideon could satisfy. Understanding little of those hungers, she let instinct take control. Her arms stole around his neck and she pressed hot breasts against his chest, knowing her pleasure would be increased a thousandfold if their bodies were bare, but little knowing how to get them that way.

Gideon's hand took over where her instinct failed. His mouth seemed to suck her inside him, while his fingers stroked her cheek, her neck, her bosom, cupping her fullness, running a thumb inside the edge of her gown, stroking the hard tip that so eagerly awaited him.

With a low moan, he did what she had been too cowardly to do. He tugged the neckline lower until both breasts were exposed to wherever he wanted to touch, to whatever he wanted to do.

He ended the kiss and bent to lick one tip, and then the other. Lightning pleasure shot through her. All reason fled, replaced by a panicky eagerness she could not control. She leaned down to kiss the hairline at his temples, to lick his skin, to taste his salt.

His hands eased down to her waist, to her hips, holding her tight against him. Her whole body throbbed. She would do anything, anything . . .

Her eyes fluttered open for a moment. She caught sight of the unlit chandelier hanging over them, of the stuccoed ceiling, of the shadows flickering about. Too, she saw the pair of them as if she were standing aside, watching with cool detachment their frantic gropings.

A small, thin voice of reason broke through her passion. This was wrong, no matter how right it felt.

"No, Gideon," she whispered, "no," unable to push him away, knowing that she must.

He held still a moment—he must not have heard her—then with a groan broke away, quickly, almost frantically, as if she had burned him with one of the coals.

Her head reeled from the suddenness and she fought for breath, the pleasure of his kiss and of his touch still rippling through her as she struggled to understand what had happened.

She had come to her senses—that was it, though it brought her little joy.

"My God," he whispered. "What have I done?"

A cold draft blew across her. She shivered and squeezed her eyes closed. He pulled her against him and held her tight.

Slowly sanity returned. Once again she had made a fool of herself with Gideon, only this time she had gone further than she had realized was possible. Other women might behave in such a way with men. But not she. Not until now.

Nothing had prepared her for the ecstasy she felt in Gideon Blackthorne's arms.

Neither had she been prepared for the degradation that followed. He liked women. He used them. Had she not been told this more than once?

She pulled herself free. He backed away, turning toward the fire, giving her a chance to adjust her gown and smooth her hair. She pulled her gloves over trembling hands, wanting to cover every part of her that she could.

Only a moment ago she had been begging for something far different. He had done nothing unwanted. As experienced as he was, he had to know it. The pitiful little *no* had been to herself more than to him.

A new wave of humiliation washed over her. Somehow she must get through the next few minutes without completely debasing herself. Somehow she must recover the Lucinda Fairfax that she had always known, reclaim once again her self-reliance, her clearheadedness, her pride.

For that, she needed to be alone.

She glanced at the desk. "The bullet," she said simply.

Gideon turned to face her. Their eyes met, and neither spoke. An understanding seemed to pass between them. What had happened should not be discussed. The feelings they had aroused in one another must not be rekindled, each having demonstrated dangerous abandon where the other was concerned.

She should have felt relief at his sensitivity, as well as surprise. Instead, she experienced a momentary desolation, as if someone she knew very well had died.

"The bullet," he said.

"What do you plan to do about it?"

He walked to the desk, standing very close beside her, and awareness of him rippled through her. His attention was focused elsewhere. Picking up the bullet, he gave it a cursory glance, then dropped it in his pocket.

"I will have to take steps to see that such an accident does not occur again."

She did not ask how such a prevention could be arranged.

"You must promise me two things," he said.

She stared at his lips. *Whatever you wish*, she almost said, but that would have been beyond foolishness, a return to insanity.

"First, mention the incident to no one."

She nodded. Whom would she tell? Who would take her seriously?

"And second, do not ride in those woods again."

"It is not something I am tempted to do."

He picked up his cape and the gloves that lay beside them.

"I will let myself out. I am sorry, Lucinda. For many things. Though what passed between us tonight I cannot bring myself to regret."

He was gone before she could say a word, leaving her to silence and to memory. Once, an eternity ago, she had thought herself strong, impervious where men were concerned, ready to face the challenges of the world. She did not think so anymore.

After a while she rang for Fenton and asked him to take word to Sir Sheridan that she had been taken ill and would he please make her excuses to her guests.

When he was gone, a scowl of disapproval on his normally unreadable face, she hurried up the back stairs to the sanctuary of her chamber, where she would have to deal with the inquisitive eyes of Alice and the accusing stare of the hound.

After bustling about a few minutes, Alice left, and eventually Baron settled by the fire. Taking off the finery she would never again wear, she held her wrapper tight over her nightgown, stepped onto the balcony, and gazed at Blackthorne Hall. Riding cross-country, Gideon would by now be halfway home.

Gideon, with his secrets and the hidden places he went and the women he knew.

She touched her lips and felt a burning in the back of her eyes. Interrupted passion had torn her, but it was not that which disturbed her now. Rather, it was another emotion, one far deeper and more complex, an unrequited stirring of the heart that, allowed to grow, would bring her unbearable pain, a suffering that might well endure for the rest of her life.

Chapter Eleven

For the next three days the skies opened and the rains fell. Trapped inside the house, Lucinda did what she frequently did at the New York farmhouse: she dusted. Outside of galloping across an open field, it was the best activity she could think of to occupy her mind.

In moving about the many rooms of Craven Manor, she stayed away from her father's private chambers. She had not been near them since that first visit. Whether his presence had been real or a product of her imagination, she was loath to go in them again.

Dusting, however, did not bring peace. Mrs. Pickering fussed, Fenton frowned, and Alice said she had never done such work before except in her lady's chamber, and even then rarely, but she would give it a try if Miss Fairfax truly wanted her to.

Mrs. Pickering was the worst.

"I'll get to it when I can," she said. "I always do. If my work is not what it should be, I'll leave and you can hire someone more to your liking. Like enough there's plenty of housekeepers ready to take the job."

Lucinda put down a figurine of two dogs facing one another. She had just begun her scandalous assault in the drawing room and estimated she had another dozen figurines to go, as well as one desk, three tables, a half-dozen chairs, and a mantelpiece clock.

"This really troubles you, doesn't it?" she said.

Mrs. Pickering sniffed. "Will you be giving me references? Such papers will help, though where I shall apply in these hard times I cannot guess."

Lucinda threw up her hands.

"You win. I'll stop. But all of this is much too much for you and Fenton to see to. We had temporary workers here for a couple of days. Can we hire any permanently?"

The housekeeper eyed her suspiciously. "What did you have in mind?"

"Help for you. How many workers do you need? If you could have all you wanted."

The woman did not have to be asked twice.

"Let's see, there's housemaids, a pair of 'em,

upper and under. The rooms get dusty, as you can see, whether or not there are people about. Then, of course, there's the kitchen maid and the scullery maid; one of each ought to do. We've been needing a groom, too."

"And a gardener. I definitely want a gardener," Lucinda said.

She could envision the frown of disapproval on Carlyle Winston's face when he heard of the expenditure. "Your father would not approve sacrificing so much of your competency," he would say.

There was no disapproval in Mrs. Pickering's expression. But she did look skeptical.

"You're not teasing me, are you, Miss Fairfax?"

"I'm as serious as I have ever been in my life."

"Lord Westcombe was not one for extravagance."

"Which of the servants would be an extravagance?"

"The gardener, if I may be so bold as to say."

"But he's the one I want most. You and Fenton will do the interviewing, won't you? Let me know how much money you will need. I'll have it added to the household account."

With that, she threw on her cloak and hurried through the rain to the stable to talk to Lancelot. Jumping and barking and throwing his bulk in wide circles around her, Baron seemed as glad to get out of the house as she.

* * *

On the day the rains ceased, she was introduced
to another upper-class custom: the calling card.
A stack of them, from the female guests at the
soiree and from a half-dozen people she had
never heard of, appeared on a silver salver Fenton had placed on the mantel in the library.

"What am I supposed to do with these?" she
asked Alice.

"Have you your own card, mum? If not, you
should do the return visiting yourself."

She shivered at the thought. "What if I don't?"

"I'm not sure how it's done in other parts, but
in Hummersby Bridge they'll be calling again,
in the afternoon, and you're obliged to receive
them, unless you lie and send word you are not
at home. That's what Lady Pettifore did—see
the guests, that is. She was a right one for doing
things proper."

As if her new mistress were not. The girl
clearly had not forgiven Lucinda for the dusting.

And that was why, on the first clear day after
the rain, when visitors were sure to come, Lucinda set out for a brisk walk on a country road
that wound off from the main highway, in the
general direction of the plowed fields that the
tenant farmers worked. Even with Baron at her
side, she would go nowhere near a particular
forest where careless hunters dwelt, a forest

near the precipice that overlooked the River Craven.

She stayed in the open where she could not be mistaken for a grouse; the only likely dangers were puddles of rainwater and patches of mud. She would be safe. Not even the Devil Duke could find fault.

She would have preferred a carriage ride into town to visit the china factory, but two things had stopped her. First, Hudson Smedley had turned down her repeated requests for a tour. A post to the banker had brought quick written assurance that the profits from the factory continued to rise and that she should harbor no concern, but still, she had an uneasy feeling about the place that would not go away until she saw it for herself.

Her second reason for avoiding town was more personal: She might easily run into someone who had witnessed her disgraceful departure from the soiree. The possibility of such encounters was what had sent her running from the calling cards.

She sighed. If they only knew how far her disgrace had gone.

Without her being conscious of the change, the road narrowed to little more than a lane, barely wide enough for a wagon to traverse. A half mile down the way the lane cut sharply to the right. She was prepared to follow it when Baron began sniffing around a clump of weeds, his tail wagging in excitement. Investigating his find, she discovered a hidden branch of the lane, a narrow path that hinted at a rural scene she had not observed before. It was this branch that she chose, feeling like an adventurer though she could not be the first person to have walked this way.

To the right lay a furrowed field, its crop of hay long ago harvested, and on beyond, a herd of sheep was scattered about a distant hillside, feeding on the October grass.

Banked along the left side of the lane was a stone fence in such disrepair it could have been erected as long ago as Roman times, although she doubted that any Roman builder would have been so imprecise in the construction. A tangle of shrubbery and brambles lay on the far side of the fence, along with a few scattered oaks and evergreens, blocking the view of the landscape, giving the whole area a shadowed, forbidding look, as if the sun shone everywhere but there.

She felt a chill but could blame only herself. Seduced by the rare sunshine, she had come out without cloak or hat or even gloves, her hair plaited into one long braid that hung heavily against her back. Her dress was one she had brought from America. She had thought the coarse wool fabric, along with exercise, would be enough to keep her warm, but she had been wrong.

Still, after so many days of confinement, she did not want to turn back just yet. Despite the thick foliage behind the fence, this was a pastoral scene—peaceful, free of human habitation. All was well. For this little while she felt free.

She continued the trek for three-quarters of a mile, the field receding on her right, replaced by the same tangle of wild growth that grew on her left, the bushes on either side so tall they blocked out the light.

Plunged into shadows, she rubbed her arms for warmth, sensing an eeriness whose origin she could not name. Her feeling of freedom fled. She had not known that such a wildness existed on her land. Or perhaps it was Blackthorne property; she was not sure.

She was reminded of the atmosphere in her father's chambers. Here in the open she felt no similar presence. But she felt threatened, as she had then, by a force unknown and unseen.

When she came to a sharp bend in the lane, she was about to turn back when a low growl in Baron's throat stopped her. Fear sent a chill down her spine. Above the growl she heard from ahead the sound of an approaching horse, the hooves hitting the ground hard and fast.

Gideon. Silly thought. It could be anyone. Whoever the rider was, if she did not get out of the way, she would be run down. She panicked. Stone steps protruded from the fence two yards in front of her. A stile, thank goodness. She took the steps two at a time, finding herself in a clearing of the shrubs.

Without hesitation, Baron bounded over the fence and passed effortlessly on beyond her. Following his lead as if she were on a leash, she hurried across the field. The more she ran, the faster her pace.

A rustling noise from behind set her heart to pounding. Someone was upon her, coming from out of the bushes beside the lane, chasing her on foot. She whirled. Feeling foolish, she realized the sound had been caused by the breeze.

She stopped and took a steadying breath. How foolhardy she had been to get herself in such a situation. The report of a gun seemed to echo around her. Imaginary though it was, at the moment the shot seemed very real, as real as her vulnerability and her solitude.

The fear struck more strongly, as powerful as it was without reason. She did not want to see Gideon, or anyone, out here like this in the middle of nowhere. So many things could happen, and none of them good. He had tried to tell her that danger lurked in the countryside. She should have listened.

In the distance she could see a line of shrubs and trees, and above it a ribbon of smoke as might come from a chimney. It must be the cottage of one of the tenants. She made her decision quickly. Lifting her skirt, ignoring the rocky, muddy terrain, she headed out at a run toward the chimney.

"Lucinda, stop!"

She looked over her shoulder to see Gideon in the lane, astride his horse, his upright figure visible through a break in the hedge. Something in his voice and in the way he held himself made him seem, for the first time, truly threatening, as though he would do her harm if she did not obey.

He called her name again. She waved him away.

"Go on with your ride," she cried out, as if he would do as she asked. "I'm all right. Please leave me alone."

With Baron barking alongside her, she tried to slow her steps, to show him she was out for no more than the leisurely stroll that had been her original intent. But her feet had a will of their own, and her pace quickened until she was once again running. She tripped and fell, her hands landing flat against the muddied ground, but she was up in an instant, mindlessly running.

Suddenly the hound stretched his long legs and once again bounded in front of her, this time slowing as he got in her path, forcing her to do the same, as if he acted in partnership with the man. She glanced back and saw the black gelding soar effortlessly over the fence and run in her direction without breaking stride.

She turned from the sight. After a few stumbling steps, she felt a strong arm encircle her waist and lift her into the air. Before she could begin to fight him, he sat her sideways across his lap, her feet dangling helplessly close to the horse's foreleg, two powerful arms extended on either side of her, holding her in place.

All of Gideon's actions seemed effortless, as if he kidnapped women every day. And her attempts to fight him were as useless as efforts to close her mind to his memory.

In truth, the will to fight had evaporated the instant she felt his hands on her. Her mind told her to resist his authoritative manner, but every other part of her had come alive.

He reined to a halt. The horse pranced restlessly in place, then at a click of his master's tongue, held still. After one sharp bark, even Baron fell silent.

"You're a fool, Lucinda," Gideon said, his breathing as ragged as her own. But he was not looking at her, instead staring straight ahead, in the direction of the hidden cottage beneath the ribbon of smoke.

Her cheeks burned at the rebuke, but she could not refute him. He had no idea how right he was.

For a moment he seemed to forget she was

there, and she felt the rigidity in him, a tension that had nothing to do with her.

He's got secrets . . . places he goes . . .

Staring at his strong profile, feeling his warmth and strength, she admitted the truth: She would have sacrificed everything to be a part of those secrets, to share in his journeys no matter where he went.

Her weakness for him was why she had run.

It was a weakness he did not share. He wanted to tell her nothing, to go his way alone.

She felt sick inside, empty, more isolated than when she had actually been in solitude. Beyond doubt, something, someone, was in that cottage. Someone who meant a great deal to him; someone he did not want her to know about. It was why he had been in the lane.

A woman. Had she not been told often enough that he kept them? It had been her ill luck to discover his secret love nest at the moment he was riding by.

She felt his eyes on her. They burned with a fire that brought no comfort. When she dared to look at him, he was studying the isolated, broken field.

"What are you doing out here?" he said. "How did you find this place?"

She tried to sit with a modicum of dignity, but with his hard thighs beneath her and his arms on either side, she failed.

"Chance," she said. "And Baron sniffing around."

"You took a wrong path. You have no idea what danger might await. I tried to warn you."

"You exaggerate, Gideon. I was all right until you came along."

His gaze slid to hers. In the depths of his black eyes were flecks of light she had not seen before. Unsmiling, his hair as wild as hers, his sun-browned granite face darkened further by bristles, there was nothing soft or yielding about him except his mouth, which was parted, promising a sweetness she had tasted before.

Damn him. He was driving her not only to immorality, but now to profanity as well.

"Were you truly all right?" he said. "And now you are not?"

She caught her breath as yearning flooded through her. What if she were mistaken in her supposition? What if he had no woman to warm his bed on cold Yorkshire nights? What if all the talk had been just that and nothing more? She had been so certain she'd heard the truth. She had never wanted more to be wrong.

"You know too much about me," she said, thinking of all that he had seen of her the last time they had been together, and more, all that he had kissed.

"Not nearly enough," he said.

She read a world of meaning into his simple words, but she knew he referred only to her physical being; he knew nothing about what blossomed in her heart.

Still, the muscles in the pit of her stomach tightened, and she felt her breasts begin to swell. She was like an obedient pet who preened and panted when her owner drew near. The thought did not change her reaction to him. Foolish though she was, she was lost enough in her growing feeling for him to feel no shame.

Taking off his gloves, he shoved them under his belt and stroked her cheeks with the backs of his fingers, then cupped her face.

"Lucinda," he said, and then, "light."

"You are the danger," she said. "You tear me."

"I should." She closed her eyes, fearful of what he might read in them. "I cannot be one of your women, Gideon."

He took a deep breath. "So you have heard about them."

At least, she thought, he did not try to deny their existence. He could have no notion of how much the implied admission hurt.

She thought of the smoke curling out of the distant woods. She ought to ask him who was warmed by the fire. Would he tell her? Did she really want to know?

She tried to match his tone. "You lead a curious life—mysterious, secretive, yet your reputation has spread."

"And you cannot be my woman."

"Not one of many."

"And if you were the only one?"

She studied the open throat of his shirt. Pride came to her rescue.

"Stop it. You don't mean it. And you know I know little about men."

"Except to dislike them."

"I dislike their selfishness."

"That is how you view me, as selfish?"

"Of course. Why else would you keep teasing me and taunting me? It must bring you a perverse kind of pleasure. You have no intention of making me your only . . . companion. And I have no intention of accepting, no matter what you offer. You must know I plan to leave before long."

He held still for a moment. She could hear the air around them move.

"I had not realized it," he said. "Though I told you that first night in the garden you ought to do so."

"I never intended to stay. You were right. I do not belong."

He kissed her lightly.

"No, you don't."

She pressed her hands against him, muddying the front of his shirt.

"I don't understand you," she said. "You seem to push me away and draw me close, as if I were some kind of toy. I don't know what it is you want."

"What an innocent you are, my dear."

"I grow less so each time I'm with you."

"And more desirable."

He kissed her again, this time more firmly, and the heat from him stirred her blood. She dropped any pretense of being offended by him. He had to know he was driving her mad.

Slipping her arms around his neck, she looked into his eyes and melted a little more. If he could play games, so could she, the only difference being the effort expended; for him, games came easily.

"You have a well trained horse," she said.

That brought a twitch of his lips. "Much better trained than his master."

She returned the kiss lightly, knowing he read the promise in it.

"Trained in what?" she asked.

"Respectability. I do not have the knack."

"That makes two of us, doesn't it?"

She felt heady, talking to him this way, teasing him when she already knew the things he was capable of, the way he could tear her apart.

"Only one of us lacks respectability," he said, "and it is not you."

"You sound far too serious. I wanted to get away from that."

"I am by nature a serious man. I wrong you, Lucinda. Even for the brief time you are here, I can make no promises."

All the lightness she had been attempting

201

turned to a heaviness of heart. A shiver ran through her, and she pushed away from him as best she could. The horse stepped about in place, sharing her disquiet. Gideon held her firmly, making sure she did not fall.

"Do you really think I am after promises?" she asked. "I am not that much of a fool."

But of course she was. Knowing she was leaving, understanding it was for the best, she wanted him to ask her to stay. It mattered not that at times she doubted him as much as she wanted him. Until this instant, she had not realized the depth of that wanting. Or the inconsequence of the doubt.

But she should have. Every woman who felt about a man the way she felt about Gideon needed promises as well as pleas. It was part of the feminine character, a part she had not known existed in her. In the relationship that had developed between them—she could think of no better word—she was learning very little about him but much about herself.

She felt his eyes boring into her.

"Please," she said, "don't embarrass me by trying to be noble. I would much rather you be the devil I heard so much about. That way I will expect little. Look at me as an American adventuress. That way you can feel the same."

Again the horse moved restlessly, rocking Lucinda in her devil's arms. A soothing click from his master settled the animal down.

She got no such consideration.

"So you want me to kiss you," he said. "I mean really kiss you."

"I want it very much."

He gave her what she wanted, in the manner in which she wanted it, gentle and then with more thoroughness, his hands firm against her back, then easing lower until they pressed against her hips. She felt his body tighten under her. As his tongue invaded, she shifted against him and he groaned.

For once she felt like the one in control, the one who could bring the desired reaction in the other. Power made her giddy, and the giddiness made her bold. She touched her tongue to his and sensed a tremor shooting through him. It passed from him to her. She clung to him, but only for a moment, until the shape of him was impressed upon her.

He broke the kiss and rested his forehead against hers.

"This is madness," he said. "You do not protect yourself."

"I don't know how. I thought I did, but not anymore."

"Then it is up to me, is it not?" He kissed her temple. "I have faced many difficult tasks in my life, but none harder than this."

At that moment she sensed such a warmth in her heart that she started to tell him how she truly felt, to put words to an emotion she had not herself named. How could she possibly part from him and keep such a powerful secret to herself?

But she had no idea how he would react. She would die if her confession brought his first laugh.

She pushed away. "I've gotten you muddy," she said, studying his once-white shirt.

"We are both in the same state," he said, with such solemnity she wondered if he meant the mud. "American adventuress or not, I can hardly deliver you home as you are. There's only one thing to do: take you to Blackthorne and give you a bath."

Before she could protest, he clicked his well trained horse into action and they took off across the field.

"Hold on," he said.

He didn't have to say it twice. Despite the burden of a second rider, the gelding leaped over the stone fence as effortlessly as he had the first time. Baron was close behind. Gideon took a winding path toward the castle, frequently turning into different lanes, almost as if he did not want her to retrace the route.

He approached Blackthorne Hall from the rear, passing cottages and outbuildings that became more frequent as they reached the shadows of the looming castle. Several men and women came out to watch them ride by, and children, too, all nodding or waving at their master, clearly holding him in respect if not outright affection.

One boy no older than eight came bounding out of the barn, calling out, "Gideon," in a familiar manner that she would have thought unlikely for a working child to a duke. He started to run after them, but a glance at the huge hound running behind the rear hooves stopped him.

Glancing over Gideon's shoulder, Lucinda got a good look at the boy. It was like staring into the face of a younger version of the duke. There was no mistaking the resemblance—the black eyes and hair, the lift of his head, the lines of the face that would grow sharper as he matured.

One of Gideon's bastard sons. He must be. She had no time to react, for the father reined to a halt, eased her to the ground, and joined her, turning his mount over to a stableboy, and taking her by the arm.

He led her through a back door, along a dark corridor, and into a small room that served as a pantry.

"Hullo," he called out.

"Coming," a familiar voice cackled.

Within seconds, Lucinda was standing before the short, stooped figure of Jenny Patchell.

Jenny, who was known to disappear for days at a time.

Jenny, who had warned her to stay away from the duke.

Lucinda hid her astonishment.

"Got yerself a mite soiled," Jenny said. "I'll take ye into the kitchen and clean ye best I can. Be off wi' ye, Blackthorne. Looks like the both of ye could do wi' a good scrub."

With a nod and a long, thoughtful look at Lucinda, Gideon did as Jenny ordered. Between the boy outside and the old woman indoors, Lucinda was struck into silence.

The silence continued as Jenny directed her into a small room off the kitchen, where she took off her gown and shoes, sat in her underclothes, and tried not to think. A blank mind proved impossible. Details that seemed unimportant when she was in Gideon's arms assailed her now. He had been greatly disturbed to find her running across the field, but when she'd tried to ask why, he'd teased her and kissed her. He had done the same when he'd ordered her from the soiree.

Was he using her weakness for him to distract her? Whatever his purpose, it was working. Any doubts she harbored, any questions she wanted to put to him, died the instant she went into his arms.

When she was dressed in clean clothes, she followed the old woman down corridors and past a hundred closed doors, always keeping her eyes straight ahead lest she learn something else that might hurt.

At last they went through an entryway as dark and gloomy as anything else about the man who owned it, down the front steps of the hall, and into the duke's waiting carriage. Lucinda climbed inside with the aid of a very proper footman.

Baron, likewise cleansed, came out of nowhere and bounded onto the seat across from her. The footman closed the door after him, then scurried to his rear perch. Lucinda looked out the window to see the duke himself striding down the stone steps toward her. He was wearing a clean white shirt, clean trousers, and polished boots, and he had added a blue waistcoat that made him appear almost formal.

His staff, including Jenny, was certainly thorough. They had done a very fine job.

"Thank you for the ride," she said stiffly, thinking he could choose which one she meant.

Here was the moment to bid him good-bye and to vow she would never see him again. It was the only approach to him that made any sense.

After a deep breath, she added, "If the weather permits, I plan to take Lancelot out tomorrow evening." She told him her route. "You may join me if you wish, though I warn you a gallop is all I plan and the only thing I want."

He looked at her without speaking.

"I mean it, Gideon," she said with more sincerity than he could ever realize.

"Of course you do," he said. "And so you should. But I wonder why you tell me."

"It is a question I ask myself."

He nodded toward the coachman, and Lucinda was borne away, leaving him standing in the middle of the drive staring after her. Or so she supposed. She did not look back.

As the well-sprung carriage rolled along, giving her by far the smoothest journey she had ever experienced, she thought back to the strangest afternoon she could ever remember . . . to the hidden lane and the hidden cottage, to all of her suppositions and fears, to Gideon's talk about a danger he never got around to explaining, to the weakness she had felt in his arms.

And there was Jenny, very much at ease in the home of the man she had warned her new mistress against.

The puzzles she was uncovering in her father's world continued to grow, only now they were worse, far worse, because her heart was involved. There was only one way to learn more about Gideon. She needed to be with him when he did not touch her. Hence, the suggestion of the ride.

A half hour later she was deposited in front of Craven Manor, again aided by the footman. Another carriage had arrived ahead of her.

Standing in the portico were Mrs. Rebecca Atterbury and Sir Sheridan Pettifore, both of them staring at the Duke of Ravenswood's crest on the carriage door.

With a forced smile, Lucinda smoothed her disgracefully uncovered hair and walked toward them, ready to receive her first post-soiree afternoon guests. With each step, it was not their bemused expressions that burned into her mind, nor even the dark, steady gaze of Gideon, but rather the happy regard of a young boy staring after his master, the lord of the manor who shared the same eyes and same face.

Chapter Twelve

"I had visitors waiting for me yesterday."

Lucinda concentrated on Lancelot's ears as she rode down a lane that was wide and un-cluttered, definitely on Fairfax land, far from yesterday's path.

"Let me guess," Gideon said. "Sir Sheridan Pettifore."

"Your coachman told you."

"No one told me, Lucinda. No one had to. I have seen the way he looks at you."

She shrugged off the ridiculous comment.

"He wasn't the only one waiting. Rebecca Atterbury joined him. They were standing on the portico and watched my arrival."

He glanced at her from beneath the low brim

of a hat, worn, he claimed, to look respectable, to show her he knew how. But there was nothing respectable about the glint in his eyes.

"They took note of the crest," he said.

"I could barely get them indoors. And barely away from the hints and intimations that I should explain why I was in His Grace's carriage with only a dog for company."

"What did you tell them?"

"That I was very glad they had come to call, and please let me ring for tea."

"I'm sure that satisfied them."

"Oh, it did. Cook is quite talented at preparing small iced cakes."

His lips came very, very close to curving into a smile. "I like a woman who knows how to skirt the truth."

She dared a quick look into the dark sea of his eyes. "Strange. I don't feel that way at all about a man."

They rode in silence for a few minutes, the only sounds the lazy plop of hooves against the hard-packed dirt, the occasional bark of Baron, investigating fields to right and left, and the faraway rasping cry of a grouse.

They had been riding thus, in silence and then in casual conversation, for half an hour, the darkness gathering around them as a comfort, shutting out the world. This was the way things should be between them—uncomplicated, friendly, their glances warm instead of heated with inner fire.

Until this evening she had not know whether such a conversation was possible. She rejoiced that it was.

"Mrs. Atterbury is interested in you," Lucinda said.

"Is she?"

"She mentioned your name once or twice, talking about what a mysterious man you are, with suggestions of violence and danger surrounding you."

"You agreed."

"About the danger, yes. The violence I'm not so sure about."

She was skirting too near topics she did not want to discuss, and she hurried on.

"She really is a very beautiful woman. And so British."

"British?"

"Like you. Men and women do like to be close to their own kind."

"I have never disagreed with you more. Tell me the truth. Are you trying to make her one of my women?"

"If you would cooperate, I believe she might agree."

"And what about you and Sir Sheridan?"

She sighed in exasperation. "You keep hinting that something is going on between us. I don't see how you could possibly think such a

213

thing when . . . well, I don't see how you could. He is nothing more than a friend."

"Men and women do not make good friends."

"But of course they do."

"Give me an example."

She thought a moment. "I'll admit I can't come up with one, but I'm sure such friendships exist."

"If you won't be my woman, then you will be my friend—is that what you're suggesting?"

I'll be your woman.

She concentrated on Baron's wagging tail a half-dozen yards in front of Lancelot. Like a metronome, it moved to the beat of her heart.

"I'm not suggesting anything."

She almost added *Your Grace*, but she knew how the formality annoyed him. It was another mystery concerning the Devil Duke, a small one, but still something unexplained. He could hardly find the honorific an insult. Most people used it with close to reverence, for the power it represented if not for the man.

"I've hired a gardener," she said.

"To work on our secret meeting place?"

"I don't think the garden was all that secret."

"Still, I rather liked it wild."

"I'm certain that you did. Tell me the truth. Have you ever planted so much as a seed in your life?"

"I thought you knew the answer to that."

It took a moment for her to comprehend what he said.

"Gideon, that was not a nice thing to say. And I'm not sure I should admit to understanding it."

"I told you I am a terrible man. That is a fact you keep forgetting."

"And that's why you keep reminding me."

He did not have to. The image of the dark-haired, dark-eyed boy running after him at Blackthorne Hall kept flitting through her mind.

More silence. A little of the joy went out of the ride.

"Actually, I'm quite good at planting," he said. "Do not frown, my light, I'm speaking of peonies and roses. You must come and see what I am able to grow."

She wasn't sure whether he was dealing in innuendo again, and she answered him in the same ambiguous tone.

"I would like that very much."

They rode on for a half hour more, gradually wending their way back to the manor house, bidding each other good night with no more than a nod. Their talk had been of flowers and fertilizer, and gradually she'd realized he really did know something about gardening. When they rode again the next evening, he brought her cuttings from a favorite climbing rose.

By the end of the week, during which they

rode every evening but two when rain kept them indoors, she could no longer deny how she felt about him. He could have a thousand mistresses stashed away and still she loved him—wildly, madly, and gently, too, in a manner that one moment set her pulse to pounding and the next comfortingly warmed her heart.

She could hardly tell him how she felt, nor could she ask him to hold her and kiss her, as she very much wanted to do. She knew that if she did, he would comply with all that she asked for and far, far more.

She was not the woman she had been when she'd set sail for London, and she was not the woman she would be when she sailed back home. For the while, she would rejoice, privately, always privately, in Gideon Blackthorne's company, in the suggestive looks and words, in the occasional touch.

And she would forget as best she could the aura of danger that surrounded him, the hints of violence, the dark mysteries that ate at his soul.

If any of her servants wondered about the exact relationship between her and Gideon, especially after the evening rides began, nothing was said. The same could not hold true of her frequent afternoon visitors. Lady Pettifore was the most direct.

"What's going on between you and the Devil Duke? Do not let him lead you astray, my dear.

Men have their needs—yes, even my precious Sheridan—and His Grace is the worst of the lot. Surely you have heard—"

"More tea, Lady Pettifore?" Lucinda asked, shoving a plate of iced cakes in her direction.

The woman's eyes twinkled. "Of course, Miss Fairfax. How kind."

And the subject was effectively changed.

It was from Mrs. Hanson, the vicar's wife, that she got the rest of Gideon's tragic history, when that lady paid her a call.

Lucinda tried not to pry, but when Mrs. Hanson brought up the story herself, recalling how her recounting had been interrupted that day in the churchyard, Lucinda did not discourage her.

Mrs. Hanson started right in. "Let's see, where was I? Oh, yes, Geoffrey's accident."

"The one that left him different."

"When he was twelve, yes, I recall exactly where I stopped. Through all those years of his growing to manhood, he really was quite wild, which his father, the late duke, was loath to admit. But finally, after a particularly ugly scene when Geoffrey almost beat a man to death over a game of cards, all the while smilingly talking about teaching him a much-needed lesson, His Grace admitted the truth."

"It must have been very difficult for him."

"I'm told it was, Geoffrey being his favorite. And of course he blamed Gideon for the fight since Gideon had been elsewhere at the time—involved in a dalliance I'm told, if you understand what I mean, though I've heard no proof concerning his exact whereabouts. I do not personally speak ill of him, you understand, but only what was the general talk."

"I understand."

"Because there was a great injury to the poor card player, the magistrate was called. To keep his son from jail, His Grace agreed to take him to a specialist in London, where he could receive help for his very tragic condition, which, truth to tell, no one around Hummersby Bridge completely understood. A faithful servant accompanied them, a strapping man as strong and healthy as the damaged son, to help in the sea voyage to London, a journey that was supposed to be an added benefit to Geoffrey's health. Or so His Grace believed. It was why he chose not to confine his son to a train."

She paused a moment. "He could not have been more wrong."

Stirring her tea, she reached for another cake.

"These are wonderful. I do hope your cook will share the recipe."

"I'll ask," Lucinda said, and then, prodding: "You said they drowned."

"Ah, yes. Sad. Very sad. A terrible storm it was that struck the seacoast on the eve of their departure. The waves buffeted the ship about, crashing the hull against the dock and bending the masts until they almost snapped. Already the three travelers were on board, not having known, you see, about the unexpected turn in the weather. They were seen walking about the deck, Geoffrey shaking his fist at the elements as if he could hold off the wind and rain, partly in jest and then in a fury as thunderous as anything around him."

She hesitated and set aside her plate. Lucinda stared into the drawing room fire and felt the chill of the long-ago storm.

"It was a part of his illness, I am sure," Mrs. Hanson said. "Later the captain declared he should have ordered the lot of them to their cabins, but dealing with a man of such high birth as the Duke of Ravenswood was not something he managed well, especially when he would be telling him something His Grace must have already realized. He seemed, it was said, quite unable to control his son."

Another hesitation.

"What a terrible time for everyone," Lucinda said.

"That it was. All three were lost, washed overboard sometime during the night. The next morning, when their cabins were found empty, a search was begun, boats sailing up and down the coast, but the sea had claimed them and was not about to return its treasure so easily."

"But you said father and son were in the crypt."

"In good time, I'll get to it in good time. The younger son was sent for and joined in the search, wandering to and fro along the beach, climbing the high cliffs, staring out to sea with his spyglass during the times he was not actually sailing upon the water. They say he was a terrible sight, his dark features stark with grief, searching and walking for three days straight without food or sleep, until his eyes were reddened and he was unable to see."

"Poor Gideon," Lucinda said softly. Unable to sit still a moment longer, she went to the hearth and stirred the fire.

"Aye, poor indeed," Mrs. Hanson said behind her. "A week later two bodies washed ashore. Gideon identified them as father and son, though their features had been destroyed by creatures of the deep. Forgive me for the cruelty of the details, but you wanted to know."

"And the third man? The servant?"

"Weeks later he was found, and His Grace, the present duke, saw that he received a proper burial in the home of his birth to the south of here."

"How did . . . His Grace identify the bodies?"

"Oh, there was no doubt. Others named them before he ever saw them, from the clothing and the jewelry and a fresh cut that Geoffrey had received in the fight that almost sent him to jail. Somehow that identifying bit of flesh had been spared, as if Providence was allowing the lad a

Christian burial under his rightful name."

Lucinda stood in hushed stillness by the fire and at last brushed away a tear, a gesture that did not get past the vicar's wife.

"You have a good heart, my dear. It was, indeed, a terrible tragedy. His Grace, the current one, was never quite the same afterwards. Always moody and private, he became more so. Rumors abounded about drinking and carousing, for days and weeks on end, though there are none to say that such sins continue, at least not the drinking. As to the other, I cannot say and would not even if I knew."

"Right away he became the Devil Duke."

"I fear 'tis so. It's a reputation he's not been able to shed. In truth, he's made little attempt to do so. I don't ask that he attend services on a Sunday, though all the Blackthornes before him were seen each week in the family pew. But he ought to pay his respects to the remains of the two that were lost. Never once has he done so, not that anyone has observed, and we are, you might have noticed, a most observant town. His night rides are well known, but they have not taken him anywhere near the family crypt."

Lucinda thought of Gideon's first visits to her in the garden, after the sun had gone down. A devil in the dark, that was what he had been, and would always be to most people.

But she was not like most people. Or so she told herself.

* * *

The next evening, when he joined her out on the road, she pretended trouble from loose stirrups and asked him to help her dismount. They were far away from signs of civilization, and a cloud had passed over the moon.

Long used to the quirks of both master and mistress, the horses and the hound remained in their respective places as Gideon dropped to the ground and walked to her side. His hands were firm on her waist. As he lowered her, she gripped his shoulders and held herself close, her body pressed to his as she slid down to stand before him.

She needed no moon to see the glint in his eye.

"Lucinda."

"I shouldn't be doing this. I'll say it before you have the chance."

"You'll have me thinking there's nothing wrong with the stirrups."

"Think what you must. They did seem to tighten up just as you reached for me."

"You play with fire."

"Yes. But I wanted a simple kiss, and I needed to inspire you."

"You inspire me by existing in the world."

She caught her breath. "You have a silver tongue."

"My tongue is something you should know

much about. You want a simple kiss? Impossible."

He covered her mouth with his and showed her what he meant. She had been days away from his lips, and she responded hungrily. If there was desperation mixed with the hunger, he did not seem to notice. The ground moved and the world around her swirled.

He ended the kiss and brushed his lips against her eyelids, whispering her name.

"It feels strange to kiss you when you're wearing a hat," she said, trying to be light, though his every touch inflamed her.

"If it bothers you, I'll take it off. I'll take off anything you want."

She still retained the modesty to blush. "What a gentleman you are."

"That I am not."

He held her tightly for a moment, and she buried her face against his chest. He was wearing his cape, but the thickness did not keep her from feeling the beat of his heart. It was at moments like this he was no mystery but simply a man, and there was nothing in the world that could ever keep them apart.

But of course, moments like this did not come often, nor did they last.

She was the one to back away. "Was that thunder in the distance?"

"Probably. It's a sound I'm used to."

She stared at him for a moment, at the lines between his eyes.

"I think you mean more than just the promise of rain."

"Do I?"

Always enigmatic . . . always a mystery.

She felt him withdraw, as surely as if he had turned his back on her and walked away.

The lovely spell that had momentarily descended over them was gone. Without either of them speaking, he helped her into the saddle, then escorted her back to Craven Manor before disappearing at a gallop into the dark.

A cold wind chilled where once she had burned. Close to the stable door, a whirlwind whipped the leaves into a dusty vortex. After seeing to Lancelot, she and Baron barely made it into the manor house before the rains fell.

Hours later, when the clouds had passed and a silvery moon shone down on the rain-drenched landscape, she stood on the balcony and stared across the miles toward Blackthorne Hall. A movement on the distant moor caught her eye. She made out a man on horseback, riding to and fro. Her heart quickened. Like her, Gideon had not yet found his rest.

She waved. With the light from an oil lamp at her back, he must see her far more easily than she was seeing him. But he did not return the wave. Instead, he and his mount held still for a moment; then he reined away from her and rode off.

It was silly to feel rebuffed, yet she could not respond otherwise. The next afternoon he sent word he would not be with her on that evening or the next, and perhaps she had best remain at home. Her reaction was the same as when he had declined to wave.

With a little of her former stubbornness, she rode anyway, not so far and not so long as when he had accompanied her, but enough to satisfy her foolishly bruised pride. When she took the same ride the following evening, she saw him in the distance. Her heart lifted. He had come after all. But when she urged Lancelot into a gallop to catch up with him, he turned and disappeared at a bend in the lane, quickly, as if an ancient god had bent to earth and swept him away.

Baron took off after him, barking, and Lucinda had to call several times for him to return. For all his determination, the hound could not conquer the will of the gods.

On the third evening, Gideon rejoined her for their ride. A mist was settling over the land, but it did not deter them from striking out slowly along a winding lane.

Right away she sensed a change in him, an uneasiness, as if he were plagued by the serious worries she'd detected in him as long ago as his first visit to the garden.

But she had worries of her own, and she put her questions to him bluntly:

"Why did you ride away from me last night? And before that, two nights ago, I waved to you from my balcony and you did not respond. I don't understand. Please explain."

She heard the audacity in her words, but she could not stop them. Surely he could see she had been hurt.

"You must be mistaken. I did not see you, and you could not have seen me."

"But I did."

"You have a fanciful eye. You could not have seen me, because I was nowhere near you on those particular nights. Ask Joseph Dent, if you choose not to believe me. I had concerns of my own."

He spoke with finality, as if her questions irritated him. Her heart grew heavy. He lied. Whatever he had been about, it concerned matters that he did not want to disclose.

She could not leave things alone. Raising issues with Gideon was very much like rubbing at an old wound, but she was helpless to do otherwise.

She stared into the dark. "You love this land."

"It's all I have."

He meant it was all he cared about. She forced herself to go on.

"If something happened to me and my property reverted to the Crown, would you be able to purchase it?"

He reined to a halt for a moment, forcing her to do the same.

"Are you asking if I am grasping enough to mean you harm?" he asked.

"I don't know what I'm asking. It's a point that has occurred to me. I have no heir and am not likely to. What would happen to all this? I simply want to know."

He must know she was lying. There was nothing in her question that was simple, nothing that did not chill her soul.

He looked into the misty night, then back at her. "I could purchase everything you own—your land, your house, the undergarments you wear next to your skin. As to whether I would, it is the latter that draws my interest most."

"That's no answer. It's a provocation."

"Believe me, Lucinda, it is an answer. As to whether I mean you harm, that is for you to decide."

"It always has been, hasn't it? Early on I told you about my father and mother, and then about my wastrel grandfather, though that's a topic I've never mentioned to anyone else. You have told me nothing about yourself."

"I did not have to. Others have said all you need to know."

And all she was likely to hear. She could not look at him another instant, not because he repulsed her, but because he broke her heart.

By unspoken mutual consent, the ride was at an end. When he halted at the stable door, he helped her down and watched as she turned the reins over to the coachman Rigg.

"I have made a mistake," he said, pushing his hat to the back of his head.

Being with her, encouraging her, allowing her to fall in love—she waited for him to confirm her most desperate fears.

"We all do," she said, tugging off her riding gloves. Willfully, she likewise removed her riding hat and shook out her long hair, daring him to call her wanton.

He did not call her anything for a long moment, just looked at her, then looked away.

"I have returned to an old custom begun a century or two ago by an ancient Duke of Ravenswood I can't even name."

Seducing women to rapture, then tossing them aside.

She held her silence.

"All Hallows' Eve comes in a fortnight."

"A night of hobgoblins and ghosts."

"So some believe. By tradition, a great feast and bonfire celebrate the occasion. At least it used to until ten years ago."

Ten years ago he had lost both his father and his beloved, troubled brother. She had been viewing his behavior as if it concerned only her. But he had unsettled troubles not yet resolved, matters that did not and never could involve her.

"The celebration is open to all the workers at Blackthorne and Craven Manor as well," he said. "You, of course, are included."

"That's not necessary. I know how much you value your privacy."

Stiffly said and priggish, but that was the way he was making her feel.

"What I value, Lucinda, matters little now. Of course you must attend. Our families have long been neighbors, and though in recent years we have not been so close, the geography of our respective properties demands we share the good times and the bad."

"Geography. I wondered what it was."

He hurried on as if she had not spoken.

"We've both had a good harvest and the sheep thrive. The workers deserve a celebration before the lambing, and I've decided they shall have it."

"Although it may be a mistake."

"I shouldn't have said it that way. Please tell your butler and housekeeper to spread the news. No matter what, we shall have our conflagration." He paused. "I ask one thing of you, one thing special."

The mist sparkled like crystals in his dark hair. She wanted very much to touch it.

"Just one?" she asked.

For a moment she thought he was going to reach out to her. But he did not.

"Part of the tradition is for the lady of the house, either at Blackthorne or Craven Manor, to dance with a worker of her choice. The next dance goes to the lord. It has been many years since a woman resided in either place. I ask that you follow tradition."

"I shall dance with one of the workers."

"And then you dance with me. Whatever follows the fire will be up to you. But before the torch is put to the pyre, we will stand before one another and let the music take hold. If, that is, you are not ashamed of being in the Devil Duke's arms where others can see."

Chapter Thirteen

Over the next two weeks there was a great bustle around Craven Manor. Everyone, from Lucinda to Alice to Mrs. Pickering down to the new scullery maid, must have new clothes. Or so Alice declared. Somehow the young lady's maid had taken charge of such matters.

And there was food to prepare, the feast being provided equally by the two houses.

Jenny returned to bake the bread, which had long been her specialty.

"They say I put a special flour in it made from moondust and milled in the mist," she said when Lucinda expressed surprise. "Believe what ye will. It do have a way o' curin' the gout."

There were others about, and Lucinda could

say no more. Later she caught Jenny alone in the kitchen, arms deep in her special flour as she hunched over the slab of marble that served as a kneading board, most of her wiry gray hair hidden beneath a white cap, her figure so short and bent she could barely work at the table.

"You were at Blackthorne Hall," Lucinda said.

"There's little use denying it."

"I don't understand. You warned me away from the duke."

"And so I did."

"Have you now changed your mind?"

"I know in me bones he'll bring trouble down on yer head. Terrible trouble. Ye should fear for yer life."

"But that doesn't make sense."

Jenny's long, wrinkled fingers slapped at the dough, turning it over a time or two, sending puffs of flour into the warm kitchen air.

"There's little in this world that does, Miss Lucinda. Little that does. Ye should listen t' what I say. Every word. I'll not lead ye astray. That's all to do wi' the matter. I'm sworn to secrecy, and old Jenny's a woman t' keep her word."

Her thin lips turned inward, disappearing in deep wrinkles, as if she swallowed knowledge she was tempted to reveal.

Lucinda was not so easily put off.

"Why were you over there?"

232

"Ye're no saying I've not the right." She punched the dough. "I'll no believe it. I've had me freedom for many a year t' come 'n go as I will. 'Twas the old master who give it t' me. The one 'ut set up the factory."

Again the lips disappeared. Jenny ignored the questions put to her, about how she had got from Craven Manor to Blackthorne Hall, her duties there, if she answered directly to the duke, and if so, was she not afraid since he was such a dangerous man?

After three-quarters of an hour, all Lucinda had for her efforts was a fine coating of moondust and a heightened sense of frustration.

Going in search of Mrs. Pickering, she found her in a small room off the kitchen that served as the housekeeper's office. Already crowded inside was the entire female staff. A lecture was just ending on how their duties were to be performed the night of the celebration, what was expected of them that evening and, equally important, on the following morning when no one would be eager to do the regular chores.

She had never heard the housekeeper so brisk, so determined, so happy. It did not require a genius to figure out the cause. She was busy doing her life's work, what she had been trained to do, what she most enjoyed—supervising a busy household. When the woman saw her mistress standing in the doorway, her face assumed its regular pinched look and she shooed the servants out.

No one met Lucinda's eyes as they scurried away.

"I feel like an intruder," she said as she slipped inside the office.

"It's your home, to be sure, Miss Fairfax. You can intrude—that is, you can come and go as you please. But you don't need permission from me for that."

The words were blunt as always, but the tone softer than Lucinda had heard before. Not friendly, never that, but closer to it. She smiled to herself.

She regarded the housekeeper thoughtfully. "That first morning, when I arrived early, you were afraid I would send you packing, weren't you? You and Fenton both. I just now realized it."

Once said, the words stood out as the simple truth. Fear made the woman defensive, almost surly at times. She and the butler had to proceed cautiously, as she put it, so that they could keep their jobs.

"I don't know what you mean," Mrs. Pickering said, avoiding her eye. "You'll pardon my thick mind, Miss Fairfax, but sometimes your American way of talking and doing is confusing to me."

"How? Please tell me."

"The work and all—setting about cleaning

when it's never been done by a mistress of the house, not to my knowledge, and not to Fenton's, either. You've a free way about you, too. Not that there's anything wrong with that, but still, we've all noticed. You speak to us sometimes as if we were your equals, which you know we are not. It confuses us. We don't know what's expected."

"Very little. A kind word every now and then. I'm not much used to being waited on, but I told you that before."

"So you did." Mrs. Pickering sniffed, once again on the defensive. "When, pray tell, was I not kind to you? I've seen to your needs, have I not?"

"Always."

"Any advice I've given has been kindly meant. There were times I wanted to say more, you can be sure."

"When was that?"

The housekeeper studied her hands, which were clenched in front of her.

"The times are past. Best leave 'em be."

It wasn't necessary to elucidate. Lucinda's meetings with Gideon Blackthorne, the nightly rides, the way she had behaved with him at the soiree, leaving her guests, staying with him in the library alone . . . all of this must be truly scandalous to a woman as provincial as the housekeeper.

Mrs. Pickering was right in her judgment. But

Lucinda would not change a moment of the times she had spent with Gideon, even if she had the chance.

"One more thing, and then I'll let you get back to your tasks. I do have ways that are not yours, and I admit it. But they should not trouble you for much longer. I don't know exactly when, but before long I'll be booking passage for a return sailing to New York."

For the first time since Lucinda's arrival, the woman looked flustered.

"Oh, my. I hadn't known . . . How long will you be gone?"

"I won't be coming back."

Mrs. Pickering stared at her open-mouthed, but the housekeeper's loss of words brought her mistress little pleasure. In truth, announcing the departure gave finality to her plan, though she still had weeks before she would actually leave.

Tears sprang to her eyes, and she looked away. "I plan to make arrangements for the care of the house. No one is to be let go. That is to be part of the news that is spread. I won't have anyone upset"—her voice broke—"over the loss of a job."

With that, she hurried up the back stairs to her chamber, interrupting Alice, who was busy with needle and thread getting ready for All Hallows' Eve. Throwing on her oldest dress and shoes, Lucinda hurried back down again to dig in the back flowerbeds with the new gardener.

The work brought additional pain, for she spoke with him of plants and shrubs and climbing roses that would bloom long after she was gone.

October 31 dawned overcast but dry, and Craven Manor was busy early on, most of the work taking place in the kitchen. At midday a wagonload of supplies left for Blackthorne Hall with Cook sitting high beside the driver hired for the day. In the back the new serving girls settled carefully between the bowls and crocks and pots, making sure the containers did not spill their contents before they could be delivered.

The gardener had gone early to help with the gathering and laying of the wood for the bonfire. As the sun was nearing the western horizon, Rigg cracked a whip high over Bessie's rump and the Craven carriage started the journey, its passengers Lucinda and Alice on one side of the interior, Mrs. Pickering and Fenton on the other.

Baron was left behind with a slab of meaty ribs to enjoy in a more private celebration. As was his wont, he cast Lucinda a baleful look when she laid the feast before him, as if she were making a terrible mistake in not taking him with her.

As for Lucinda, she would have gladly settled

down beside him in the stable with her own plate of ribs and spent the hours listing all she had to do before she set sail.

She had not seen Gideon since the night he'd announced the celebration, when he'd asked her to save him a dance. As if she would not save for him all the dances through all of the years she had left to live.

She was dressed more like one of the workers than mistress of a grand house. She wore a dark blue blouse that draped off the shoulders and a matching skirt that Alice had embroidered with brightly colored thread around the hem. A red sash was at her waist and a red shawl thrown over her shoulders to ward off the night chill.

Her hair was pulled back and curled, and there was a red ribbon pinned in her locks.

"I look like a gypsy," she said when she stared at herself in the mirror.

"That's what I had in mind," Alice said. "Oh, don't you look pretty. You're a gypsy princess, that's for sure."

For herself, the lady's maid chose white, likewise gaily embroidered. Mrs. Pickering and Fenton stayed with unadorned black.

When Lucinda arrived, the festivities were already under way in a cleared field behind the castle: games and music and dancing, tankards of ale passed freely, as well as rum and pitchers of lemonade.

In the light from a hundred flickering torches

Lucinda recognized few faces, and she was content to stay in the shadows sipping a glass of lemonade. And so an hour passed. Gideon's lookalike son played Pick Up Sticks with a group of children beneath one of the torches, but his father was nowhere in sight. Neither was Mrs. Littlewood, for which she was grateful.

One adult very much in evidence was Mrs. Pickering, who seemed to draw great pleasure from watching the children.

Like the housekeeper, Lucinda tried to let the spirit of the night cheer her, but she could not stop looking for the host of the celebration. No matter how much she felt herself warming to the people, nothing seemed interesting without him. It was just as well. Drawing pleasure from the evening would make her yearn to be a part of Yorkshire just as she was preparing to leave.

Away from the others, the brawny bailiff Joseph Dent strolled into view. Gesturing with his hands, he shifted, and there was Gideon, listening to his animated discussion. Her heart leaped and liquid warmth rushed through her at no more than the sight of him.

For the evening he had put on a loose-fitting coat, which he wore unbuttoned. His white shirt was open at the throat, and her eyes traced the long column of his neck and down his shirt to the buckle of his belt, the fitted trousers, the high black boots.

All this she took in at a glance, all of him achingly familiar. A whimper of longing caught in her throat.

A third man joined them, a stranger to her, thick-necked and as big as the bailiff. He put in a word or two, drawing Gideon's attention as much as Dent had done. The two men seemed to be arguing about something. They held their duke's interest. He did not look her way.

And then he did, suddenly, as if he heard her silent calling out to him. She started to smile, but something in his expression, visible even at a distance, killed the urge, and she simply returned his stare. If he looked at her as carefully as she was looking at him, he must surely see the love in her eyes.

He would probably interpret it as hunger, but that was all right. She hungered for him, too.

He turned back to the two men and began to speak. His voice was too low to hear, but now she could see anger coming through in the set of his mouth and the hooded darkness of his eyes. His listeners did not interrupt him. At last he clapped a hand on the bailiff's arm, and the three men disappeared into the dark.

Gideon did not glance back at her.

Despite the crowd of celebrants close by, laughing and talking, she had never felt so alone. It was time to leave. How could she have ever believed she might feel herself a part of Yorkshire?

It took a quarter hour before she found Rigg

beside a barrel of ale, mingling with the new gardener and a half-dozen Blackthorne men.

He saw her and drew himself apart.

"Faith, what's ailing ye, Miss Fairfax? Ye look pale as the moon."

"I'm sorry to bother you, but I'm feeling a little faint. Perhaps I could sit in the carriage awhile and then you could take me home."

"I'll take ye home now."

"No, really, I just need to rest. I guess it's all the excitement."

"Could ye have had a wee bit o' ale? It's a strong brew, made on Blackthorne land. A frail thing like yerself might not take to it as was meant."

He was grinning at her.

"It was only a small sip. I thought no one saw." The lie was a benign one, the kind she was getting good at.

She had only to argue another minute and he led her to the carriage, which was set apart at the edge of the light. Bessie grazed nearby. Sitting in the darkness of the interior, the red shawl pulled tightly around her, she rested her head against the high seat back, closed her eyes, and thought of how Gideon had looked at her and then looked away.

"You owe me a dance."

She jerked upright and stared out the carriage window into eyes as black as sin.

"How did you find me?"

Evelyn Rogers

"I'll always find you."

"When you want to."

"I'll always want to."

She could have thrown herself at him through the window. Instead, she looked away.

"Don't tease me, Gideon. I've been accused of drinking ale, but I think you're the one who's besotted."

"I'm besotted with you. I want our dance."

He opened the door and eased inside next to her, took her in his arms, and covered her mouth with his, all quickly, smoothly done, giving her no chance to object. She tasted the ale on his tongue and it made her drunk; desire flowed through her like wine. She did not pull away; there was not enough strength in all the world to free her from his arms.

He broke the kiss and held her close.

"Lucinda," he whispered, drawing out her name. "If this is the night for witches, you have me bewitched."

"Only for the night."

"If we could have it all to ourselves, safe, alone, I would be a happy man."

He seemed to believe what he said, but she knew that, like his so sweetly expressed desire, his happiness would last no longer than All Hallows' Eve.

It was a sobering thought. She managed to push away. "I'm supposed to dance with another. Isn't that what you said?"

"Choose him carefully, Lucinda, lest I tear out his throat."

He startled her. He was teasing again. He had to be.

"Please, no bloodshed," she said. "This is a celebration."

"Yes," he said, more somber than she liked, "I had thought it was."

Remembering the two men and Gideon's anger, she put on a smile.

"And so it shall be. I'll have my dance, and then you shall have yours with me. I will show you I do not object to your holding me in your arms where others can see. There's probably not a soul on this hilltop who doesn't know where we are right now."

She shoved at him. "Now help me out before you bring me completely to ruin." She spoke carelessly, jesting about the most serious consideration of her life. He did as she asked and led her into the light.

"Whom do you suggest I ask?" she asked.

"If you're asking whose arms should hold you, I would choose old Peter, who is eighty-three and blind and walks with a cane."

"He sounds delightful. And probably lonely."

"Of course he's lonely, or at least alone. He's also got breath to turn the stomach of a goat."

As she looked around her, she caught the eye of a handsome farmer with the muscles and browned skin of a seasoned laborer. He was standing with a group of men beside a barrel of beer, and his head was thrown back in laughter.

"Anyone?" she asked. "I will not be turned down?"

"Even old Peter is not so blind. You have been the center of every man's attention since you first arrived."

"How do you know?"

"I know. If I have not told you before, I tell you now that you are a beautiful sight. You glow, my light. You put the torches to shame."

"Have you been at the ale?" she said, trying to sound saucy, but his words pleased her more than he could know.

She handed him her shawl and made for the farmer. By the time she got to him, he had already stepped away from the others and was grinning at her in a way that must have turned many a maiden's heart.

She did not have to say a word. He took her hand, lightly held her waist, and they whirled in time to a lively fiddle. Around and around they went, and she felt her carefully combed curls flow wild as the red ribbon fell to the ground.

She had thought she would be stiff and unyielding, unused as she was to dancing, but after the first turn she closed her eyes, dropped back her head, and let dizziness take control. When at last the music stopped, her head kept spinning and she had to cling to her partner to keep from falling.

Still light-headed, she felt herself passed to another man. She looked up into Gideon's smoldering eyes.

"My turn," he said huskily.

"Yes." Now and always.

He wrapped her shawl around her waist and pulled her hard against him. As if she had done so a thousand times, she wrapped her arms around his neck.

The music quickened. She had thought the dance fast before, but it was nothing like the pace Gideon set. Her feet barely touched the ground as around and around they went. Somehow, in the skillful, graceful way he had, he maneuvered her away from the watchers, away from the flickering torches, into the dense shadows close to the hall.

"Lucinda," he whispered.

She thought he would again cover her mouth with his. Instead, with only the barest light to guide him, he kissed her with no more than his eyes, touching her lips with his hot gaze, her eyes, her throat, the swell of her breasts and, with a moan, her lips once again.

"Tell me to go away," he whispered hoarsely.

"Stay."

"You know not what you say."

"I know."

"I would take your innocence."

Her answer was a touch of her tongue against his lips.

An animal sound came from deep inside him. He swept her up in his arms, and she found herself being carried in the dark along the cold stone wall of the castle, through a door somewhere toward the back, down a dark corridor, into a dark room. He rested her on a long couch, and she sank into its softness.

He knelt beside her. "I must start the fire," he said.

"You already have."

"Outside, I mean. I'll be quick."

She brushed her fingers across his mouth. "Is quickness what I want?"

He stroked her cheek. "Do not leave me. Not just yet."

She took his hand and kissed his palm. "No, not just yet. You wanted one night. Surely we can have that."

He kissed her cheek and was gone.

She shivered in his absence. Sometime during the dance the shawl had gotten lost. A woolen blanket lay across the back of the couch. She wrapped it around her and waited for him to return.

One night, or the portion of it they could steal for themselves—she would take whichever she could and feel no regret. Cruel day would come soon enough, and with it reason. And judgment. And separation.

For now, she would be the wanton he had once accused her of resembling. It was a role she knew not how to play. For now, she could act the brazen, but in the end she would put herself in Gideon's hands.

Chapter Fourteen

"I left you in the dark and the cold."

Gideon closed the door and walked toward her. Lucinda could barely hear his footsteps on the rug as he rounded the couch and stared down at her.

Her heart twisted. Something was wrong. She knew it right away, though he was little more than a dark shape blocking out the rest of the room. But she could fill in the hidden details and she sensed a hesitancy not in him before.

He had changed his mind. It was all she could think of. He did not want her anymore.

She felt hollowed out. Clutching the blanket up to her chin, she forced herself to sit up. What she was supposed to do now, she had no idea.

"I'm not cold," she said. "I welcome the dark."

He had no idea how much she spoke the truth. In the light, she would have to face realities for which she was ill prepared, whether or not she had her one night with him.

"Was the bonfire suitably brilliant?" she asked, not caring if it had burned out of control across the moors. The question was merely something to fill the dreadful silence that lay between them.

"I scarcely noticed."

She could see the outline of his hands loose at his sides. He should be touching her with those hands. Anywhere he chose.

"I'm glad about that." She was rattling on, sounding like an idiot, but she could not stop. "You were supposed to be distracted."

"I told Rigg I would see you home." He could have been speaking to Mrs. Pickering, for all the emotion he put in his words. "He seemed concerned about your health. I said you were not quite yourself."

"If I understood what *myself* really was, I would know if you spoke the truth."

Now was the time for Gideon to kneel beside her as he had before and teach her the things she needed to know. Everything she said and did was an invitation. Already she had slipped out of her stockings and shoes, to make the situation easy for him, less awkward, as if he could ever be awkward.

All she'd accomplished was to make things awkward for herself.

He did not come to her. Instead, he went to the fireplace and, sitting on his heels, began throwing logs across the grate, letting them lie haphazardly the way they fell. He struck the fire and watched it kindle into flame.

Something troubled him, far more deeply than she had at first realized. She shifted to where she could see the light flicker across his face. It was not a gentle face, a loving face, the face of a man about to bring a woman to ecstasy. He looked carved from hot granite. If he burned inside, it was not because of her.

This was all wrong, this night of love. The air was close, the shadows oppressive at the moment when she had hoped to be transported to a cloud. Silly, virginal idea. The truth was that her lover had turned his back on her. She felt hurt and hungry at the same time. The hunger won.

She tossed the blanket aside. "Something happened outside, didn't it?"

He poked at the fire. She wondered if he heard her.

"You've changed your mind. It's something to do with your brother, isn't it? Tonight is to honor his memory. Ten years since his final troubles began, that's what I was told. If there is a ghost here tonight, it is his. You should be thinking of him, not . . . what you were planning with me."

He laughed, the first time she had heard him do so, but it had a raw, hard edge to it, and it chilled her.

"My God, is that what you think? You could not be more wrong. Go away, Lucinda. Run while you can. It's not too late to let your coachman take you home."

"Oh, yes, it is, Gideon. It's far too late."

She walked to him. He did not look away from the fire. She realized the depth of her vulnerability. He was a dangerous man, used to power, comfortable only when he was in control. He could do anything to her he wanted, and there would be no one to come to the defense of the crazy American.

If she had not loved him so completely, she would have been terrified. But the sense of danger served only to heighten her need.

"I do not ask anything of you," she said. "I've already said as much. But I do want one night. I know I'm being very selfish right now. But I also know it's all I will have."

Taking off the red sash, she dropped it beside her bare feet, pulled her blouse free of the skirt band and dropped it on the floor beside the sash. She wore a thin camisole. In an instant it lay beside the blouse.

Half naked, she shook out her hair. It fell against her bare shoulders and back. Her breasts felt full, heavy for the first time in her life, and the tips were hard and pointed. In the dimness they took on the color of dark roses. She felt as voluptuous as she ever could, and very much afraid, not of his touching her but of his leaving her alone.

Kneeling before her, he watched, very still, very quiet, and there was something about him that gave her confidence.

"Tell me to go away now," she said. "I don't think you can."

She closed her eyes. Surely he could sense her trembling; surely he could hear her heart. If she were wrong—if he did not want her now—he never would.

A twig snapped in the grate, the noise sharp against the sibilant rush of their separate breathing. Nothing else stirred the silence. Nothing.

With a cry, she grabbed up her clothes and ran for the door. He caught her by the wrist and jerked her back against him. Her clothing fell in a heap on the rug. Hot lips burned the side of her neck; an iron arm wrapped around her waist, pinning her to a hard body; a callused hand cupped her breast.

It happened so fast she could barely respond to all that he did. The hollowness inside her filled with heat. She curved herself against him, pressing her lips against his, wanting him to absorb her so that neither existed without the other. She yearned to welcome the thousand new sensations he aroused and never, ever suffer a coherent thought, except that the man she loved taught her sweet lessons she would carry in her memory all her life.

"You should have run," he said huskily against her tight skin. "I told you to. Now it's too late."

He spoke harshly, as if he were angry. She knew he was not. She felt his wildness. He would not let her go.

A feeling of joy raced through her, killing the shame of how she had presented herself to him, kindling prickles of longing that came close to pain, and a rush of anticipation and frustration because she needed to hold him the way he was holding her.

His embrace eased, and she turned to grab hold of him, fearing nothing more than that she might swoon and disgrace herself. He tore off his coat and shirt, baring himself to the waist as she was bared.

"Oh," she said, staring at the taut contours of his body. The sweat-soaked shirt she had once seen on him had given only a hint of what lay beneath. She'd had no idea of his magnificence, no concept of the effect it would have on her.

With a small cry, she buried her face in his chest, rubbing her cheek against the short dark hair, her palms making small hard circles around his nipples. She was going on instinct, doing what pleased her. His flesh had an earthy, primitive feel to it, hard and soft at the same time. She could smell the fire on him, and the fire in him. She wanted to consume him in every way she could.

When she pressed her breasts against him, she heard a rumbling build inside him; it came out as an explosive sigh.

"You're driving me insane," he whispered.

"Good."

"I wrong you."

"Then why does everything feel right?"

Thrusting his hands in her hair, he kissed her, then whispered against her parted lips, "Because it is the only thing in the world that is right. If only the world would leave us alone."

She backed away. "Then let us banish the world and be just Gideon and Lucinda. Speak no more of right and wrong. For us, those concepts do not exist."

He stared at her nakedness. "You make me believe the impossible."

"I did not know I had such power."

Slowly his gaze rose to hers. "You've always had it. Make me forget. Make me think of only you."

"Show me how."

"You know how. Already you have begun." He ran a fingertip across the tip of a breast. She came close to collapsing. "Do I have power over you?"

"You always have," she said.

"Then we must do as you said and banish the world."

He completed the undressing of her, letting the skirt fall and then the petticoat, past her hips, her thighs, his eyes lingering on what was revealed. His movements were steady, sure. Tossing her clothing aside, he gave her no chance to be shy.

"I please you?" she asked.

"You cannot know how much."

She turned her back to him and stared into the flames. "Then do the same for me and take off your clothes. I'll not face you until you say you have done so."

"If you think the view you now present is any less pleasing, you are very much wrong. You are dangerously close to being taken from behind."

"Oh," she said, not understanding completely what he meant. She dropped to the floor fast, before her legs gave out from under her. She was so ignorant. She would do this wrong.

His boots fell. Her heart pounded wildly. She heard the rustle of his clothes, and then he was down beside her, pulling her into his arms, both of them lying to face one another on the rug in front of the hearth. She got no more than a quick glimpse of his long, strong body—the muscled legs, the flat abdomen, the expanse of his chest, before he lifted her chin and burned his gaze into hers.

"Forgive me, Lucinda," he said.

"There's nothing to—"

He licked the tips of her breasts, and the words died in a sigh.

Everything went crazy after that. He kissed his way down to her abdomen, where his tongue played in the private hairs. Hidden places throbbed in an astonishing kind of frenzy. He gave her no time to feel embarrassment or shame. She had no room in her heart for anything but the craving he aroused.

If he had truly desired her to be wanton, such was the woman she presented to him. She touched him wherever she could, her hands gripping his powerful arms. He must have lifted a million boulders on his land to get such arms. His skin was brown in the flickering light. He did not always work fully clothed. The image of the sun kissing his flesh made every part of her throb.

She wanted to run her fingers along all the bunched muscles of his body, parts the sun could and could not reach, but she did not know how to tell him, and she doubted he would listen if she did.

It was Gideon who knew what to do. He played her body like the master he was, kneading her buttocks while he kissed her thighs, his hands stroking downward to the backs of her knees, bending her legs. He kissed the inside of her calves, licking her ankles in a sudden un-

257

expected gesture that was as erotic as anything else he did.

And then he kissed his way back to the tender place between her legs.

"I want to drink you, Lucinda." His tongue touched her. "I want to eat you."

He sucked at her. She could not keep herself from writhing beneath his lips and his tongue.

He stopped too soon, or so she thought, moving up the length of her, rubbing his body against hers as he did, thrusting his tongue between her lips.

"Do you taste yourself?" he whispered. "Does it seem as sweet to you?"

He gave her no chance to do more than return his kiss, to tease her own tongue against his until he took it inside his mouth. His own taste was the dark dampness of desire.

His erection pressed hard against her stomach.

"Open your legs for me," he whispered.

"Anything," she said in a voice she did not know. "Anything."

He positioned himself between her legs. She stiffened involuntarily, as if he would hurt her instead of continue the pleasure. She did not want to stop him from what he was doing. She needed him to hasten everything he did. But she could not keep from stiffening.

"Do not worry," he said, brushing the hair from her face.

"I don't."

The throbbing between her thighs became so intense it did indeed feel like a pain. She felt his sex rub against that pain, and such pleasure jolted through her as she could never have imagined. Her whole body coiled tightly, ready to spring into sweet release. She closed her eyes and her mind turned to black velvet, no coherent thoughts allowed, only dark sensations that threatened to burst into light.

"I need you," he whispered against her hair. "God may condemn me, but I cannot wait."

The pressure she had been fearing came, a slight hurt, a tightness despite the wetness of her body. He eased inside her, then slipped free again. He trembled. This could not be all, she told herself. She felt so stupid, but she knew it could not be all. And then he was inside her again, deeper than before. He groaned and plunged again and again into her narrow slickness, each penetration following faster than the one before, until the world shook and a tremendous shudder took hold of his body.

He cried out and held her tight. "Lucy," he whispered again and again. "Lucy, Lucy." He had never called her thus—no one ever had—and it sounded thrilling on his lips.

And desperate, too. He made her want to cry, not for herself but for him.

His shudders slowly died, but her own body continued to throb. She buried her face in the

259

crook of his neck and kissed his damp skin. If she did not feel the complete satisfaction that seemed to ripple through him, she experienced something that was equally thrilling.

She had brought him to this state, this total dependence on her and what she could do for him. The masterful and solitary man known as the Devil Duke was no devil in her arms, and his title was as nothing. He was a man. It was all she wanted and all she would ever ask him to be.

He eased himself off her, but he held her close as he positioned himself between her and the fire. It was as if the heat passed through him and into her. She wanted to store his heat and never be cold again.

Wrapping her arms around his middle, she laid her head against his chest.

"Do not leave me," she said, then added hastily lest he misunderstand, "not just yet."

"No, Lucinda. Not just yet."

There it was again. The hesitancy, this time mixed with tension, had returned. She had not been able to hold it at bay for very long. In that moment she learned how a woman could find complete happiness and utter misery mixed in one mad emotion.

"What's wrong, Gideon?"

He answered quickly, too quickly, his attitude close to glib.

"I did not bring you to the satisfaction you deserve."

"You . . . satisfied me. But do not now treat me like a child."

His hands covered her buttocks and he held her against him, his skin as warm and slick with sweat as hers.

"A child?" He tightened his hold. "No woman has ever made such an accusation. I doubt you can do it now."

The words stunned her for a moment. He spoke of other women. Now. With her.

Crying out, she scrambled away and grabbed the blanket, holding it between them like a shield. But it could not protect her from his words. It could not heal her heart.

"What else did I do that no woman has ever done?"

"I would give up my life to tell you. If I could."

She would have laughed, but she was too close to tears.

He sat up, unconscious of his nakedness. The flickering light kissed his sleek skin. She would have been aroused more wildly than ever, if she could think beyond her pain. She had known it would come, but not so quickly, so unexpectedly. Her body had not yet forgotten the intimacies of his touch. They played in her and on her like a haunting melody.

She was obsessed with him. He was all she would ever want, ever need.

But still, there was the pain of his words, devilish, as if on purpose, in place of the love words she longed to hear. He could have driven a fist into her middle and not hurt her more.

"I have asked you to forgive me," he said. His eyes never left hers.

"Was that a forever kind of forgiveness? I should forgive everything you will ever do?"

"I hurt you."

She pretended to misunderstand.

"Only slightly," she said. "I expected discomfort the first time."

"If only that were all. I told you —"

"I know. You are a terrible man. I had not realized how far you would go to prove it."

Awkwardly she pulled herself to her feet and stared down at her clothing scattered about the room. She sensed him standing close behind her.

"No one has ever done for me what you have done," he said. "You cannot know what tonight has meant."

"Tell me. The night is not yet past."

"You come to me too late. Or is it too soon? I do not know."

She turned to face him. He was still naked. She could not look at him for long. The fire was safer. It burned with far more gentleness.

"I did not come to you," she said, watching the flames. "You came to me. Or perhaps you have forgotten the first few times we met."

"I have not forgotten."

"I'm trying to understand you. But it's like climbing a high wall with broken glass across the top."

"I am not worth the trouble. My greatest fear is that you will learn how terrible I truly am."

He reached for his clothes and pulled them on quickly. He gave her no choice but to do the same. While she dressed, he went to the window and peered into the night.

"A few revelers remain."

"Is Rigg among them?"

"I will see you safely home."

He left her attempting to tie her sash in place and straighten her hair. He returned carrying a heavy cloak and the cape that was as familiar to her as her name. He wrapped the cloak around her, his fingers brushing against her throat as he fastened the closure.

"It's too big for you. You are so small."

She had thought that tonight she was voluptuous. She had been wrong about many things. She had expected to be happy in the afterglow of lovemaking. In that supposition lay the worst of her mistakes.

No. There was another, far more torturous. She wanted him again. And again. And again.

He led her through the door and down dark corridors. She realized with a start that she could describe nothing about the room where she had given herself to him. She could, of course, recall in detail everything about him.

They went through a doorway she did not recognize and were suddenly outside, on a deserted side of the hall. And there was Gideon's black horse waiting for his master, as if everything had been planned.

He mounted and reached down for her, lifting her to sit across his lap as he had done one misty day in a field she could never again find.

"Hold tight to me, Lucinda. And do not fear. I know my way in the dark."

With all her wounded heart, she wished she could say the same.

Chapter Fifteen

Gideon brought her all the way to the manor house kitchen door.

As they walked down the garden path, the final portion of the long journey from the shadowed castle room where they had made love, a sharp wind whipped their clothing and clouds passed over the moon. He had held her tightly as the horse thundered through the dark night, right up to the garden's back gate, where she slipped from his embrace to her own turf.

She walked separately from him now. Only their cloaks touched.

"I'll see you inside," he said.

"No. Please, no," Lucinda said. He was trying to be kind. She was not in a mood for kindness.

What did she want from him? She closed her eyes, and memories washed over her. The answer was easy: She wanted what she could not have.

Did he think of what they had done? Other than the kindness, he gave no hint that he did. She could think of little else.

She had no weapon to fight him or the way she felt, nothing but distance, and secrecy, both strategies more suitable to a military struggle. Both were strategies her lover knew well.

They reached the door. She brushed a strand of hair from between her lips.

"Tell me, Your Grace, what does etiquette demand? Do you thank me? Do I thank you?"

She could feel him withdrawing, as if she had shoved him away. Which, of course, she had. It was one of their mutual strategies.

"I would say the gratitude is on my side," he said, "but it is not gratitude I feel."

Neither was it love. She wanted to hear him speak of nothing else.

She thrust the borrowed cloak into his hands.

"Good night, Gideon," she said, backing through the open door. "Whether or not it is the thing to do, I thank you for giving me what I was obviously begging for tonight. Virginity is such a pesky condition, isn't it? I assure you I do not miss it now that it is gone. I am certain I never will."

She closed the door quickly, before he could

respond, and turned her back to lean against it. He did not leave right away. She could sense him standing alone in the dark. It was the milieu he preferred.

She waited. The air was heavy with his nearness though she could neither see nor hear him. And then he was gone, like the passing breeze, leaving her in emptiness, leaving her hollow inside.

"Gideon," she whispered, "I love you."

The declaration brought no satisfaction. She must one day, before she left, whisper the words in his ear.

Lighting a lamp, she started for the back stairs, then stopped as if an invisible hand had raised itself to bid her do so. Something, a summons from an irresistible force, drew her toward the main corridor that ran the length of the ground floor, toward the far corner of the house, to the room she had visited only once before.

A shiver ran through her, but it was not nearly strong enough to stay her from the beckoning course. This was a night for strangeness, for exploration, for risk. Despite all her previous fears, she could not ignore the silent call.

She walked past open doors, so different from the closed doors of Blackthorne Hall, across the wide entryway, and past more doors. She did not stop until she stood before her father's private rooms.

The hour was long past midnight. All Hallows' Eve was over; the time for ghosts was done. Besides, she had already given herself to the devil. Surely that made her safe from further harm.

Taking a deep breath, she stepped inside and closed the door behind her. With the lamp held high, she stared at the central feature of the room, an ornately carved wooden border framing the fireplace. Together the border and hearth occupied most of the opposite wall. It was curious she had not noticed that feature on her one and only previous visit. On that afternoon, frightened, she had not lingered long.

All else was as she remembered—the high, wide poster bed, the dark furniture, the heavy drawn draperies.

And her father, of course, William Fairfax, sixth Viscount Westcombe, whose worries he had taken to an early grave. She felt him in the musty air. His spirit brushed across her skin.

But she did not tremble. She had been through too much tonight to run as she had before.

"Good evening, Father."

Silence. She had expected nothing else. Old tales of moaning specters and clanking chains were just that, old tales. Lord Westcombe's ghost was of a subtler sort.

"It seems strange to call you that, but I know of no other name to use. It has the benefit of being accurate if not necessarily affectionate."

Stepping deeper into the room, she rested the lamp on the table beside the bed and looked at the shadows it cast on the high stuccoed walls.

"I have no idea what you know of events beyond this room, or if you care. I've not come to confess my transgressions. They are none of your concern. But I do say that, while I cannot forgive or forget your abandonment of the kindest, most gentle woman I have ever known, I now understand the call of this land where you were born."

She closed her eyes a moment, unable to go on, not because she felt foolish speaking out in this manner, but because she knew her words, difficult to say, did not go unheard. She must choose them carefully.

Glancing toward the covered window, she thought of what lay beyond the confines of the abandoned chamber. Her heart warmed at the pictures in her mind.

"I have ridden across the moors and fields and I have watched the people at work and play. There is much I do not understand, but there is also much to admire and to love."

She pulled her attention to the cold hearth, the dark corners of the room, the high feather bed. She could sense her father nowhere in particular yet everywhere at once.

"During the past two months I have come to understand something that has troubled me since I was a child. I now know how Mother could love you when you did not love her in return. This was a lesson not easily learned. And it was not learned without pain."

She thought of Gideon's arms around her, and then of the almost brusque way he had led her from his home, as if he were two men in one body, wanting her and not wanting her at the same time.

"I must also tell you that no matter how much I wish to do so, I will never understand men."

If she expected a whoosh of air or low moan of protest, she did not get it. Silence. All was silence.

"You must also know that England can never be my true home. You have made me a wealthy woman, something I did not expect or desire. As soon as possible, I will take a portion of that wealth and return to the country of my birth. It is where I belong. I know it more tonight than I ever have."

As if he had spoken out in protest, she hurried along with what she had to say.

"Craven Manor will be taken care of, as will Fairfax land and the people who work on it. In the event I find myself the mother of a son, I will tell him what awaits him here. I assume legitimacy is not a condition of his inheritance. Carlyle Winston mentioned no such stricture, though I doubt he would have considered a bastard heir possible. I am not . . . I *was* not a woman likely to take a lover to her bed."

She wrapped her arms around her middle.

"Of course, it is highly unlikely I am with child. It will certainly be some weeks before I know. Which must tell you something of what happened tonight. Rest easy knowing your grandson or granddaughter will bear noble blood. That is something I know you value very much."

Suddenly the lamplight flickered and the air grew chill, as if the window had been blown open by an early winter wind. At last, after all her impudence, the spirit had grown angry with her, reminding her she should direct that same anger toward herself. She had behaved without shame, yet she felt no regret. She had disgraced the Fairfax name. As if it had not been disgraced long before.

In life her father had not been kind. In death he was no different. If she had expected some sort of consolation from him, a settling of old hurts, she did not get it. Instead, she got judgment. And rejection, again.

With a low cry, she fled the room, struggling with the door, forgetting the lamp, running in the dark toward the window front stairway, up the steps past the landing window, not stopping until she came to the sanctuary of her room.

Hurriedly she locked the door and tossed the key aside, hugging herself, still cold, grateful to find that Baron was not awaiting her. She had suffered too much of this world and, more, whatever it was that lay in the vast beyond. She wanted nothing but the solitude that Gideon craved so much, away from him and his temptation, away from whatever evil lurked downstairs. The truest words she had spoken to that cruel, lifeless presence was that she did not understand men.

Quickly she undressed and threw herself, naked, under the covers. She ought to scrub away all marks that her lover had left on her body. She still felt him on her breasts and between her legs. She cursed the weakness that made her want to hold the feelings as long as she could. It would take only a moment's consideration to make her throb for him again.

She touched herself where she felt him most, then jerked her hand away as if she had done another terrible wrong. Only Gideon could move his fingers across her in the intimate way that drew her into erotic sweetness. Only he had the right. Because she gave it to him. Because she gave him her love.

Tomorrow would be soon enough to wash his touch away. If only, she thought as she stared into the dark, tomorrow would never come.

Sleep was a long time coming and brought her no rest. She dreamed of a bonfire gone wild, its flames licking through the windows of Blackthorne Hall. Sparks burned through her undergarments, all that she wore. Screaming, she slapped and tore at the sparks, but they blazed dark circles in the flimsy cloth, searing her skin.

Again she screamed, turning, turning, trying to escape but finding nowhere to run. The fire surrounded her. Gideon, safe in a suit of armor, stood nearby and laughed.

She awoke in a fit of coughing. Smoke filled her bedchamber and stung her eyes. She could not see, could not breathe. Fire! Her nightmare had come true.

She leapt from the bed, but the smoke was thick and she could not find her way. She clasped a hand over her mouth to keep from drawing smoke into her lungs and lurched toward the door, remembering how she had stupidly locked it the night before when she had desired nothing but privacy. More stupidly, she had tossed the key aside.

Her fingers groped frantically around on the floor, but she could not find it. The seconds seemed like hours. She pounded the thick wood and tried to cry for help, but her efforts proved feeble. No one came to save her.

Stumbling backwards, she tripped and fell. Panic took hold. Her lungs screamed, ready to burst. She knelt on the floor and closed her eyes against the stinging smoke, scarcely aware of her nakedness.

"Gideon," she called out weakly. A foolish cry.

He could hardly have heard her had he been in the room.

She must get up. She had to save herself. The dressing room. She must get to the dressing room door. She threw herself in its direction. The wood was hot, ready to burst into flame. The blaze threatened on the other side, only inches from where she stood.

She fell back in panic. The balcony. Why had she not thought of the balcony?

Even as hope came, her strength ebbed, and her head reeled from lack of air. With a sob, she slid once again to the floor. She needed to rest. That was it. Here, next to the carpet, the air was almost sweet. She had only to lay her head down a moment and all would be well.

"Gideon," she cried to herself. "Help me."

Her answer was a crash of glass, hard footsteps, strong arms lifting her. There was shouting, too, from far, far away, but the arms that cradled her were all that she needed. Slumping against their strength, she dropped into oblivion.

When Lucinda awoke, she was lying on clouds and listening to distant voices, calling to her from the void. She tried to determine where she was and who was speaking, but her eyes saw nothing in her surroundings except darkness.

With a cry, she tried to sit up. An insistent hand eased her back to the clouds.

"You'rc all right, Lucinda."

Gideon.

He lifted a cloth from her eyes, and she blinked up at him. The room was dim, but she could make him out, sitting at the side of the bed.

"Mrs. Pickering wanted to make sure your eyes were not damaged by the smoke."

Smoke. The fire. Suddenly she remembered everything.

"My room. Where am I? Is Craven Manor—"

"Damaged, but nothing that cannot be repaired."

The smell of smoke hung in the air, nasty, acrid, bringing back unwanted memories. With a trembling hand, she reached up to touch his face. "You were there."

"Almost too late." He spoke angrily.

She pulled back. Adjusting to the dimness, she could make out the details of his form, the sunken eyes, gaunt cheeks, grim mouth. She had never seen him in such a state.

"How long have I been unconscious?"

"A half hour. No more."

She closed her eyes. Other than a rawness in her throat, she felt no ill effects from what she had been through.

Except for the memories. Always memories.

She looked at the man who had saved her. He had never seemed so distant or harsh.

"How did you get into my room? I remember

glass shattering but little else. Mostly I was trying not to breathe. I think that was why I passed out."

"The balcony."

"How on earth did you get up there?"

But he was not of a mind to answer any more of her questions. "You are all right," he said. It was as much a command as a question.

"I am all right."

Striding to the door, he threw it open.

Mrs. Pickering and a dozen others stood on the far side.

"Is she—" the housekeeper began.

"She is alive. I go to prepare a room for her at Blackthorne Hall. Gather her belongings. All of them. I will send for her in the afternoon. She will not return."

"Gideon," Lucinda called out.

He spared her a parting glance. "You will remain with me until it is time for your return to America. Don't ask if it is the right thing for you to do. It is the only thing." He hesitated, but only for a second. "I have business that must be seen to; otherwise I would take you to Blackthorne myself."

He was gone before she could reply.

Mrs. Pickering and Fenton hurried into the room, closing the door to Alice and the other servants crowded in the hall.

Lucinda sat up and dropped her feet to the side of the bed. Someone had covered her nakedness with a nightgown. She wondered if that someone had been Gideon.

I will send for her.

He was keeping her close by his side, by his order. He gave her no choice. Her head reeled. She should refuse. Honor demanded it, and dignity as well as pride. But to be with him was what she wanted, more than he could ever know.

Her heart should have soared, except that the closeness between them would last only until she made arrangements to sail home.

"Miss Fairfax, you cannot go with him," Mrs. Pickering said.

Lucinda scarcely heard her. She stared at the door. "He said he came in through the balcony."

It was all she could think of to say, that detail the one she most wanted to clarify.

"The ivy is quite strong," Fenton said. "It held his weight."

"He climbed the wall?" She looked stupidly at the butler. "Did he put out the flames as well?"

"For that, give thanks to your staff. The fire began in the kitchen and went up the back stairs. It did not go farther than your dressing room. We are looking into its cause."

"There's little need for that," the housekeeper said. "I can tell you how it began. The devil himself was lurking nearby, ready to rescue our mistress and carry her away."

"But kitchen fires are not infrequent," Lucinda said.

"And the blaze that took your father's chambers?"

She stared at the woman, again feeling stupid. She rubbed her temples. There seemed so much to take in.

"There was a second fire?" she asked. "Far from the first?"

"All was ruined within your father's room," Fenton said, "but no other damage resulted. The flames were contained there."

She felt an inexplicable sadness that had not come with the loss of her own chamber. Did ghosts burn? Did they linger in charred ruins? It seemed unlikely. Her father must be gone. He had left her once again. And this time because of an accident.

Or was it? How could a fire occur in an abandoned room?

She stifled a cry. "I just remembered. The lamp. I left it on the table."

"You were there?" Mrs. Pickering said. "In your father's room? Whatever for?"

Lucinda looked away, silent. She could not tell the truth. The woman would think her mad.

"I just was. When I returned home, I could not go to bed right away."

"This is a strange night indeed," Mrs. Pickering said, echoing Lucinda's thoughts of earlier. She shook her head sadly. "I've not wanted to tell you, though I've given hints enough." Her voice was the voice of doom. "His Grace was close by when your father fell to his death, same as he was close by on this dreadful night."

Lucinda stiffened. "That proves little."

"I tell you no more than what is generally known. Like the rest of us, at the time of Lord Westcombe's . . . accident, His Grace did not know of your existence. 'Twas generally thought Lord Westcombe had no heirs."

"Which would have meant nothing to Gideon Blackthorne."

Or would it? He could have bought her land. She had once raised the possibility herself.

"There's few of us can guess at his purpose in doing what he does, riding about in the dark, keeping to himself. Except that the devil needs no purpose other than evil. If you put yourself in his hands, there's little knowing what will become of you."

"He will not harm me."

Mrs. Pickering sniffed. "You've fallen under his spell. Right from the start. I told Mr. Fenton—"

"Enough, Athena." The butler spoke sharply, with a depth of emotion he had not exhibited before.

"But—"

"I said, enough." He turned to Lucinda, his tall, thin figure bent. "We speak only from concern, Miss Fairfax. Accommodations can be made while the damage to the house is repaired. You will be comfortable, if that is your worry. There is little reason for you to leave."

He looked so solemn, so concerned, she thought for a moment he would reach out and take her hand. As a father might have done. Or so she supposed.

Her heart warmed. How foolish she was, close to crying at such a simple show of caring.

"I doubt I will be at Blackthorne Hall for long."

"But the gossip—" Mrs. Pickering said.

"I'm sure I have already scandalized Hummersby Bridge. If I were staying, perhaps it would be a consideration. But I will be making arrangements soon to go home, before winter sets in."

The servants exchanged glances.

"Oh, miss," Mrs. Pickering exclaimed, "we do not want you to return to America. None of us, Mr. Fenton and myself most especially. Craven Manor should be your rightful home."

Lucinda looked at her in wonder, then at Fenton, who nodded his agreement. She needed a moment before she could speak.

"That is very kind of you." Her voice was thick.

"Kindness has little t' do with it. We've grown fond of your Yankee ways."

"Even the dusting?" she said, managing a smile.

"You tried that no more than once. If you've a mind to try it again, I'll do my best not to object."

Lucinda looked around the bedchamber, so similar to her own. Even after the terrible events of the past hour, it did not look so regrettably dark and forbidding as she had first thought. All the manor house needed was a touch of paint here and there, open windows, lighter draperies, and it would be quite livable.

Foolish, foolish thought.

"You have no idea how much you tempt me. Or how grateful I am." She smiled, and her eyes burned. "But I must leave. And though, as you say, it will bring shocking gossip down on my head, I will go to Blackthorne Hall. For a little while. And then I will go home."

Mrs. Pickering blinked and looked away, though she was not done with her arguments.

"You can't go with him. You have no clothing. Everything was burned except the nightgown Alice left on your bed."

"Then I'll borrow something from one of the servants." Lucinda stood. "I'd like a bath, if that is possible. And tell Alice to pack her things. She is going with me. And, of course, Baron. And Lancelot, later. In the next day or two."

She got no argument, only a sad shake of Mrs. Pickering's head.

When she was alone, her thoughts returned to Gideon. Mrs. Pickering was completely and totally right in her objections to Lucinda's leaving. In the housekeeper's eyes, as in those of most everyone else, he was a danger. At the very least, her mistress would be ruined. Mrs. Pickering had not even mentioned the fact His Grace had not *asked* her but, instead, had given orders. And he'd offered no explanation why he had been so near the manor when the fires began.

What business took him from her now? She could not begin to guess, and he would never tell.

Did secret dangers truly threaten?

What would happen between the two of them when she moved to the castle on the distant hill?

Only the last question could she begin to answer. What would happen was anything he wanted. Anything at all.

Chapter Sixteen

"So he's got you under his roof, has he? I should have known he would."

Irene Littlewood stood in the doorway to Lucinda's new bedchamber and clucked her disapproval. Baron stood by the hearth and growled.

Lucinda glanced at the door that led to Gideon's adjoining room.

"His Grace was most kind to offer me refuge while my own home is under repair," she said, stroking the hound's massive head.

"Kind?" The onetime nursemaid to two infant boys laughed sharply. "Is that what they're calling it these days?"

Lucinda pictured the woman the way she had

appeared weeks ago, a dead chicken in her hand and ugliness spewing from her mouth. She lacked only the chicken to look the same.

"It's what I call it." She smiled brightly. "His Grace has done several favors for me which I consider extremely kind. Now, if you don't mind, I really would like to rest a few moments before dinner. I'm sure you understand."

Alice, who had been standing aside looking as though she weren't taking in everything, started bustling about the room, smoothing the lace cover on the canopied bed, then hurrying back to the open trunk, feverishly searching for something her mistress needed right away.

Mrs. Littlewood's pinched lips flattened, and she left without another word. Alice closed the door behind her.

Lucinda collapsed on the nearest chair.

"It's not my place to say so, but that's an evil woman," Alice said.

"An unhappy one, for sure."

Baron nuzzled his head in Lucinda's lap. She stared down at the rope burns circling his neck. While she had been at Blackthorne for the All Hallows' Eve celebration, someone had managed to drug the poor dog and bind him to a post in the stable. The fire had awakened him to a frenzy. Gideon, on one of his nightly rides, had heard the barking and had come to her.

This he had admitted. It was why he had arrived so quickly after the start of the blaze. It was the only explanation she had heard, the only one she would accept.

Alice stared down into the trunk. "Begging your pardon, Miss Fairfax, but you've pitiful few clothes for such a place as this. There's only the one dress you're wearing now, and that an old one put downstairs for repair, else it would be cinders now." She rolled her eyes. "We won't even mention the state o' your drawers. The dressmaker must be waiting for you to call."

"She knows of my burned wardrobe? Don't answer. Of course she does."

The thought of traveling into town, ignoring smirks and all-too-knowing stares, turned her cold.

"Go for me, Alice."

The girl looked as if she were going to protest; then her pretty young face brightened into a smile.

"You'd trust me?"

"The dressmaker has my measurements, and she knows my taste."

"Aye, and aren't I as familiar with it myself," Alice said glumly.

"You don't approve of what I wear?"

"The green dress, that was a lovely thing, and the riding clothes. As for the rest, they could have done with a bit more trim."

"You can't wait to do this, can you?"

"It's my duty."

"And your place."

The girl's smile broadened. "If you say so, Miss Fairfax."

"I need just about everything, as you well know. Don't worry about the money. Spend what you think is necessary. And while you're at it, order something pretty for yourself."

"Oh." Alice's eyes filled with tears. "Oh, mum."

Lucinda was close to joining her in crying. What she suggested was no more than she should have thought of long ago. What was money for if not to make people happy?

It had not made her father happy. But he had not spent it. He'd hoarded it.

Alice curtsied. "I'll go down, if you don't need me, and see about a ride into town. Already it's afternoon and chances are I won't be going until the morning, but I need to find out for sure. You don't suppose I would be riding in His Grace's carriage with the crest and all on the side? No, that would be too much."

She went out chattering about the crest, closing the door behind her, and Lucinda was alone for the first time since the fire. She ought to get right up and start learning a little something about her temporary place of residence. Much of what she had already seen of Blackthorne Hall was similar to Craven Manor, only larger, darker, colder.

She did not want to consider what such a home said about its owner.

Where was he? What was he doing right at the moment? Was he thinking of her?

The idea was presumptuous. He could not possibly think of her as much as she thought of him, or he would think of nothing else.

Leaning back in the chair, exhausted, she closed her eyes and thought of him some more. She dozed, for how long she had no idea, then jerked awake when Baron stirred at her feet. He lifted his head and stared at the door. In an instant her mind cleared. She sat up to watch as Gideon entered. She could not breathe.

Your bed or mine?

She did not say the words. It was likely that having had his one time with her, he did not want another.

He took off his cape and tossed it over his shoulder. For all the tension she could see in him—the gauntness, the sunken eyes, the bristles that darkened his cheeks—he looked very, very good.

"Are you well?" he asked.

"I'm well."

"I see you brought your protection."

"You mean Baron? Yes."

"I'm sorry he was injured."

"*You* didn't bind him."

"I imagine you could find someone who swore they saw me riding around last night with a rope."

"Probably."

"But you would not believe him. Or her."

"No, I would not."

He gazed at her without speaking. She gripped the arms of the chair.

"Is your business done?" she asked.

He looked away. "My business is never done."

"I should not have mentioned it," she said.

"It is of no matter." He hesitated. "We'll have to get rid of the dog."

"If you mean permanently—"

"For a few hours. He's got a man's eyes in a hound's face. I do not want him watching."

Her heart caught in her throat. "Watching what?" she asked.

"I want you."

"We had our night. It's daytime now."

"The better to see you."

"Someone might come in."

"No. No one will."

"You seem sure of yourself."

"I am sure of my people. Your housekeeper and coachman are downstairs making certain you have not fallen victim to a sex-crazed beast. They are too wary of me to venture upstairs until I give them permission. Thus far only your maid has that. And she is gone."

"Mrs. Littlewood—"

"Mrs. Littlewood is occupied, killing something for dinner, I believe. You seem filled with worry. Tell me to go away. I will leave. You have only to say the words."

"Are you a sex-crazed beast?"

"You have made me so. Does that frighten you?"

Her body thrummed. "It gives me hope." She looked at the bed. "I haven't even sat on it yet."

"I had not planned for us to remain in here. I want you in my bed, Lucinda. I want you to want the same."

"Is that why you put me in an adjoining room?"

"There's a door between. You can lock it on your side."

"And you can lock it on yours, I assume. In case I should become a sex-crazed beast."

"It is my most fervent wish."

He had no idea how difficult it was for her to stay upright in the chair and coherent. He had no idea how much her body already throbbed.

"Take down your hair," he said.

She did as he asked, slowly, letting the curls unwind and fall to her shoulders, running her fingers through them the way she wished him to do. He looked on in a manner that served both to satisfy and to stimulate.

She looked down at Baron. "You are going to be a good boy and stay here while I go away for a while. And I"—she looked up at Gideon—"am going to be a very good girl."

"You're turning saucy on me."

She stood. Her shabby skirt fell around her in folds. "Not so much. I have not the vaguest idea how to get from in here to in there without feeling awkward."

He was across the room in two strides, the cape tossed aside. He swept her up in his arms and cradled her close to his chest, as if she weighed no more than a whisper. Her arms moved swiftly around his neck.

"Kiss me," he said.

She pressed her lips against his cheek.

"Where would you touch if I said fondle me?"

She stroked his hair. "Anywhere I could reach. You are a man ripe with temptations."

"Did you know you are driving me to madness?"

"You are as sane as any man I have ever known. A dangerous man, they say. Perhaps I have driven you to gentleness." She touched his lips. "For a while."

"No one has ever accused me of being gentle."

She looked into his eyes. The stark hunger she saw there sent a shiver of anticipation through her.

"It is not an accusation. It is a plea."

"I think you will not always want gentleness."

He had her in his room in an instant, the door closed firmly behind him, leaving Baron sitting and watching the door on the other side.

With her arm stretched along the width of his shoulders, she stroked his cheek, then looked around at the dark corners of the chamber, the dark draperies, the heavy furniture. One piece in particular caught her attention.

"That is the biggest bed I have ever seen. We could roam over it for an hour and not touch one another."

"No, we could not."

He set her on her feet. She went to the window and threw open the draperies. Afternoon light spilled across the carpeted floor.

"You can see Craven Manor from here," she said.

"It has drawn my attention of late."

"And I have looked at Blackthorne Hall."

She faced him. He stood in sunlight, close to the bedpost, wearing shirt, trousers, and boots as she had seen him so many times, tall, lean and muscular, his hair wild, his face sharply drawn, his eyes dark and deep. She came close to bursting with love.

"I undressed first for you last time. You—"

He had his shirt half off before she could say the rest. She looked at him, and her hands began to burn.

"This time you're not warning me to run," she said.

"I am a selfish man. Do not leave."

"I won't." Not yet.

She walked to him and licked the hollow of his throat. He took her by the wrists and rubbed her hands across his chest, then brought them to his lips and kissed her palms.

"You really are well," he said.

"Except for being unable to breathe. Or think."

He eased her arms around to her back and pinned her wrists in the grasp of one hand.

"This time is yours, Lucinda. If you do not understand, I will show you."

Bending his head, he bit at her breasts through the fabric of her dress . . . gently, provocatively. Her back arched. He ran his hand down her side, then eased his fingers between her legs and began to rub, slowly at first, teasingly, then faster. Her body burst into flame.

"I can't stand this," she whispered hoarsely.

"You have no choice."

"You're cruel."

"You have no idea how cruel."

He tugged at her skirt, working it high on her legs until his hand rested against her bare thigh.

"You wear no petticoat, Lucinda."

"Everything burned in the fire."

"Are you naked beneath your dress?"

"Find out for yourself."

His fingers worked their way to the wiry hair low on her abdomen.

She whimpered.

He let out a heavy sigh. "You were right, my light. You are very, very good."

"You have no idea how good." She licked his lips. "Release my hands and I will show you."

He was quick to do as she said. One hand

traveled quickly to the hard thickness between his legs. Her fingers teased him as he was teasing her.

He groaned. "You must stop, else this will end too soon."

"Make me."

He kissed the corners of her mouth. "I should take you now."

"Standing?"

"The ways of making love are infinite."

"Let's try them all."

He eased his hand from her body, and her skirt dropped back in place. He took a moment longer to remove her hand from his hardness.

He undressed them both quickly and toppled her back onto the bed, stretching her hands above her head, where he held them in place.

"You keep imprisoning me," she said.

"Would that I could."

With tongue and lips and hand, he began an exploration of her body. She writhed beneath his touch.

"Gideon, please, stop. I can't endure it."

He pulled away, though he did not release her hands.

"No," she said urgently. "I didn't mean it. Don't stop."

He returned to where he had left off, pressing his lips against the sensitive skin above her private hair.

He moved lower, and lower still, his lips and

tongue working until her body threatened to burst.

"I can't stand it," she said.

He freed her hands. "Then stop me."

She could not, and he knew it. She could do little else but rub his shoulders and back, as far and low as she could reach, feeling the bunching of his muscles and the slickness of his skin.

He had a magic tongue. He placed it where she wanted to feel it most. He brought her close to madness, then moved his lips swiftly up her body, urged her legs apart, and plunged deep inside her. Blood roared in her head and her body throbbed as his plunges quickened, the room in a whirl, the two of them suspended in honeyed heat.

The world exploded. She cried out his name and surrendered to ecstasy. He stiffened in her arms, then shuddered once, twice, moaned "Lucy" and fell against her, holding her tight until at last he grew still, the only sound his ragged breathing as it mingled with hers.

She held him in a frenzied embrace, fearful he would move away and leave her to memories. She did not want him in memories. She wanted him here and now.

Refusing to loosen her hold, she let her mind and body slowly drift into the sweet ache of afterwards. She did not speak, unwilling to break the spell that completion had cast over her, wondering if this strange interlude was the same for a man.

The seconds drifted by, marked by the beating of her heart. He held her with a fierce gentleness that matched her embrace of him, as if he understood her need, as if he shared it.

"I did not know it would be like this," she said when she could find her voice.

"Only with you and me, Lucinda," he said. "Do not doubt me now. I mean what I say. Only with us."

This time he did not speak of other women. She felt a second satisfaction, less explosive than the first, but just as pleasing.

He eased off her and somehow maneuvered them both beneath the covers, where he held her against him, their legs in a tangle, her head resting on his chest.

She ought to keep quiet and take whatever it was he offered, to feel at peace, to welcome contentment. But she could not. Not just yet.

"Why did you bring me here?"

"You have to ask?"

"Was it just for this?"

"I had hoped it would be enough."

She raised herself up and leaned on her elbow, her fingers brushing the damp hair away from his face.

"It is, for me. I was thinking about you."

He looked at her for a long while, as if choosing what to say.

"You have a way of drawing trouble," he said. "This is the only way I can make certain you are safe."

But I'm not safe. I have fallen in love.

"You are my greatest trouble, Gideon."

It was the closest she could come to revealing the truth.

"I wish that were so."

He pulled her down against him and kissed her, hard, then pressed her back onto the bed and kissed her again.

"Make love to me," she said. "I'm not sure I did everything right."

"I could argue with you, but it does not seem in my best interests to do so."

She grinned, luxuriating in his attention. For a while, she was his business. For a while, he was hers.

"All right," she said, "I was perfect. Let's see if I can be perfect again."

"You have a man's hunger in a woman's body."

"Is that wrong?"

He gave his answer with his hands and lips. She could do nothing more than answer him in kind, showing her love through her touch when she could not put it into words.

Chapter Seventeen

He left sometime after midnight, carrying her very satisfied body to her own bed, assuming she slept, little knowing that she kept a dozen burning questions to herself.

When he was gone, she put on her nightgown and crawled beneath the covers to stare up at the dark folds of the canopy and remember.

She awoke late, aching in places that had never ached before, and began to stir. Alice was in the room and by her side in an instant. She must have been waiting right outside the door. Stretched out on the hearth, Baron thumped his heavy tail against the bricks.

It was not the morning greeting she would have preferred, but she felt the affection of both the maid and the hound. On this morning, they warmed her.

"I found your dress on the foot of your bed early this morning and did my best to make it presentable." Alice smiled broadly. "The dress-maker said she would have more garments ready by tomorrow morning, even if she had to take on extra help and work through the night. She's got a new machine that should hurry things along. I said I'd pick them up early."

She giggled. "She was quite shocked when I told her of the state of your undergarments. She made sure I had petticoats and drawers and such. She even added a pair of scarlet knicker-bockers. They're flannel and warm for the York-shire winter, she says, though I've never worn 'em meself."

While Alice saw to her mistress's bath, she chattered on about the clothes she had or-dered—"I hope you don't mind all that I pur-chased in your name, nor the colors, which she said were all the thing"—and in general kept Lucinda's mind occupied.

With Gideon gone, she took her own tour of the house, and no one—not the solemn-faced housekeeper nor the butler, who resembled more a tenant farmer than he did her own John Fenton—told her nay.

The castle was built in a square, each of the four sides opening onto the large center garden, at each corner a high, round turreted tower copied from medieval times. Only two of the sides and one of the towers were finished and open. If open was the right word. They were furnished and ready for habitation, but nothing outside of the two bedchambers Lucinda already knew and the kitchen area looked as if anyone had used them in years.

The front door opened onto a huge hall, its stone walls hung with giant tapestries depicting battles of old. A trestle table ran down the middle, a dozen chairs lined along each side. A mammoth stone fireplace occupied the center of one wall, and at the end of the room, a modern stairway wound its way upward into darkness.

Doors on either side of the hall led to a drawing room, library, kitchen, and a smaller dining area. The arrangement was not too different from Craven Manor, except that the proportions were larger and the atmosphere even more somber, something she would have thought impossible.

The upper floors, she assumed, consisted of extra bedchambers, the nursery where Gideon and his brother had been raised, the schoolroom, and quarters for the unloving, unnurturing nanny. But the floors were closed off, and she could do nothing but guess at their makeup.

Everything considered, it was a cold, drafty place, filled with shadows, reminding her of the man who owned it. She got the feeling that inside Blackthorne Hall it was always night.

Only in the garden did she find a touch of day. It was beautifully kept, with rows of well tended shrubbery and autumn flowers, and beds that promised a glorious profusion of color in the spring. It was Gideon's work. She knew it. Hidden from the world, it was his secret, hints of which he had revealed to her on their evening rides.

She treasured those hours more than ever now. Riding beside him, talking about roses and farm crops and sheep, she had felt as close to him as she did when she lay in his arms.

He did not return to Blackthorne until night, after she had eaten a tasteless meal prepared by his tight-lipped cook. She stood alone by the foot of her bed, wearing only her nightgown, having dismissed Alice a short time past. Even Baron had been taken outside.

Gideon knocked once, then strode into the room, pulled her into his arms, and kissed her. With only a whisper of her name, he picked her up and carried her into his chamber, elbowed the door shut, set her on her feet, and leaned her against the wall. His body pressed hard against hers.

It was if she were caught in a whirlwind. She started to protest. She needed to. Nothing else made sense.

Instead, breathing in the earthy scent of him, feeling the roughness of his clothing rub against the softness of her gown, she went wild.

He thrust his tongue between her lips. She answered by working at his belt. Her movements were frantic, his the same. When his trousers dropped, he lifted her nightgown, then lifted her. As if she had done so a thousand times, she wrapped her arms and legs around him. The tip of his sex rubbed against her wetness. She sucked on his tongue. He entered quickly and shook the wall.

The explosion came almost immediately, for him as well as for her, a frantic climax to the imperatives that drove them both. With a thousand shudders rippling through her, she clung to him as feverishly as he was clinging to her.

She squeezed her eyes closed against the burn of tears. No more than a minute or two had passed since he'd walked into her room. He had wanted her, he had taken her, and she had rejoiced. What had she become? A love slave. It was a term she had heard only once before Yorkshire, years ago in a snickering play-yard conversation among the bolder girls at school, and one she had not understood.

She understood it now. The depth of her passion frightened her, so completely had it taken hold. She should feel degraded, but she did not. Something that felt so right could not be wrong.

Her love directed itself to the man in her arms, to him and only him. He had cast his spell and made her his. She drew a particle of pleasure from knowing that in a much smaller, more temporary way, she had cast a spell over him.

Slowly he lowered her to her feet, smoothed her gown, brushed his fingers through her hair.

He kissed her eyes, and she wondered if he tasted tears.

"What am I doing to you?" he whispered, his forehead pressed to hers.

"I did not fight you."

"It would have done little good."

"I think it would. But fighting did not enter my mind."

"This was not what I planned," he said. "I saw you and I could not help myself."

"It was the same for me."

He picked her up and laid her on the bed, then saw that she was snugly covered. Fastening his trousers, he went to the window and stared out. She longed to reach out to him, but she did not know how.

"You know I can give you nothing," he said.

The words stung.

"So you have already told me. You insult me by saying it again. I am not here because of anything you might bestow upon me."

"My name." He said it softly and twisted a knife in her heart. "It is not much, but it is all that is truly mine. And I cannot share it with you."

The knife kept turning.

She sat up in the bed, the covers held tightly against her body like a shield.

"The only thing I would ask is that you tell me things I do not know."

She looked around the room, at the richness of the appointments, at the fancy bed, the fancy carpet, the expensive carvings in the ceiling.

"This is not yours?" she asked. "I do not understand."

"Nor should you."

"Do not misunderstand me, Gideon. I am not a venal woman. When I came here, to claim an inheritance I had not expected and did not entirely welcome, I wanted only to get by. Now I find myself wealthy."

Taking a deep breath, she stared at his back and wondered if he understood what she said.

"Anything I might ask of you would have little to do with material possessions. And nothing to do with a title. One far less grand than yours brought me nothing but suffering."

She was quiet for a moment. Still, he did not turn.

"All that I want is more of what you have already given me. And a chance to relieve whatever it is that tortures your soul."

Her voice broke and she fell silent. If he were ever to tell her of his troubles, now was the time.

At last he faced her. "*You* torture my soul."

"And nothing else?"

"My thoughts, my body, all that you see before you. I can think of little else but you."

It was a lover's answer, but not that of a man in love. He did not choose to share with her anything other than what had already passed between them. His words, though warmly said, were like the closing of a door.

She looked away, lest he see the blurring of her eyes.

"Then I should leave."

"Not now. Not yet."

"Even though I torture you."

"It is a sweet torture. You give me light, and I give you . . ."

"Nothing? Is that what you believe?" She forced the sorrow from her voice. She would take what she could. "You are wrong. You proved it last night, and you have proved it again just now. Would that you would continue to do so."

It was an open invitation. He did not misread what she meant.

He moved slowly to the bed, undressing with each step. Joining her beneath the covers, without a word he took her in his arms and gave her all that he could.

It was not enough, and yet it was the world.

Over the next week, and then the next, life settled into a routine that she both hated and loved. Gideon absented himself most of the day, but when he returned it was only to her. He had told her that lovemaking came in an infinite number of ways. He had not lied.

They both tempted fate. She felt certain she could not escape impregnation, but she showed no sign she was with child. At her insistence, when the monthly flux came, their lovemaking was forestalled.

Still, he came to her and talked about his work on the land, the approaching lambing, the comings and goings of the tenant families.

It was almost as if they were a family themselves, a man and his loving wife. Almost.

Each night, when he thought she was asleep, he left. She did not know when he ate or when he slept. With each passing day he grew more gaunt, his eyes more darkly sunken. She had no idea of the cause. If it were she, her presence did him little good.

Lancelot was brought to the Blackthorne stables, but one of the workers always accompanied her on her rides, remaining a dozen yards behind, his presence very much felt. She kept the outings short.

She had more clothes than she had ever owned in her life. Alice had indeed gone wild, but she looked so pleased that her mistress, studying her new wardrobe, could do nothing but exclaim how satisfied she was.

The womanly side of her was indeed satisfied. The day dresses were of varying hues, the styles very chic, according to the lady's maid, all with fitted bodices, sloping shoulders, and full sleeves that ended in tight bands at the wrist. Flounced skirts and plain, both were trimmed with piping or small ruffles. There were crinoline petticoats, lace-trimmed drawers, slippers, gloves, and a black velvet cloak to replace the plain one that had burned.

Two evening gowns, one of apricot velvet, the other of flesh-toned silk, made her feel rather like a queen . . . or a duchess. It was a concept she hastily brushed aside.

Mostly she concentrated on the riding habits—three, in black, brown, and gray, for which she was grateful. Alice must think she did little else but ride.

It was, in truth, mostly what she did, even though the rides were short.

With her permission, Gideon arranged for workers to begin the repair of the manor house. Once, Rigg came to take her and Baron to view the progress of the work.

She grew restless. She needed to go into town, she told Gideon one night, to confer with Carlyle Winston on how her expenditures affected her estate. The next morning, a cold and dreary Yorkshire November day, the ducal coach awaited her in the front drive.

She had not been completely truthful with him. It was not the banker she wished to see. Too long, Hudson Smedley, manager of the china factory, had barred her from exploring what he considered his domain. She was done with trying to arrange a meeting with him. If nothing else, her Devil Duke had taught her to be bold.

The factory lay at the edge of Hummersby Bridge. From blocks away she could see the thick, black smoke rising from its chimneys, beyond the steeple of the village church.

"What are you doing here?" Smedley said the moment she entered his office. His skeletal body blocked the door that would lead to the workers; his pale gray eyes were lit by a steel glint that should have sent her away at a run.

What would Gideon do at such a turn? She knew, and she proceeded to do the same.

"Good morning, Mr. Smedley," she said. "Perhaps you have forgotten who I am—the late Lord Westcombe's daughter and only heir. I have come to see exactly what it is that I own."

When she tried to go around him, he moved to bar her way.

"It is an unfortunate time." His tone had turned from anger to a whine. "As I told you before, the heat from the ovens can be dangerous for one as delicate as yourself."

She fixed a cold eye on him, took off her cloak, and tossed it aside.

"I won't break and I won't melt, sir. Neither will I fall in a swoon. What I will do, if you continue to stand in my way, is call on the constable to see that you are removed from the premises. Immediately."

He lifted a hand, and for a moment she thought he would strike her. She was surprised that a man of so little substance could summon such rage.

Reason, or perhaps it was cowardice, took control of him, and he stepped aside, mumbling something about how a woman should never own so much as the clothes on her back.

She walked past him, proud of her strength, scornful of the mean and narrow mind that judged the feminine half of the world with such hatred.

The pride lasted no longer than the time it took her to enter the long, sparsely lighted room where the workers created their beautiful wares. Strolling the length of the room and on to the smaller rooms beyond, past the kilns, into the storage and packing areas, she looked around in disbelief. Image after image flew at her, each one uglier than the one before.

Nothing had prepared her for what she saw.

One thought struck above all others, even the realization of the intensity of the heat. She had walked into hell.

An hour later, her pretty new gown clinging to her sweating body, her velvet cloak thrown over her arm, she made her way into the cold air of midday. Smedley was nowhere to be seen.

The carriage awaited. She ignored it, preferring to make her way into the main part of town by foot. She saw little along the way, her mind still burned by a hundred images, mostly of eyes, wide, haunting, lost. They would stay with her all her life.

Without realizing she was doing so, she made her way to the bank. Carlyle Winston was gone for the day, a tight-lipped clerk informed her. He looked her over in a manner that was far too forward, as if he had the right, as if everyone did. It was her first encounter with the results of her disgraceful liaison with the duke.

Wealthy though she was, she had put herself beyond respect.

But there was a far more disgraceful situation than hers not one mile from the clerk's comfortable and orderly desk. If he knew of it—and he probably did—he did not care.

Outside the bank, just as she had done before, she encountered Sir Sheridan Pettifore, this time in the company of the lovely Rebecca Atterbury, who clung possessively to his arm.

"Sir Sheridan," Lucinda said. "I need to talk with you." She glanced at the widow. "And you, Mrs. Atterbury, if you will give me the time. I need help and I don't know where to turn."

"Has he hurt you?" the baronet asked.

For a moment she did not understand whom he meant.

"Oh, Gideon. Of course not."

Sir Sheridan looked almost disappointed.

"Of course he hasn't hurt her," Mrs. Atterbury said. Her regard was narrow and assessing, like that of a cat studying an unexpected mouse. "But she does appear to have been put through a rather demanding time."

For the first time, Lucinda realized what she must look like after her hour in hell, her dress limp, her hat askew, her once carefully coiffed hair in disarray beneath it.

She slipped the cloak over her shoulders and straightened her hat.

"This has nothing to do with Gideon Blackthorne. It's the children, the poor, poor children, that I must tell someone about."

Sir Sheridan's regard was not nearly so friendly as it had been on their previous encounters, but he had the good manners not to rebuff her completely.

"Tea," he said. It seemed his answer for everything.

In the tea shop, with the help standing nearby in open curiosity, she did not try to keep her voice down.

"They were as young as six. Babies, little more."

"Who?" Sir Sheridan asked.

"The workers." The words spilled out, tumbling one on top of the other. "Boys, mostly. They carried molds from the potters to rooms they called stoves, close to the ovens. Small, airless places. The temperature rose so high I felt my eyes singe." She buried her face in her hands. "And others, carrying heavy loads, sweeping, cleaning. Whatever was demanded of them."

This would not do. She had to get control of herself. But the memories were too sharp. Looking from Sir Sheridan to Mrs. Atterbury, she did not try to keep the tears from falling.

"When I questioned them, they did not want to answer at first. One bold lad spoke up and said they work up to sixteen hours a day. *Sixteen*. He was so thin I wondered how he could summon strength to do more than stand."

"It's obviously not against the law, or it would not continue," Mrs. Atterbury said. "Did this boy complain of the work? Did he complain of his wages?"

A chill began to steal up on Lucinda. The woman looked so lovely in her blue silk gown and matching cloak, a feather in her hat, not a hair out of place. But her eyes had a distant look. Had she gazed into hell, as Lucinda had done, she would not have cared, except for what it did to her appearance.

"He makes half a crown a week, at most," she said. She looked at Sir Sheridan. "Half a crown. No, he did not complain. He seemed glad to get it."

His handsome face showed not a single frown. "Are these not conditions that can also be found in the United States? I am sure it's so."

A sharpness had come into his voice, as if he grew impatient with her complaining. Sheridan Pettifore, pleasant and harmless, was not so pleasant and harmless now.

"I have heard rumors, yes. But I did not see such conditions for myself. Nor did I imagine how horrible they could be. I do not defend my country. What is wrong here is wrong there." She rubbed the tears from her cheeks. "But there I did not profit from the sweat of the children. Here my father did. And now so do I."

But she could see that her tale of horror did not move the handsome pair who sat before her sipping their noontime tea. Mrs. Atterbury reached for a small, crustless sandwich of soft cheese and watercress. Lucinda wanted to slap the woman's hand and run with the food back to the factory.

She stood. "I will talk to Carlyle Winston. He can tell me what to do."

Sir Sheridan rose gracefully to his feet and looked at her pityingly. "Do you think he does not know? I should imagine he has visited the factory more than once, in your father's interest and now in yours. He was appointed trustee of the Fairfax estate, was he not?"

"Of course," she said stiffly. "You are right."

She turned her attention to the door, unable to look at either the man or the woman for a second longer.

"Most of them are foundlings," she said, as if

anyone within listening distance cared. "Rather than go to a workhouse, which one of the women potters described"—she shivered involuntarily—"families take them in and see that they are put to work. For the money they bring in. Half a crown a week. I suppose it's all they can make. They are so young. And so thin."

She hurried outside to the waiting ducal carriage. Everyone in Hummersby Bridge must be watching. By coming into the village like this, she was flaunting her relationship with the Devil Duke. An unprincipled Yankee, she dared to break society's rules.

And now she dared to judge the English on their morality.

A new horror struck. Was Gideon aware of the working conditions in the factory?

No, surely not. And yet . . .

A worse thought came. What if one of the foundlings was his? A child he did not know about or had chosen not to protect. More than once she had seen the young boy who was his son scampering about the grounds of Blackthorne. There could be brothers not so fortunate.

Falling back against the carriage seat, she was scarcely aware when the return journey to Blackthorne Hall was begun. She had trusted Gideon in so many ways, when the world condemned him. But today had aroused questions about him whose answers she did not want to know.

Chapter Eighteen

Lucinda descended from the carriage at the front of Blackthorne Hall but found herself reluctant to go inside just yet. She felt the urge to walk awhile, to think.

There was no end to her puzzle. It played out, then looped back onto itself in a knot, very much like a hangman's noose. She could order Smedley to hire only adults, but the children he let go would end up in the workhouse, a fate apparently worse than the factory.

Yet she could not leave matters the way they were.

And there was the question of Gideon. Always she came back to him. What did he know about the workers? Had he brought any of those brave, struggling foundlings into the world and then abandoned them? She could not think so, though she had no proof.

It was with a heavy heart that she set out on foot, inclination taking her along the winding driveway to the side of the hall, around to where the stable and a half-dozen other outbuildings were clustered within the stone walls.

Baron met her at the corner, at the base of one of the rounded high towers. Tail wagging, he jumped excitedly in place, then pranced—there was no other word for it—in front of her, drawing her farther down the path.

Following, she stopped beside the hound in front of the stable. A squeal of delight drew her inside. At this time of day, the horses, including her beloved Lancelot, had been put out to graze. At first she saw only Jenny Patchell, her bent figure at the opening to one of the back stalls. The old woman was grinning in a way Lucinda had never seen before.

With Baron in the lead, she went to join her.

The source of Jenny's pleasure was immediately apparent. A mottled black and brown dog lay on a pile of straw in the center of the stall; attempting to get to her teats was a litter of six black newborn pups, their short legs pumping, squeals of impatience filling the small space as they fought for their rightful place at the dinner table.

Kneeling beside the mother was the young

boy she had just been remembering, the one who bore Gideon's face and eyes.

He looked up, and his dark eyes flashed. "Look, miss, look what Lady's gone and done. I can keep one. For myself. Gideon says I can."

He glanced at Jenny. "Sorry, I mean His Grace. I'm not to call him by his name when strangers are about."

Strangers. Deftly, and innocently, he had put Lucinda in her place.

Tossing her cloak and hat aside, she knelt beside him, unmindful that she might soil her new gown.

"The pups look quite healthy," she said. "They can't be very old."

The boy shrugged. "No more'n a few hours. They was here when I come in. I've been waiting for them to get here ever so long, but Lady went off by herself, which Jenny says is the way o' dogs, and had 'em alone."

He stretched a hand toward the squirming mass, then pulled it back. "Jenny says I'm not to touch 'em until Lady lets me know it's all right. But I've picked out my pup. He's the little one, down underneath. There, you can see him now. Jenny calls him the runt, but he's a fighter. Anyone can see that."

He looked beyond Lucinda to where Baron stood, panting, his tongue lolling over his huge, sharp teeth.

"That's your dog, ain't it? Do you think he

might be the sire? That's what I'm to call him, Jenny says. The pups have his look. Hard to tell. Fathers ain't inclined to hang around."

He seemed not to realize what he said.

"Baron does indeed look like the sire," Lucinda said. "And he seems proud. Some fathers do hang around, I suppose."

The boy went rattling on about the name he might bestow upon his chosen pup. A shadow fell across the scene. She looked up to see Gideon standing behind Jenny, his dark eyes on her. She looked from him to the boy, then back at him, but he did not change expression. Indeed, he showed no expression at all. He simply stood in the immovable way he had and watched her watching him. He had played this scene with her a hundred times, but usually when they were alone.

The walls of the stall moved in on her. Hurriedly she stood and without a word backed away from the boy and ran toward the door to the stable, and on, not stopping until she was halfway down the driveway.

She stopped to catch her breath, then turned to face Gideon. He had followed, as she knew he would. He stood far too close, in shirtsleeves and black trousers, her cloak over his arm.

"You've met John," he said.

She stared at him, trying to read the thoughts behind his deep, dark eyes.

"I've seen him before, but you must have known I did. He has no mother?"

"She died of a fever shortly after he was born. She was, as you might have guessed, the daughter of a tenant farmer on the estate. And no, she was not wed."

Lucinda looked beyond him to the stable door. "You take care of the boy, but you do not claim him."

"I take care of him. That is enough. He is well tended. And content."

He spoke flatly, as if he would dismiss her concern, but he badly misjudged her state of mind.

"Are there others you take care of? Still others you do not know about? Boys who must take care of themselves?"

Her voice carried all the anguish she had felt over the past few hours. Listening, staring, Gideon could have been carved from stone. She wanted to strike him with her fists, pound his chest, shake him into some kind of reaction— anger, laughter, ridicule, anything but the granite coldness he presented to her now.

With a cry, she turned and ran down the drive, away from the house, her vision blurred by tears. He called her name, but she did not stop, not until she was through the gatehouse and across the field, abandoning the road, stumbling across stubbled autumn grass, little noting what she passed or wondering what might lie ahead.

She topped a rise. The moor stretched out before her, blanketed by mist rising from broken ground. At the moment, it seemed like a refuge. She hurried down into the dampness, with each step feeling the spongy ground give way beneath her feet. She moved slower now, unsure of herself in the blinding swirl, catching her breath after the long, mad run.

The farther she walked, the thicker the mist became, until it was more like a dense fog, the kind that sent ships at sea onto unseen rocks. If she closed her eyes and concentrated hard enough, she might be able to hear, as she had on her first night in Yorkshire, the waves on the shore twenty miles away, where the late duke had met his death, along with his favored son.

Foolishness. The only thing she could hear was the pounding of her heart.

She walked on, able to make out her hand in front of her, her skirt brushing the ground, but little more beyond. She stopped and listened. Someone was close by. She knew it, though she could neither see nor hear him. Her skin prickled, and her heart caught in her throat.

"Who's there?" she cried out, turning in place, staring into a world of unrelieved gray, the sky no different from the air.

She rubbed at her arms.

"Hello," she called, this time louder.

The word echoed back on her.

She warned herself not to panic. That would be the worst thing she could do. But she could not forget the sound of a long-ago gunshot, nor the fire that had almost taken her life.

She had to get away, it did not matter where. Picking up her skirts, she took off at a run, straight into the all-too-solid figure of a man. With a cry she jumped back, ready to scream for help. His eyes stopped her. They stared at her out of the mist, and the scream died on her lips.

"Gideon," she gasped.

"I brought you this," he said, holding out her cloak. "I did not want you to get chilled."

They might as well have been standing by the steps in front of the hall, for all the emotion he showed.

She let out a long, slow breath, ignoring the cloak. "You frightened me."

"As you have frightened me a hundred times."

She shook her head. He spoke nonsense, more for effect than truth.

"Go away, please. Leave me for a while. This thickness will not last long. In fact, it seems to be lessening now. I can find my way back."

"It is unlikely," he said. And then, more sharply, "What happened today?"

She brushed at her unkempt hair, heavy with the mist. "Nothing." Nothing she wished to reveal. Not to him. Not now.

"Did someone insult you?"

The words were harsh, frightening. She had never heard him speak with such fury.

"Insult me? Because I stay with you? It was nothing I had not expected. In truth, it was less so."

"Do not lie to me."

She wanted to laugh. "The way you lie to me? Deny that John is yours."

"I will not speak of John."

"Of course not. You will not speak of anything that strikes to the heart and soul of who you are and who you have been."

"What happened today? I must know."

He spoke low, but the words were hard and struck her as loud as a shout. On this eerie afternoon, he was a man who would not be denied. He was a man who might kill another man. He truly frightened her, not for what he might do to her but for how he might destroy himself.

Cold and desolate, she closed her eyes and hugged herself.

"Then I will tell you. I went to the factory." The words came out as half sobs. "I saw the children there, working in conditions that the devil himself would find intolerable. Foundlings, most of them, I was told, but none looked so much like you as John. They broke my heart."

He took her by the arms. If he meant to be

322

gentle, she did not give him the chance. Fury overcame her. She pounded her fists against his chest.

"No one cared," she cried and hit him again and again, as she had not been able to strike at the fashionable couple who took her to tea, at the clerk in the bank, at Hudson Smedley, at all the unseen people behind the dark windows of Hummersby Bridge.

The blows were weak—she knew it—but she could not end them. He did not move or try to stop her. At last she fell against him, exhausted.

"No one cared," she said again, but this time it was close to a moan.

He held her tight and she felt his lips against her hair, her face, her tear-stained cheeks.

"Do not cry," he whispered, and she imagined agony in his voice.

The worries of her world lay upon her so heavily she could scarcely stand. He dropped her cloak on the soft ground and laid her on it, spreading it wide so that he might lie by her side, and then he held her in his arms and continued to kiss her face.

The earthy smell of turf and damp air filled her nostrils, and the mist lay lightly upon them, hiding them from the world as no blanket could have done. Her lips sought this. They were sweet and soft, soothing at the same time as they provoked her to deepen the kiss. She could see only him, could feel nothing but his solid body against hers, his strong hands on her back, his mouth taking possession of hers.

"Make me forget," she whispered when at last the kiss was broken.

He unbuttoned the front of her gown and slipped her breasts free. He licked the tips, and the forgetting began. By the time he had explored them thoroughly, had flattened her crinoline petticoat and lowered his trousers, had thrust himself into her, she could think of nothing but the joining of their bodies. He was her opiate. He was her love.

If her wildness came more from desperation than passion, he did not seem to notice. Or if he noticed, he did not show he cared.

They did not speak again, not after the love-making, not while he gave her time to straighten her clothes, not on the long walk back to Blackthorne Hall. She had not realized she'd run so far. The air was still heavy, but he moved unerringly through it, a creature of the mist as well as of the night.

He followed her to her room. When he had closed the door, she turned to face him. How pathetic she must look with her wet, tangled hair and tear-streaked face, her dress soiled, her once-beautiful velvet cloak stained with sod from the moor.

From the look of him, his clothes scarcely

wrinkled, he might have been out for no more than an afternoon stroll.

Except for the worry she saw deep in his eyes. If worry it was. She could not be sure.

"You must think I went mad today," she said.

"I thought no such thing."

"Oh, but I did, for a while. I should not have struck you. It was as wrong of me as it would have been if you had done the striking. But I have returned to sanity. In my own way." She looked down at her hands, then back to him. "I am still a woman obsessed."

"You are the most caring woman I have ever known."

"Soft in the head, you mean. I am obsessed with you, but that is something I have demonstrated time and again. And now I have a new obsession."

"The factory."

"The children. I do not know how I can help them, but I will think on it and do what I can. The profit means nothing to me, but to close the place down would put good people out of work and send the foundlings to places they should not go."

"Lucinda—"

"Please, let me finish. Since children are much on my mind today, I have something I need to say to you. This is not easy, and I ask you not to interrupt. I truly do not believe I am with child, but should I find myself so, I will

325

make no demands upon you. When I came here, I thought I was strong, but that was not true. I am strong now. Knowing you has made me so."

"And what will this strength allow you to do?" His voice was razor-thin. "Should you bear my child."

"Return to New York and raise him in the same loving home my mother provided me, the main difference being I shall be rich. It is a powerful condition. We will thrive."

He stared at her for a long time, the torture back in his eyes. "Damn me and damn my world," he said, and there was anguish in each word. "For all I have done, I am cursed. And you, an angel, have chosen to give yourself to the devil himself. Would that we had never met."

Then he was gone, the door closed, his final words echoing in the still air of her chamber, crushing her heart.

She did not see him again that evening or the next or the next. There was no one to ask where he was, where he slept, how he passed his time. After the third day, she did not want to know.

Would that we had never met.

His parting words were enough to destroy all peace. They drove her to despair.

And yet, there were still the children. She wrote to Carlyle Winston to ask his advice on what could be done about the china factory, but had not received a reply. She was not surprised.

On the fourth day, she summoned the ducal carriage and with Alice and Baron along for companionship, she went to see how the repair work progressed at Craven Manor.

Mrs. Pickering, Fenton, Cook, even the coachman Rigg met her with smiles and, where the women were concerned, hugs and tears, a greeting as different from her first as day from night. The housekeeper and butler took her to her room while Rigg went to gather vegetables from the garden and Cook went to prepare a meal.

"We've got a ways to go," Cook said, "in making the kitchen the way it was, but I can still put food together on such a special day."

Alice stayed with the other servants, regaling them, Lucinda was certain, with tales of life in a ducal mansion, more likely dwelling on her almost daily shopping trips to town. Baron explored the grounds.

Much had been done upstairs, the burned and smoked timber removed, the chamber stripped of furnishings, fresh paint applied to the walls. It needed new draperies and carpet, which she was supposed to pick out herself.

"You can go to York, if you've a mind," Mrs. Pickering said with a sniff. "They've fine goods there, as fine as any you'll find in London."

Lucinda nodded, unable to consider such a task right away.

"My father's rooms. How are they?"

"Stripped, they are, and the work begun."

"I would like to see them."

"Oh, miss—" Mrs. Pickering began in protest.

"Athena," Fenton said, "we must do as our mistress wishes." He led the way downstairs.

At the door to the chamber, Lucinda paused. "I'd like to go in alone."

She could feel the protest bubbling within the housekeeper, but a glance from the butler quelled any talk.

When they had departed, she entered and closed the door behind her, breathing deeply, waiting for the presence to make itself known. But all was still. Her father's spirit had gone. The bed, the chairs, the tables—all were gone as well. The floor was bare, and the freshly plastered walls needed a coat of paint.

She might have been anywhere, in anyone's refurbished room, and not in the private quarters of the late Lord Westcombe. Her disappointment was bitter, though she was not surprised at the absence. She had wanted to tell him what she thought of the factory.

She turned to leave and found she could not move. She caught her breath. She had been wrong. Whatever remained of the spirit had weakened, but it held sufficient strength to hold her in place.

She found herself staring at the once ornately carved fireplace. Now it was only brick and mortar, its beautiful facade destroyed in the flames. She went closer to stroke the cold surface, her hand guided by an unseen force. One brick felt loose; she shook it, worked it back and forth, and with two hands pulled it free from the wall.

Setting it aside, she reached into the narrow space behind it in the wall. Her fingers fell on a small object. She managed to work it out. It was a leather-bound volume with the initials *W F* embossed in gold on the front, along with the family crest of facing dogs. William Fairfax. Her father's private journal. She fingered the lettering. This was as close to him as she had come.

And he had guided her here.

A packet fell to her feet. It must have been inside the book. She opened it to find letters, yellowed, worn from frequent reading, and a second stack, bound separately from the first, this one smaller, newer in appearance, as if the letters had never been posted.

The first were addressed to her father and were postmarked from the United States. Her hands trembled. They were letters her mother had sent, letters she had never told her daughter about.

Three letters were in the second stack. They were all addressed to Miss Lucinda Fairfax. She stared at them in wonder. She did not understand.

She returned to the journal. A shiver ran

through her as she opened to a page at random. The first thing her eye fell upon was her name.

As if in a trance, she sat on the floor and, turning to the first page, she began to read.

As the half-century mark of my life approaches, I begin this journal with dark thoughts and the need to unburden myself.

Those dark thoughts during his last years had been the cause of much speculation. Perhaps now she would find their root. She closed her eyes for a moment, felt a shiver of anticipation as filled with hope as it was with dread, and continued to read.

Chapter Nineteen

She read quickly—the journal was not long though its first entry was dated years before—then returned to the beginning to read again the words her father had sent her from the grave.

I should never have left my wife and child.

It was a sentiment he expressed on the first page and repeated, in various ways, throughout the rambling work.

I will make it up to them somehow.

And then later, after Anne Fairfax's death: *Too late, too late for that precious woman, but not for the daughter she gave me, the daughter I tossed aside.*

The only explanation for his misdeed: *I fell heir not only to my ancestral land and title, but also to the weakness that made me revel in them.*

He had come to America a younger son without prospect of inheritance, he wrote, his sole intent to increase the exports of fine Fairfax bone china to a growing market. He had met and married Anne. Then the letter that changed his life had arrived, the death notification of his father and brother that both saddened and excited him.

The excitement had eventually dominated. He had not handled the change of his circumstance well.

He was harsher on himself than Lucinda had ever been. He wrote of what he had substituted for love: money. He hoarded it like a miser, counting his pence and pounds, never having enough, always demanding more.

Blackthorne will not let me work the farmers harder. Hudson Smedley is a different sort. I do not like him, but I will use him to further the profits from the china business.

Beneath the substance of the text, she could read the nature of his obsession, an all-consuming one that took command of his life. Obsession was a condition she was learning much about. Profit had been her father's, as Gideon was hers.

Hudson Smedley had got that profit from the sweat of children, profit that her father had gathered for his only child. The bitter irony of the situation brought tears to Lucinda's eyes.

In the end, William Fairfax had begun to doubt himself.

Do I proceed as I should, hoarding riches that I might never be able to pass on to my daughter? Would it be better if I went to her and told her of my regrets? I am a coward, Lucinda. I can tell you of my anguish only through these written words. They are composed with much heat and all of my heart. I pray you do not read them as cold.

It was the first time in the journal he directed his words to her, and the last. He had written no more. For a reason she would never know, he had hidden the journal away, perhaps planning to pull it out again when his thoughts became clearer. The fatal fall had interfered. No one knew of the slim volume's existence, until he led her to it today.

She turned to the letters addressed to her. They expressed the feelings he could not tell her in person, that he had loved her when she was a child; though he knew her not as a woman, a fact he bitterly regretted, he loved her still.

He spoke of his daily existence, his plans for the manor house, for the factory, the unexpected demands placed upon him by the deaths of his father and brother. What had kept him from mailing the letters that would have brought her such comfort? He gave only one hint:

I have written these same sentiments to your

mother and asked that she pass them on to you. When I have heard from her that you understand, perhaps communicated to me in your own blessed childish hand, I will see that you learn of them from me.

Her mother had indeed told her such things, but Lucinda, as stubborn as either of her parents, had believed them to be little more than apologies for an unforgivable abandonment.

Do not hate me, nor anyone else, for what has passed. The blame for the unfortunate separation weighs heavily on my shoulders, and my shoulders alone. I was the man in our small, once loving family. I should have acted like one.

What could he have meant by *nor anyone else?* Surely he did not refer to Anne.

Puzzled, she turned to the faded letters composed so long ago by a wife for her absent husband. The first was dated a year after his departure:

I cannot come to you as you ask. Our beloved daughter remains too ill to make the long sea journey, but we talk of you each day, and each night you are in our prayers.

And later: *All is well. Lucinda continues to grow stronger. Tend to your family affairs as it is right and necessary. You have provided for us. That is all I ask. I would not be a burden on you for the world.*

She could picture her mother writing the words, filled with pride, wanting her husband to sail back and sweep her into his arms, unwilling to ask that he do so, needing the urge to be his. But nothing in his journal indicated he was the romantic sort to toss all aside and do such a thing. He had ever been a practical man. It was a trait Lucinda had once been proud of in herself.

Perhaps her father had been as stubborn as his wife. Perhaps he wanted her to want him enough to come to him as he had clearly requested.

At one point, some ten years after the separation had begun, he had obviously written offering her a divorce, if that was what she chose.

You say you have not found another, Anne wrote, *and that in the offer of a dissolution of our marriage you seek nothing but that which will give me comfort. I decline. You are my husband. My vows were made not only with my lips but far more deeply with my heart. I will, however, understand if you wish to seek another wife. I have made a home here with Lucinda and we are happy. The funds you send are far too generous. Please save them for needs that are greater than ours.*

So much was clear. Pride had wrung those words from her mother, a killing pride sprung from the sting of her husband's offer to free her. She had thought he wanted another. She would make no demands upon him.

William Fairfax, a man grown lonely despite

his wealth and position, had asked his daughter to blame him, and so she had. He had not known the difficulties his wife and child faced. He had not known that his wife loved him until her dying day. She had not told him.

Slowly Lucinda rebound the letters and slipped them into the journal, which she held for a moment against her bosom, then slipped into the pocket of her gown. This was what her father had wanted her to find. She knew why his spirit had not found rest.

Sitting on the floor of the empty chamber, she looked around her. "I'm sorry, Father, that I did not know you. I am sorry that you did not know me."

A breeze blew through the open window, brushing against her cheek, soft as a kiss, then quickly died, and she knew that at last, he was truly gone. She wished him the peace he had not found in life.

She sat awhile, her heart heavy and full at the same time. And she thought about what she must do.

A bark stirred her from her reverie, and she looked up to see Baron's long black face at the window, his monster paws resting on the windowsill. Beyond him lay the rolling landscape that was Fairfax land, and farther still, Blackthorne Hall.

"You're right," she said to the hound. "It's time we went where we belong."

This time she did not mean America.

She arrived at Blackthorne Hall late in the afternoon. Instead of Gideon, two letters awaited her, one from the banker Winston, the other from her cousin in New York. It was a day for correspondence.

Irene Littlewood handed them to her with a smirk.

"Bad news, I'll be bound. Nothing good can come in a life of sin."

Lucinda took them without comment. She seldom saw the woman, and when she did she made their contact brief.

Hurrying to her chamber, where she could read in privacy, she chose the banker's first. She read it twice before collapsing into the chair and reading it again.

The facts were simple, the implications immeasurable. Sometime over the past few days the Duke of Ravenswood had gone to face Hudson Smedley. Reforms were under way. The young workers at the Fairfax China Factory had been removed from the families that had put them to work in such deplorable conditions and placed in homes throughout Hummersby Bridge and the surrounding countryside, a temporary arrangement pending a final decision on where they would go. Training was immediately begun to prepare the adult replacements to take over their tasks.

Smedley was continuing in his present position on a temporary basis. If it was determined that he could not make the working conditions more amenable for all, he would be terminated. Lucinda was not disturbed.

His Grace, Winston wrote, had acted as if he had Miss Fairfax's permission to speak in her stead. The banker wanted assurance in writing that this was so, since the salaries for the new workers would be substantially higher than those paid to the children. His Grace had assumed the expenses that came with the boarding of the foundlings in their new temporary homes.

Lucinda held the letter to her heart. His Grace had more than just her permission. Her spirit soared with love.

She turned to the letter from America. Early on in her time in Yorkshire, she had written her cousin to say she would be returning to New York, though not to the farm. And she was most definitely not interested in any marriage that might be proposed for her.

The cousin wrote to say, in terms most blunt, that Lucinda was to stay away. Abraham Lincoln, enemy of the slavery that had been tearing the country apart for the last decade and more, was the newly elected President of the United States. A number of states were threatening to secede from the Union. War seemed inevitable. Sad times lay ahead.

The news was indeed tragic, and she wanted

to weep for her country. A week or two ago, she would have taken the news as tragic on a personal basis as well. Her route of escape was cut off.

Not so on this evening.

She opened the door of her chamber to find Alice waiting outside in the hall.

"Will you be needing me tonight?" the lady's maid asked dispiritedly, as if she awaited her usual nightly dismissal.

Lucinda smiled. "Oh, yes."

Alice's eyes widened. "Go on with you. Meaning no offense. But of late I've not been earning me keep."

"No offense taken. You'll earn it tonight. First I'd like a hot, soaking bath. Then dress me more carefully than you have ever done. It's time I wore that silk you picked out for me. The one the color of my skin."

Alice's eyes turned from wide to glinting, with more than a trace of triumph in the glint.

"Gor, I knew you'd take to that one. And I know just the way to arrange your hair. It's a style right up to the mark. I saw it in a book at the dressmaker's only yesterday. I've been studying these things, in case you became a duchess."

"Oh, no, that's not—"

But the girl would have none of her mistress's protest. She entered the chamber with a militant stride. Her thoughts still in a whirl, Lucinda could do nothing but put herself in the maid's hands. And then it would be Gideon's hands, as well as his heart, most on her mind.

She dined in her room as she so often did, splendorous in her finery, feeling foolish. The food grew cold on her plate as she waited for the lover who did not return. Why she thought he would come on this night she did not know, except that since early in the morning this had been a time for momentous occurrences. She wanted only one more to make her day complete.

For that, Gideon had to be very, very close.

She was sitting by the dying fire when she heard him enter the adjoining room. Nervously she stood and smoothed the silk gown over her hips. Too, she tugged the neckline lower to reveal all but the tips of her bosom. He had never before needed such inspiration to want her, but she had not seen him in a while. She would do whatever it took to hold him in her arms and say what she had to say.

She faced the door between the two chambers and waited for him to enter. She heard him moving about. Then all was quiet. Had he left? No, it could not be.

She reached for the knob, half fearful the door would be locked. It opened easily and she stepped into his chamber. The first thing she saw was his cape thrown carelessly atop his bed. And then she saw him across the room, standing with his back to her, staring out an open window into the dark.

His shirt was wrinkled, slept in for days, and his thick black hair unkempt, as if he had raked his fingers through it a thousand times. Slowly he turned to face her. The gauntness of his face startled her, the bristled cheeks, the devil lines deep between his sunken eyes.

She had seen him in such a state before, but tonight he looked worse, as if he had descended into a special kind of hell. Filled with love for him, she came close to tears.

Neither spoke for a minute. How foolish she was, dressed more for a ball than the tryst she had been imagining, her gown too fine, her hair arranged in the mass of curls that Alice had insisted on. She was far too obvious in her approach to him. But when had she ever been subtle where he was concerned?

The longer she looked at him, the less she thought about herself.

"I have missed you," she said.

It was the simplest way she could approach him, the closest she could come to asking why he had stayed away, and what it was that drove him to despair. The situation was intolerable, yet he gave her no choice but to go on.

Her stomach hardened into a knot, and the blood pounded in her ears so fiercely she could scarcely think. Why didn't he speak? Why didn't he rush to take her in his arms?

"I heard from Carlyle Winston," she said. She began to close the distance between them. "Thank you for doing what I did not know how to do."

He held still. He did not come to her. And so she had to go to him.

"We will have to decide exactly how the children should be treated. I understand the homes are only temporary. But I am ignorant of what more permanent choices for them might—"

"Lucinda."

He spoke as if he had to force her name to his lips.

She tilted her chin. "It won't do any good pretending I'm not here, or that I will turn and go away," she said.

She took another step toward him. Her silk gown rustled as she moved, and the heat from her body seemed to heighten the lavender scent of the fine-milled soap Alice had brought her from town, until it filled the air with a sweetness he could surely not ignore.

And yet he did not reach out for her; his despair remained. Tears formed; the droplets clung to her lashes. She tried to blink them away.

"I missed you," she said again, "and if you do not understand what I mean, I will tell you. I missed your lips, I missed your hands on my body, I missed—"

She was in his arms in an instant. His fingers thrust into her hair, pins fell, and the carefully combed locks tumbled free. He cradled her face in his hands and he kissed the lashes, the corners of her eyes, the corners of her lips.

She could not breathe.

He was trembling. It seemed impossible that this proud, private, all too elegant man, who kept his heart separate and alone, should tremble. Yet it was true. She wanted to stroke his cheek and assure him all would be well.

He gave her no chance for gentleness. He held her tight, his hands slipping over silk and flesh, stroking her bare shoulders as he bent to kiss the hollow of her throat. Dropping her head back, eyes closed, she offered all that she had and everything he might want.

"Lucy," he said, "dearest Lucy."

She burned, the heat racing along the surface of her skin and into her thick-coursing blood. He lifted his head, and his lips hovered over hers. Her heat became a kind of triumph. He was hers. She knew it. Her lips parted, curving into a smile. Now she would say what she had come to say. And he would listen.

Her spirit soared. This was right. "Gideon," she whispered, lifting her eyes to his, expecting to see the same heartfelt longing and happiness reflected there.

What she saw turned her blood cold: regret, anguish, desolation, all too visible in their depths, deeper now that he held her in his arms. She had not made things better for him; she had made them worse.

She gasped, and he let her go. Swaying, almost stumbling, she forced herself to stand erect.

He held his hands wide, else he might take her into his arms again. And that, his actions told her, would be a terrible mistake.

"No," he said, despair shredding his voice into a ragged whisper, and then, more firmly, as if he had reached a decision that rent his soul, "No more."

He backed away from her, stared hard, then looked away. He swept up his cape from the bed, the blood-red lining flashing in the gaslight from the wall sconce, and was gone.

Lucinda stood in the whirling room, the sudden silence deafening, his denial of her echoing in her shattered heart. Staring at the closed door, she whispered the words she had tried to say, the declaration he had not stayed to hear.

"I love you, Gideon Blackthorne. I always will."

It brought her little satisfaction. Empty air did not respond.

She looked around at all the dark corners of his private chamber. She should have known this moment of denial would come; so much of what he had said and done told her that it would. Her foolish fantasy of happiness with him had been just that, pure fantasy, and far too short-lived.

The strength ebbed from her. She had to force herself to put one foot after the other and return to her room, the rustle of her dress mocking her with each step.

Firmly she closed the door and turned the lock. She loved him, but she must not allow him to hurt her again, though how she was to manage such a feat she had no idea.

A scratching at the hall door drew her attention. She opened it and knelt to bury her head against Baron's strong, broad side.

No. No more.

The words still crushed her. She had not known he could be so cruel. With the realization came the edge of rebellion.

How dare he say such things, when she had offered him all that she was and ever would be, and without a single demand? Hope, ah yes, she had possessed hope enough, but no demands. A coward, that's what he was, riding off when he could not tell her to her face the truth behind the anguish in his eyes.

She ought to cry; she carried within her enough tears to flood the moors. But her eyes remained dry.

How dare he? Did he think her such a weakling that he could do whatever he wanted with her, to her, and then leave, and she would do nothing in return?

Of course he did. Not once had she given him cause to think anything else.

Until tonight. She was not Anne Fairfax, content to settle for what life handed her. She was Lucinda. Gideon called her his light, yet he continued to keep her in the dark. She had let him, but no more. Too much was at stake, her happiness and his.

Whatever it was that caused his torment, she would share it. Tonight.

She lifted her head and looked into Baron's eyes.

"Can you take me to him?"

The hound's tail wagged.

"You know what I mean, don't you?"

The tail wagged harder.

Quickly she stood, already unfastening her gown, hurrying toward the wardrobe that held her riding clothes. She fairly flew out of one outfit and into another, pulling on her boots as she headed for the stairs, her ruined velvet cloak tossed carelessly over her shoulders, not bothering with hat or gloves.

She had to run to keep up with Baron, down the winding stairs, out the rear kitchen door, along the pathway to the stable. She was probably seen and heard by a dozen of Gideon's people, but she did not care. No one, not the devil himself, could have stopped her on this night.

No matter what else happened in the next hours, she would at last find out the secrets that the Devil Duke was determined to keep from her. No matter how much the secrets hurt, they could not wound her half so much as his parting words.

Chapter Twenty

Baron led her on a winding path, down well-used roads, across fields, along narrow hidden lanes, running all out, his long, strong legs choosing without hesitation the path he wanted her to take. It seemed as if in all his time with her, he had been waiting for this night.

Her hair blew wild in the wind, and the crushed velvet cloak flapped around her as Lancelot followed close on the heels of the hound. The landscape to right and left passed in a blur. She focused straight ahead.

At last the dog began to slow, and she reined Lancelot to a trot, taking a moment to look around. They were on a lane that had a familiar feel, a path so narrow that two riders would have difficulty in passing. A stone wall ran down one side, and on the other lay only a moonlit field. Rounding a bend, she could see in the distance a single light, one that might shine in the window of an isolated dwelling.

Suddenly she knew where she was. This was the lane along which she had been walking when Gideon had come upon her. She had crossed the stile and dashed across the broken field, but he had pursued her. When he carried her away, she had wondered if the distant cottage might be the home of a woman, a mistress he wished her not to meet.

And if it were? Did he leave her each night after their lovemaking and return to another's arms . . . another woman important enough to bring the despair she had seen tonight in his eyes? Such a woman, innocent though she might be of duplicity and ill will, would crush the life from her.

But on she went.

When she came within twenty yards of the front door, she reined in and eased to the ground, signaling to Baron to hold back and keep silent. Gideon's horse was tethered nearby. He bobbed his head, but he did not whinny, as if he understood the need for quiet. Even the moon went behind a cloud to hide her presence. All the elements cooperated with her on this night, all but the man she came to see.

The cottage was small, thatch-roofed, its

presence hidden by thick shrubs, except for the one well-lighted window. It looked peaceful and very ordinary, sitting out here in the midst of fields and moors. Only one detail jarred: the iron bars that crossed over the window. She had not seen them from the lane.

As she walked closer, voices issued from inside—angry voices, two men caught in a fury that broke the stillness of the night. She could not make out the words, but the tone was clear enough. Both sounded like Gideon, or maybe it was that all angry men sounded alike.

She peered through the bars and saw the thick-necked worker who had been with the bailiff James Dent and Gideon on the grounds of Blackthorne the night of All Hallows' Eve. He appeared to be watching the argument, taking no part, his features twisted into a scowl.

Drawing in a deep breath, she hurried forward and threw open the door. Her eyes took in everything at once. Stunned, she held on to the door frame for support.

Two men heartbreakingly familiar faced one another in the center of the room, mirror images of each other, dressed the same, hair black, eyes black, both tall and lean, their bodies taut, their strong, gaunt features caught in a moment of rage.

She looked at one. "Gideon?"

And then at the other, "Gideon?"

The truth took a lifetime in coming.

"Geoffrey," she whispered.

One bowed, and his expression of rage softened in an instant into polite regard, as if he had slipped a mask over his face. Chilled, she held her cloak close about her.

He brushed the hair from his eyes. "Ah, Miss Fairfax. My brother has too long attempted to keep you from me, though"—this with a smirk—"you and I know he failed. At last I am allowed to present myself as who I am."

Incomprehensible. She looked at the other. He stood rigid, watching, the emotion in his eyes shuttered as she had seen all too often when she wanted most to know his thoughts. This was the man she loved, a man she did not know.

"You have found me out," Gideon said. His voice was brittle. He wore no pleasant mask. "Allow me to introduce the real Duke of Ravenswood, Geoffrey Blackthorne. As he said, I have kept you from him far too long."

Struck dumb, she could do little more than stare from one man to the other. Mostly she stared at Gideon.

"Come, come," the brother said, "you are not usually so mute, Lucinda. At least you are not when I have come to you in the night."

"Enough," Gideon snapped. "Leave her be."

But Geoffrey was not done. His eyes raked over her. "You spread your legs sweetly, for me and for the man who would be my keeper. But

352

who keeps whom, I ask? And who pleases you the most?"

She gasped and covered her mouth with her hand.

"I said, enough!" Gideon roared, and threw himself at his brother. His hands went for the neck, clutching, squeezing, Geoffrey flailing at him, fists landing wherever he could reach.

It all happened so quickly, she could do nothing but cry out, "No," and again, trying to get closer, "No! Stop!"

But Gideon was beyond hearing. His hold broke, and the brothers fell with a crash, still scuffling, arms and legs lashing out. It was a scene from hell. She looked beyond them to the thick-necked onlooker. He stood grim-faced, his hands thrust firmly in his pockets.

"They'll kill each other," she cried.

He shook his head, once, and remained in his place.

She looked around for something, anything, that might help her stop them. But it was over as quickly as it had begun. Gideon—she thought it was he—looked up at her as he knelt on the floor. His brother lay supine beside him, his eyes closed, his chest heaving with ragged breaths.

They stared at one another. "Lucinda," he said, as if only to say her name would make everything right.

She shook her head, stumbling backwards.

She had to get away, to think. Geoffrey lived. And he claimed to be her lover as well. It could not be. Her head throbbed. She backed through the door and turned, in desperation needing to run, to put distance between her and the cottage and the ugliness within.

Gideon caught her by the wrist and pulled her against him. She jerked free and faced him.

"He's dead," she said, knowing how stupid she sounded. "You buried him."

"I buried another man."

She looked at the bars. "And kept this one prisoner." She shook her head. "For ten years. It can't be."

"If you care for me, Lucinda, trust me now. I must get you away from here."

"Why? To take me to your bed and silence my questions? To continue your charade as Duke of Ravenswood?" She heard the hysteria in her voice, but she could not stop. "You are the younger brother, are you not? Irene Littlewood told me so."

"She must also have told you I was evil. Did you believe her?"

Her heart wrenched. "I don't know what to believe." She stepped away. "Leave me be, Gideon. Leave me be. I have to think." She rubbed at her temples. "It's so hard to think."

"I can't leave you. It's too late."

"No, no," she said.

She shook her head, then turned to run,

mindless, fleeing as if the hounds of hell were at her heels and not just Baron, barking furiously, keeping close. Behind her she heard a shout and then ominous silence, but she did not stop, instead dashing across the misty field by the cottage and into a thick woods, unaware of her direction, running blindly, gasping for breath in the wet air. With each step the turf gulped at her boots, and her heart thundered in her ears.

Branches grabbed at her, caught in her cloak, ripped the fabric, but could not slow her. The leaves, heavy with moisture, splashed water on her as she brushed against them. She stumbled once against a dead limb; it snapped loudly and fell to the ground. A gunshot, she thought at first, and almost screamed before coming to her senses.

Her side burned with a sharp pain, but still she ran on, stumbling, righting herself, knowing nothing but to run. She would have gone to the ends of the earth to get away from what she had seen. Lies, all was lies; she knew not what was real and what was false.

At last she broke through the trees into a clearing. Baron's sharp bark brought her to a halt, and in that instant the moon came from behind a cloud to light her way. She stood at the jagged precipice where her father had died, staring down at the shallow, fast-moving river at its base. Another step and she would have suffered the same fate as he.

Shaking, she turned and saw a man approach her through the woods, near the place where she had almost felt the death sting of a bullet. Gideon? Geoffrey? She could not tell in the moonlight. Mist and moonlight, she thought, almost giddily. Tonight was like the first in her inherited home. Except that much had changed. She was not the woman she had been. She did not live in the same world.

She stared at the man who had made it so.

"Gideon," she said. It had to be. Only he would follow her.

"Be careful." He reached out for her, though he was a half-dozen yards away. "Come, take my hand."

How calm, how reasonable he was. She could not be the same.

"Why didn't you tell me? I gave you so much and all I asked for was the truth. I don't know you at all, not at all, and I have loved you for so long. You should have let me comfort you. I do not understand. Your brother drowned. And yet he lives. Which one of you did I kiss?" The words tore from her. "Which one did I love?"

"Take my hand," he said again, as if she had not spoken, as if she had not opened her veins and bled for him.

"Tell me the truth," she managed, her voice broken, all energy spent. Her hands hung limply at her sides, and she let the tears flow. "If I mean anything at all to you, tell me. Please tell me now."

He laughed, and beside her Baron growled and snapped.

Her tears dried, and her blood ran cold.

"You're not Gideon." She spoke softly, though she wanted to scream.

"My brother is a fool, and a weak one at that. He was always so. He has let you stir his mind. He has let you turn him away from me. I have the power to ruin him, but he keeps forgetting." His voice turned wheedling. "Give yourself to me and I will study the matter. If I have not killed him already. The blow I dealt could very well have been fatal."

"No!" she cried out.

He laughed, his change of mood as frightening as anything he said. "He should have choked the life from me when he had the chance."

"I must go to him." She took a step forward.

"Call off your dog, and I will let you. When you see him fallen, weak, puling, you will know which brother to choose."

"Gideon would not be in such a state."

"Go to him. See for yourself I speak the truth." He smiled. "But first the dog."

He gave her little choice. Gideon needed her.

"Baron," she said, barely able to speak, "down. Stay."

The dog whined and sat on his haunches.

She looked up. "There. You are safe. Baron will not harm you."

Geoffrey was on her in an instant, grabbing her arm and twisting it sharply behind her back, pulling her hard against him, one hand smashed across her mouth to keep her from crying out.

"Struggle too much, my dear, and we both fall to our death."

She froze.

"It's easy to die here, you know," he said softly in her ear. "Your father, the fool, saw us there in the woods. He thought onc of us a ghost. He stumbled and . . ."

His voice trailed into silence.

Lucinda had time only for the living. Her mind raced. She had to get to Gideon. She must not think of her father. She must not think of the rocks that studded the side of the scar. She must not think of herself.

"Let her go, Geoffrey. I am the one you want."

The brother's hold on her eased, and they both looked toward the edge of the woods where Gideon stood. He bore a deep cut on his brow. Blood trickled down his cheek.

But he was alive. Blessedly alive.

Geoffrey took his hand from her mouth, but he wrenched her arm higher and she could not stifle a cry of pain. Gideon's eyes narrowed into slits.

"My, my," he said coolly, sounding more like

Geoffrey than himself. "At last you have found an opponent worthy of your prowess."

"I will do much to her to arouse a different cry. Or does she scream when she is satisfied? Perhaps it is that she has never been in such a state."

"You know I cannot let you touch her."

"I touch her now."

"I do not think she is much satisfied. Let her go. Take care of me. And then do what you will."

"I have only to threaten you with disclosure."

"That has long ceased to be a threat. Tell the world what you will. I can no longer live a lie."

"You do not mean what you say. You like the power of control."

"No, never. But I loved Blackthorne and its people. I could not let you bring it all to ruin." He looked at Lucinda. "And then I loved you. It made all the difference."

Unexpected joy filled her. She tried to tell him so with her eyes, but Geoffrey would not let them have even this brief, bizarre moment to think of one another.

"You speak nonsense. You have always protected *me*."

Geoffrey sounded hurt, puzzled by the alteration in his world, a reasonable man struck by unreasonable change.

Gideon's eyes softened. For a moment, he looked a little lost and more than a little sad.

"That was when I could look upon you as the

boy you were, a part of me as much as I was a part of you. That boy is no more. I see you as the man you are. You are ill, Geoffrey. You need more help than I can give you, though God knows I have tried."

Looking from one to the other in the damp moonlight, Lucinda saw them as they must have been, as she had been told, twins alike and different, one carefree, the other somber and responsible, the two of them against the world far too often, one needing the other as much as he was needed. She could have wept for what had been lost.

Geoffrey eased his hold on her arm. She held herself still, lest he be reminded of her. But he was caught in his talk with Gideon.

"You promised not to lock me away. You promised I would never leave Blackthorne land. My land."

He whined, a child who did not get his way, not the arrogant, abusive man he had been only seconds ago. She saw the madness in his eyes.

"You will be the recognized duke, as you should be," Gideon said. "But you must have help."

"No." Geoffrey spoke sharply. Letting her go, he backed away, going closer to the edge of the scar. "I like the life I lead. I would not have it change."

"Then kill me. You tried just now at the cottage and failed. Try again. It is the only way you can go free."

Geoffrey turned his eyes on Lucinda. "You are to blame. He is my brother no longer. I shot at you once, to make you go away. And the fire. But it was no use. He was mine. Now he is yours."

A growl sounded in Baron's throat.

Geoffrey laughed. "Even the dog finds offense in me."

He looked at Gideon. "And you. All is indeed ended." He spoke simply, the madness gone from his eyes. "What a foolish waste a life can be. My head hurts so, dear brother. I must make the pain go away."

Gideon dashed forward but could not reach him in time. Geoffrey stepped over the edge and was gone. Lucinda turned to Gideon and buried her head against his chest. He held her and stared into the abyss.

Chapter Twenty-one

"You should not have followed me."

Lucinda did not look at Gideon as he spoke. Instead, she stared into the fire and sipped a cup of tea. They were in the room where they had first made love on All Hallows' Eve, beside each other on the sofa where she had waited for him with eager anticipation.

The moment was not joyous. Geoffrey's body had been recovered and brought to the hall. The constable and a doctor had been summoned, but they had not yet arrived.

The hour was close to dawn. This was the first time they had been alone since returning from the cottage with their tragic news.

On the ride to Blackthorne, neither had spo-

ken, and she had known Gideon was lost in
grief. How deep it went she did not know, but
she was sharply aware that what happened over
the ensuing minutes and hours would affect the
two of them for the rest of their lives.

"I had no choice but to follow," she said. "I
could not be my mother, though I loved her
with all my heart."

She felt his eyes on her, and she knew he
waited for further explanation.

"She married a younger son, untitled, a working man, and then he became a viscount,
wealthy, propertied, in a land that frightened
her, so different was it from her own. I realized
none of this until I came here."

She edged a little closer to Gideon. "She let
him leave and did not go after him. She regretted it always. I could not do the same."

Setting her tea aside, she fell silent. Her story
was simple; she had told him all she could. Dec-
larations of love must wait, for them both.

He did not speak for a while. When he did,
his voice was low, each word thought over carefully.

"I believed he had drowned, along with our
father."

Her heart flooded with relief. He had decided
to talk.

"All evidence said so," he went on. "By the
time I arrived, the ravaged bodies had already
been identified—my father by his ducal ring,

the other by scars Geoffrey had received in a recent fight. The general size and shape of their remains were also right. There was no reason to doubt the identifications. Perhaps I should have, but I was . . . not myself. I had the bodies transported to the family crypt, and the proper words said over them."

Again a moment of silence.

"Weeks later Geoffrey came here, to my room, at night. I believed him to be a ghost, but his laugh was far too real. And harsh. In so short a time I had forgotten how harsh he could be. He was proud of his trickery. He could not allow himself to be taken to London; he could not see the specialist our father had engaged to examine him. He would be locked away, he said, and I knew he was right. His course appeared simple to him. When a storm struck the ship, opportunity arose. He threw our father overboard, knocked unconscious the servant accompanying them, mutilated him with wounds similar to his, then sent his body to join the first."

A shudder went through him, but he did not stop.

"Luck was with him. He safely swam to shore. The bodies of the other two did not surface for days, not until the sea and its creatures had done their work. To Geoffrey it seemed provident, as if all the forces beyond him were on his side. He hid, close by, waiting for the moment to reveal himself to me."

Lucinda took his hand and stroked the long, strong fingers. They tightened around hers.

"While I was deciding what to do with him, another body surfaced, a poor soul whose identity I never knew. I came to the decision that has haunted me ever since. God forgive me, I said he was the servant and buried him in grand style. I was thought to be magnanimous. Sometimes I wonder if his family waits for him, and worries."

"You did what you had to do."

"I did the only thing I could, or so it seemed at the time. For too long, I had been Geoffrey's protector. He could not help what had happened to him. He could not alter what he had become. And I could not reveal his presence. If I did so, at best he would be imprisoned, at worst, hanged. Justice would demand it. He had slain two men, one of them his father."

She thought about the bars on the windows.

"And so you imprisoned him yourself. For ten years."

"They seemed forever, one much like another. It was my life. I could accept no other. Geoffrey had seen to that. I was a criminal as much as he. And he was my brother."

He fell silent for a minute. She did not speak.

"Sometimes we rode together, always at night, and at others we talked about the early days, He was himself again. But such times became more rare. In his delusions and lapses into rage, Geoffrey thrived. I became the prisoner."

"Who knew he lived?"

"The bailiff, a few farmers, good men all. Irene Littlewood suspected the truth, but hatred of me consumed her to such a degree, she could not think the matter through."

"Why have you kept her here?"

"Penance for my sins."

"And Jenny Patchell?"

"Ah, Jenny. She knows everything. She has been a source of great strength. She did not condemn me. For that I owe her more than I can ever repay."

"The night I first met you in the garden, she warned me against the duke, saying he was a danger to me. When she called you by name, she spoke only of your lust. I did not understand. I thought you were one and the same man."

At last he looked at her, and she saw that for the moment she filled his mind.

"The lust was real enough," he said, his voice not quite so unsure. "I wanted you from the moment I saw you in the village, standing helpless yet brave in the middle of the road. I was in an ugly state. Geoffrey had been particularly difficult. Then you were there. You seemed like a miracle to me, a rescuer. It was why I came to you that night, and returned, again and again, knowing I was cursed. My world was dark, and you brought light. I could not stay away."

"I did not want you to. I found life bleak for a long while, except when you were near."

"I feared I frightened you."

"You did." She smiled. "I had never met anyone like you."

She looked away from him, into the fire. There was so much he still had to say, else the grief might harden in his heart. If she kept him in her gaze, she would soon hold him and kiss him and the talking would cease.

"The man at the cottage," she said. "I saw him once before, on All Hallows' Eve. Who is he?"

"The watchman I hired. On that night, a time of celebration, Geoffrey had been particularly difficult, threatening to ruin everything."

"The watchman could not handle him?"

"Not that night. He came to me for help. The trouble was, Geoffrey had charmed him, as he has charmed so many others. Too many times he allowed him out, to walk unaccompanied, to ride. But my brother was clever. He made certain the two of us were never seen together. Whatever he did on his solitary rides was thought done by me. Even the women brought to the cottage were mine. They thought so because Geoffrey told them the truth, that he was the Duke of Ravenswood. I did nothing to end the talk. It served a purpose. I was the Devil

Duke, too evil even to be called upon."

"The boy John—"

"My nephew, not my son."

"You took him in and let the world think he was yours."

"Do not make me out a saint. Geoffrey has accused me often of reveling in the title and wealth that should have gone to him. He is right, in part. The title means little, but Blackthorne land and the hall, these I welcomed. I have told you more than once I am not an honorable man. I could have killed Geoffrey when he threatened you. Each time he came close to hurting you, I told him so. Tonight I almost did."

His voice trailed off, and he seemed close to slipping into a private reverie. That, she could not allow.

"I was told of a man who disappeared on the estate."

"The itinerant. Do not soften your words. You were told I killed him. The truth is that Geoffrey, in sport, beat him when he wandered too close to the cottage. I paid him well to leave and keep the beating to himself. He was a poor man. He seemed pleased with the bargain. I told my brother if he ever did such a thing again, I would turn him over to the constable. As far as I know, he never did."

"Tonight, when you left, you said *no more*."

"I had gone to tell Geoffrey the charade was

done. I could not stay away from you, or send you away. Nor could I be certain of protecting you as I should."

"That was the argument you were having when I came through the door."

"You should not have come. You almost lost your life. Instead. . . ."

"Instead your brother took his own. He was thinking clearly when he did so, Gideon. You must always remember that. The end was of his choosing. His suffering is done."

She smiled. "And you have his son. Adopt him and call him yours. Let the world think what it will. In a way, Geoffrey will live on in the boy."

"You make everything seem simple. And inevitable."

"Perhaps it has been just that. Even my coming here and standing in the road."

"Still, you should not have come to the cottage."

"That's how we started out our talk this morning, with you lecturing me." She made her voice light. "It is not the first time you have done so."

"You have seldom listened."

"I'm listening now." She lifted his hand to her lips and kissed the fingertips. "I will do whatever you want."

"He never touched you. No matter what he said. The end would have come much sooner if he had."

"I knew that was so. I would have known if

another tried to make love to me. That first time, at Blackthorne, I thought you had changed your mind, and then afterwards, I thought you were done with me."

"The truth was I had just begun." He pulled her into his arms. "I have loved you from the first. You must tell me what is in your heart. Can you ever forgive me?"

"For what? For being a man who can care? For being a man who can suffer? These are the traits in you I love most."

"I can be most burdensome."

"I assumed that was a trait of all men. And have I not driven you to distraction more than once?"

"Constantly. But it is not the trait in you I love most."

She thought a minute. "I am a sex-crazed beast. Is that it?"

He laughed, and the sound was like sunshine in her soul.

When he looked down at her, the laughter died, but not the glimmer in his eyes.

"I have called you my light, and so you are. I have lived in the dark so long I did not think anyone such as you could be possible for someone such as I. You change me. You give me hope."

She reached up to smooth the lines between his eyes.

"Please, don't change too much. Promise me

you will not entirely forsake your devil's ways. They have become most dear to me."

He kissed her. The kiss deepened, and she was ready to give herself to him once again in front of the fire. A knock at the door stopped her.

He eased her away and stood.

"That will be the doctor. And the constable."

She stood beside him. "We will talk to them together."

"They will want to see me alone. There is the possibility I could be put under arrest. I have, you must realize, committed several crimes."

Before she could reply, the door opened and two men, stern and businesslike in appearance, walked in. She could do nothing but stand and watch as Gideon led them from the room.

Chapter Twenty-two

Two weeks later a hearing was held before the magistrate in Whitby, the seaside town from which Gideon's father and brother were to have sailed a decade before.

At his request, and after making strong objections, Lucinda agreed not to accompany him.

"I will send for you if the news is not good," he promised.

He was trying to spare her the public spectacle that the hearing would become. His request meant much to him. She could do nothing but let him go alone.

In his absence, a winter storm raged. On the day of his return, the sun broke through.

She was standing in the Blackthorne garden, looking in dismay at all the bedraggled plants, trying to concentrate on their replacement, when he came to her. She stood in the center of the path and watched as his long legs brought him to her side. He looked particularly elegant in a morning coat. He even wore a cravat and the blue waistcoat. Standing tall before her, he was very much the duke.

As always, his eyes were unreadable, but his words were plain and direct.

"Marry me."

She shook her head. "What did you say?"

"Be my wife. I love you more than life itself. Bear my children. Stay with me here in Yorkshire. Do not go back to America."

She broke into a smile.

"You're free," she said. "There are no charges against you."

"I am not free until I hear you answer yes. I should tell you first that after the scandal of the trial, mine is not an honorable title. You should be aware of that."

"An honorable man holds it. That is all that is important."

"Do not speak too quickly. My name is tarnished."

"It always was. Dear, dear Gideon, you ask me to marry you, yet give me reasons I should not."

"It seems I have a conscience after all."

"I hope it does not get in the way of your be-havior too often." Her smile became a laugh. "Of course my answer is yes. You knew it would be. I am not nearly subtle enough for your devious mind."

He took her in his arms and kissed her. The kiss lingered until they both, reluctantly, drew apart.

Her heart fluttered. She wanted to dance down the path and let happiness whirl her around and around.

She managed to keep it within her. For a little while.

"Now that that's out of the way," she said, "tell me what happened."

"Out of the way?"

"You know what I mean. I told you I was not subtle."

Surely her eyes were twinkling. Surely he saw that her lightheartedness was a show for him. He needed it in his life more than he knew.

"So tell me." She grew solemn and took his hand. "It must have been difficult for you."

"It was not pleasant."

"Do you want to talk about it?"

"Later." He stroked her hair, which she had been wearing loose every day, waiting for his return. "Much later."

She sighed in relief. They had gone through so much confession, so much recall. There would be other times when they would go through the same again.

But now she had just agreed to be his wife.

"So what do you want to do?" she asked.

"Celebrate."

He whispered in her ear.

Her face grew hot and she pushed him away. "Have we ever done that before?"

"I do not believe so. It may take some practice."

"Whatever you say." She looped her arm in his. "I suppose we ought to go upstairs right now and get started."

"If we do not, I will have you here and now in the nearest flowerbed."

She waved her hand airily. "Let's wait for that until spring. Things will be sweetly scented then."

He kissed her again. She came close to changing her mind about which bed they should use.

"I've been thinking," she said, striking out once again toward the garden door, making certain she had a tight hold on his arm. She was not nearly so chipper as she appeared. He must realize that.

"Ah," he said. "Thinking. You make me shudder."

"It passed the time. I believed I would go mad the first days you were gone. Everyone hovered over me. Oh, by the way, Irene Littlewood suddenly remembered a sister in the south of Yorkshire. She's gone to live with her." She hesitated. "Where was I?"

"Thinking."

"Oh, yes. It's hard to do with you so close. The children. The foundlings from the factory. They need a permanent place to live, at least until they can strike out on their own. I am sure there are others in a similar predicament. I would like to make Craven Manor their home."

"An orphanage?"

"I'd like to think of it as more than that. School, training in some kind of trade, a chance to learn to ride, to garden if a boy or girl chooses. I've certainly money enough, especially with the profits from the factory. When I can, I would like to take up where my father left off so long ago in his plans to export to America."

"You really have been thinking."

"Bone china is a fine product. I've been studying the whole process, from books I found in the Craven library. I even went into town once, just to see how Hudson Smedley was getting on. You must have frightened him terribly. He was doing fine."

"You throw too much at me. Let's start at the beginning. You're turning your ancestral home over to the children."

"With supervisors and teachers, of course. And Mrs. Pickering to watch over them. Fenton, too, and whoever else wishes to stay. I know

Evelyn Rogers

there will be government regulations and inspections and lots of problems thrown in my way. They won't stop me. The solution has a nice bit of irony to it. The manor house has been too long without children. And, strangely enough, I think my father would approve."

"If you think so, then who am I to disagree?"

"Who indeed."

This time she was the one to kiss him, leaning him against the closed back door of the hall, easing her hands beneath his coat and rubbing them over his chest and around to his back, letting them roam lower, back and front, until she was considering tugging his trousers down to his knees.

And he a peer of the realm. So elegant. So hard.

He moaned against her mouth.

She licked his tongue and returned the moan.

Taking her hand, he pulled her along the dark corridors, to the winding stairs, picking her up and carrying her to the hallway in front of his chamber door.

She kissed his ear. "There's one more thing."

He kissed her throat. "Be brief, Lucinda. I am only human."

Which of course he wasn't, not in the ordinary way of men, but that was something she would tell him later, when they were both naked and in bed.

"I've been thinking about Baron."

378

"Baron?"

"Where did he come from? I arrived, and suddenly he was lifting a paw to me."

"He had been seen around here for some time. He never got close to a human, though I suspect there is a bitch or two he gifted with his favors. We've the evidence scampering around the grounds right now."

"It's as if he had been waiting for me."

"I understand his feelings."

She thought of her father. Had his spirit somehow arranged—

No. Impossible.

And yet—

She could not forget the facing hounds on the gateposts leading into Craven Manor, so like her mystery dog.

Gideon shouldered open the door, set her on her feet, and began to undress her. She forgot about Baron. She forgot about everything but returning the favor. She did not move quickly, nor did he. When at last she looked up at him, after a careful study of the real elegance that lay beneath his clothes, the devil lines were gone.

"I love you, Gideon Blackthorne. I'll probably make a terrible duchess, knowing nothing about the part, but I will make you a very fine wife."

Taking his hand, she led him toward the bed to show him what she meant.

She stopped by the bedpost. There was one

thing more important than physical love, though at the moment he might find the point debatable.

"I not only love you, but I respect you and I need you. All my loyalty and devotion I place in your hands. I know you will guard them well. You are, dearest Gideon, the best man I have ever known."

Enter a tumultuous world of thrilling sensuality and chilling terror, where nothing is as it seems, and dreams and nightmares blend into heart-pounding encounters too enticing to be denied, too frightening to be forgotten. In our new line of gothics the most exciting writers of romance fiction explore dark secrets, forbidden desires, the hidden part of the psyche that is revealed only at the midnight hour by...

Candleglow

Coming in March...

The Scarletti Curse

by Christine Feehan

Strange, twisted carvings and hideous gargoyles adorned the *palazzo* of the great Scarletti family. But a still more fearful secret lurked within its storm-tossed turrets. For every bride who entered its forbidding walls seemed doomed to leave in a casket. Chosen by her feudal lord, Nicoletta knew she must accept her fate as Don Scarletti's bride-to-be. The only question was whether he would be her heart's destiny or her soul's demise....

Available March 2001

0-505-52421-X

THE SCARLETTI CURSE

CHRISTINE FEEHAN

There was complete silence in the room. A cold draft seemed to come out of the very walls and swirl around Nicoletta so that she shivered. Deep within her heart, she heard her own cry of unspoken protest. There was evil walking in the *palazzo*. She stared up at Don Scarletti, her gaze locked with his. Fierce. Intense. Soul to soul. She couldn't even feel the hand of her companion, Maria Pia, in hers. She and the don were the only two people in existence. He was watching her closely, his mind in hers. She *felt* him there. He was waiting in silence for her to condemn him.

Unbidden came the image of his scraped knuckles, the small, incriminating droplet of blood on his otherwise immaculate clothing. Nicoletta felt her heart pound. His gaze continued to bore straight into hers, and she couldn't turn away from him. She knew he was waiting for it, knew he expected her to denounce him. Don Scarletti, *Il Demonio* of the *palazzo*. The curse. The whispers. The rumors. Still, Giovanni Scarletti stood tall and straight, his black eyes fathomless, his features carefully expressionless.

Nicoletta took a breath and let it out slowly. "Will you send your men to search the maze for Cristano? It is possible he wandered in and could not find his way out."

Was that what had happen to her former suitor?

The don bowed slightly. "At once, *piccola*. And I will send them into the hills to see if the young man was injured on his way home." He said the words deliberately to remind her of the numerous times others had set out traveling and fallen victim to wild animals, the harsh terrain, or even to robbers. But his voice sounded incredibly gentle, and a warmth brushed at the walls of her mind, so that she felt almost comforted.

Nicoletta swallowed the hard knot in her throat. It was difficult to think straight with the don watching her so intently. She could sense Maria Pia's gaze on him now, accusing.

"Don Scarletti, you were the last person to see

Cristano alive." Maria Pia said what Nicoletta would not. Her very tone was a declaration of his guilt.

"We do not know that he is dead, Donna Sigmora," Giovanni pointed out softly. His voice held a thread of menace, as if his patience was fast wearing thin. "If the young man met his demise in the maze, the scavengers would be present overhead."

Relief swept through Nicoletta. "That is true, Maria Pia," she said. But a terrible dread was slowly creeping into her mind and heart and soul like a dark shadow. She would know if someone was hurt, wouldn't she? Surely she would know.

Maria Pia faced the don bravely. "The wedding should be postponed until the young man is found," she challenged. *If you are exonerated.* The words were left unsaid, but they shimmered there in the room, as vivid and alive as if Maria Pia had uttered them aloud in condemnation.

The black eyes gleamed ominously. "Nothing will stop the wedding, Donna Sigmora. Not you, not this rebellious young man. For all I know, he disappeared with every intention of bringing a halt to the wedding plans. We are to be married on the morrow." It was a decree, Giovanni's dark features an implacable mask.

For a moment Maria Pia looked mutinous, but the don's words seemed to sink in. She

385

knew Cristano well. He had a shocking temper and, if humiliated, could sulk for days. He was quite capable of disappearing and causing alarm to get back at Nicoletta for not marrying him as he had demanded. Maria Pia looked at her young charge. She had the feeling Nicoletta was in terrible danger, and she wanted desperately to drag her from the *palazzo*. "It is possible I am worrying over nothing," she said softly, looking at the floor in defeat. Giovanni Scarletti was not going to give up her beloved Nicoletta; she could see that in his masculine aggressiveness, his possessive posture each time he was near the young woman.

Giovanni reached out to capture Nicoletta's hand, taking it right out of Maria Pia's firm clasp. He carried her fingers to the warmth of his mouth. It was a blatant gesture, claiming her, branding her as his own.

His black gaze was locked on hers so that Nicoletta had a strange feeling of falling forward, to be trapped for all eternity in the depths of his eyes. Time stood still. Her heart beat for him. She felt the rush of blood, of heat, of liquid fire.

Don Scarletti released her reluctantly, his touch lingering for a moment before he glided away. "I have kept my visitor waiting far too long, and I must arrange for my men to begin the search for your young friend."

Nicoletta stood dazed, as if in a trance, staring at the closed door after the don left the room.

Maria Pia sighed heavily. "Do you believe him, Nicoletta? Really believe him? Because I am not certain I do. It is possible Cristano is hiding out in the hills. When he was a boy and angry with his *madre*, he did such things. Or it is possible he is hurt and needs help." She was watching Nicoletta closely as she spoke.

Nicoletta's teeth teased nervously at her lower lip. She should know if there was someone in need, and Maria Pia was well aware of it. Nicoletta had always known. And the bird would come to her. She looked at the older woman. "I must go outside, where I can feel the wind on my face. I want to look at the sky."

"What do you have in your hair?" Maria Pia reached around her and picked strands of a spider's web from her long tresses. Nicoletta shoved a hand through the unruly black waves.

"Something is wrong here, *piccola*. When I am in this house I feel the echo of your *madre*'s screams as she was thrown over the balcony to her destruction. I can feel the spirits of the dead. They are uneasy in this *palazzo*." She made the sign of the cross and kissed her crucifix. "May the good Madonna save you from your enemies."

Nicoletta did not protest. She knew she had enemies at the *palazzo*; she just didn't know why. She felt eyes staring at her in disapproval each time she left her bedchamber. "I must go outside," she said again. Her heart felt heavy in her chest. She opened the door, turning back toward Maria Pia as she did so. "How did all of this start, so long ago? When did they first start to whisper of the curse on the Scarletti *famiglia*? Is it possible there is a strain of madness in the Scarletti blood?"

Maria Pia glanced past Nicoletta to the waiting guards. "It is not a good thing to speak of in this place where the walls have eyes and ears." She lifted her chin. "Come, let us go out to the courtyard. We will see if the don kept his word and sent his men looking for Cristano."

"I can imagine many things about Don Scarletti, but he lives by his word. He would not tell me one thing and do another," she said, to her own surprise, defending him.

Maria Pia looked at her sharply. "It is possible you are already falling under his spell. I told you to be careful. He can make you say things you do not wish to reveal. You must be strong, Nicoletta. Until you know more of the don . . ."

"The man who is to be my husband," Nicoletta whispered. "We are to be wed on the morrow. I will live with him, and this *palazzo* will be my home. I have no choice in the matter. You said even the Holy Father would not go against him."

Maria Pia twisted her hands together as they moved down the long corridor to the stairs. She leaned on the banister and uttered a soft cry, once more crossing herself devoutly. "Look at this, Nicoletta! The artwork on his stairs. A serpent coiled around a tree branch! What manner of man is he?"

"He inherited the *palazzo* and the title from his *padre*. What should he have done? Refused to live in it because he did not like the artwork on the stairs? It is beautiful, Maria Pia. If you look at some of the work, it is truly remarkable."

Maria Pia resorted to clucking as she often did when she was agitated. "He has cast a spell over you, *bambina*."

Nicoletta glanced over her shoulder at the silent guards following them at a circumspect distance. "Where is little Sophie?" The don's niece, who had doted on Nicoletta since she came to the palazzo to help heal her, would be upset that her beloved mentor had been trapped in the *palazzo*'s maze of secret passageways while looking for her.

"The child was sent to her room, *signorina*," one guard replied instantly.

Nicoletta looked at Maria Pia. "Come along with me. I must go to Sophie. She will be so frightened. By now she will think *il fantasma* has gotten me."

As they started back up the stairs, the guard shook his head. "The child was removed from the nursery and is on the first floor."

Nicoletta smiled at him. "Thank you." She

knew the exact hideous room the child had been banished to. She ran along the corridor toward the chamber, Maria Pia trailing behind and waiting outside the door.

Sophie lay facedown crying on the big bed, so small she could barely be seen among the covers. Nicoletta rushed to her and pulled her into her arms, rocking her while the child sobbed as if her heart was breaking.

"I thought I killed you!" The child hiccupped the words, her tears soaking Nicoletta's neck. "I am sorry, Nicoletta."

"*Bambina*." Nicoletta hugged her even closer. "You did not do anything so wrong."

Sophie lifted her head, looking forlorn. "*Zio* Giovanni told me never to go into the passage. He said it was dangerous. Now I have to stay in this scary room forever. I have to be punished." She wailed the last dramatically and looked as pathetic as possible.

Nicoletta laughed softly. "Maria Pia shall stay with you, and I will go talk to your *zio*. Perhaps he will think you have been punished enough. But you must heed his warnings. I do not think *i fantasmi* guard the passageways, but you could get lost in there and endanger your life. You must promise me you will never go in there again."

Sophie nodded vigorously, willing to promise Nicoletta anything at all.

"Dry your tears, *bambina*. I will get you out

of your prison." She ruffled the child's hair and
beckoned Maria Pia into the room to comfort
Sophie while she was gone.

Nicoletta hurried back along the hall, but outside the don's study, she hesitated, her courage
suddenly faltering. She was interrupting his
work, intruding on his time. She was all at once
unsure of herself. Don Scarletti had been kind
to her, but he had a certain reputation, and, a
very powerful man, he had probably earned
that reputation many times over. She bit her lip
in an agony of indecision. He and his important
visitor had already been interrupted once so he
could rescue her from the secret passageway.

She glanced over her shoulder at the guards,
then rapped on the door quickly before she
completely lost her nerve.

Giovanni opened the door to find a very ner-
vous Nicoletta gazing up at him. He wrapped one
large palm around the nape of her neck as he
moved out into the corridor, closing the door to
his study behind him, obviously affording his visitor privacy. His thumb tipped her face up to his.
"Once again I find you without your companion,
cara mia. How is it you manage to elude Maria Pia
so often? She looks quite capable to me."

That faint betraying shiver began again, from
deep within her. Helplessly she glanced at the
guards. They were no help, moving away to give
the don privacy in dealing with his errant bride-
to-be. Giovanni urged her closer to the hard

strength of his body. "What is so urgent, *piccola,* that you would dare *il demonio* in his lair?" His thumb was now feathering along the delicate line of her jaw, lingering over her frantically beating pulse.

Her dark eyes were enormous as she looked up at him. "I do not think of you as *il demonio,*" she denied.

He quirked an elegant eyebrow at her. "Is that so?"

"I might have before I met you," she conceded reluctantly, unfailingly truthful.

His black eyes gleamed at her, a wicked amusement dancing in their depths. "I may have become one since I met you," he answered her suggestively.

She frowned at him. "I think you like to scare me with your wickedness, Don Scarletti, but in truth, I am not so easily frightened." It was almost the truth. No one else seemed to frighten her in quite the way he managed. He looked so implacable. Dare she argue with him? "I . . . I have a need to speak with you . . . about your order to have your men taste my food and drink. I would not wish anyone to be inadvertently ill on my account," she said haltingly.

Giovanni shook his head gravely. "I will not rescind my order, *cara mia,* not even to please you. But you already knew that. I suspect you had another reason to seek me out."

He was watching her with such intensity, she

wasn't certain she would be able to think straight much longer. "I . . . I would like to take young Sophie with me outside into the courtyard. She is very sorry for her disobedience, and I have lectured her on the danger of the passageway."

He stared down at her for so long, Nicoletta thought she might melt. She was mesmerized by the hot intensity in his black gaze. She was very aware of his powerful body so close to hers; she could feel the heat of his skin. There seemed to be a current arcing between them like a lightning bolt, sizzling and dancing so that her skin became sensitive and ached with an odd, unfamiliar need. His gaze dropped to her mouth, and her knees went weak. Butterfly wings brushed at her stomach, and heat pooled deep within her.

Then, suddenly, his mouth fastened to hers, hot and exciting, sweeping her away. It was a dark promise, erotic and sensual, his tongue demanding rather than asking for her response. She melted into him, boneless and pliant, her body molding to his, so that she felt his fierce arousal. Instead of pulling away as she should have, Nicoletta reveled in her power, wanting more, suddenly craving his dark secrets, aching with a need so strong she burned with it. Liquid fire. Molten heat.

Her breasts swelled with need, pushing into the heavy muscles of his body, straining for his

393

touch. The thin material of her blouse seemed all at once too much of a barrier between them. Her mind was suddenly filled with sensual images—her hands on his skin, his palm cupping her breast, his mouth blazing fire along her throat, lower, across bare skin to close, hot and moist, over her aching breast. She wanted him more than she had ever wanted anything in her life.

Giovanni lifted his head, his hand still curled around the nape of her neck, her body resting against his. "I need you, Nicoletta." His voice was husky and sensual. "*Dio*, I do not think I can wait one more night. Go take the child into the courtyard, and do not get into any more trouble. Keep Dona Sigmora with you at all times. She is your only protection from me."

She could feel his strong body trembling with the effort to allow her to go. A good girl would have been appalled at his conduct, shocked and horrified at her own conduct, but Nicoletta suspected she wasn't as good as Maria Pia would have liked. She wanted the don's hands on her body. And she knew he wanted her. She made him nearly as weak with wanting as he made her. She gazed up at him, trying desperately to find a way to breathe.

He groaned softly. "You cannot do that, *piccola*. You cannot look at me with such need in your eyes." He kissed the top of her silky hair. "I am not to be trusted. . . ."

WICKED
Evelyn Rogers

Gunned down after a bank robbery, Cad Rankin meets a heavenly being who makes him an offer he can't refuse. To save his soul, he has to bring peace to the most lawless town in the West. With a mission like that, the outlaw almost resigns himself to spending eternity in a place much hotter than Texas—until he comes across a feisty beauty who rouses his goodness and a whole lot more. Amy Lattimer is determined to do anything to locate her missing father, including pose as a fancy lady. Then she finds an ally in virile Cad Rankin, who isn't about to let her become a fallen angel. But even as Amy longs to surrender to paradise in Cad's arms, she begins to suspect that he has a secret that stands between them and unending bliss.

___52359-0 $5.50 US/$6.50 CAN

By the Bestselling Author of
The Forever Bride

If there is anything that gets Conn O'Brien's Irish up, it i
a lady in trouble–especially one he has fallen in love with a
first sight. So after the Texas horseman saves Crystal Brade
from an overly amorous lout, he doesn't waste a secon
declaring his intentions to make an honest woman of he
But they have barely been declared man and wife befor
Conn learns that his new bride is hiding a devastating secre
that can destroy him.

The plan is simple: To ensure the safety of her mother an
young brother, Crystal agrees to play the damsel in distress
The innocent beauty has no idea how dangerously charmin
the virile stranger can be–nor how much she longs t
surrender to the tender passion in his kiss. And when Con
discovers her ruse, she vows to blaze a trail of desire tha
will convince him that her deception has been an error of th
heart and not a ruthless betrayal.

__4262-2 $5.99 US/$6.99 CA\

Dorchester Publishing Co., Inc.
P.O. Box 6640
Wayne, PA 19087-8640

Please add $1.75 for shipping and handling for the first book an
$.50 for each book thereafter. NY, NYC, and PA resident
please add appropriate sales tax. No cash, stamps, or C.O.D.s. A
orders shipped within 6 weeks via postal service book rate.
Canadian orders require $2.00 extra postage and must be paid in
U.S. dollars through a U.S. banking facility.

Name_____
Address _____
City_____ State _____ Zip_____
I have enclosed $_____ in payment for the checked book(s)
Payment <u>must</u> accompany all orders. ☐ Please send a free catalog

Christine Feehan
Dark Magic

Young Savannah Dubrinsky is a mistress of illusion, a world-famous magician capable of mesmerizing millions. But here is one—Gregori, the Dark One—who holds *her* in terrifying thrall. Whose cold silver eyes and heated sensuality send shivers of danger, of desire, down her slender spine.

With a dark magic all his own, Gregori—the implacable hunter, the legendary healer, the most powerful of Carpathian males—whispers in Savannah's mind that he is her destiny. That she was born to save his immortal soul. And now, here in New Orleans, the hour has finally come to claim her. To make her completely his. In a ritual as old as time . . . and as inescapable as eternity.

__52389-2 $5.50 US/$6.50 CAN

Dorchester Publishing Co., Inc.
P.O. Box 6640
Wayne, PA 19087-8640